After marrying her husband Richard and raising two children, Sally Wragg completed an English degree at the University of London and has since turned her hand to writing. Sally began with short stories in women's magazines, and has also written *Maggie's Girl*.

PLAYING FOR KEEPS

Generations of the Vernon family have been involved with Rislington Rovers Football Club, otherwise known as the Rogues. But now the Rogues are not only faced with relegation but also an ongoing investigation into the club's financial affairs. The mayhem within the club is matched only by the turmoil of Vernon family life. Eleanor Vernon, wife of Rogues stalwart Landon, hates the influence the game has on her family, but things are about to get much worse. The Rogues are seeking a new chief executive and the shock appointment threatens the very core of Vernon family life . . .

Books by Sally Wragg
Published by The House of Ulverscroft:

MAGGIE'S GIRL

SALLY WRAGG

PLAYING FOR KEEPS

Complete and Unabridged

ULVERSCROFT
Leicester

First published in Great Britain in 2010 by
Robert Hale Limited
London

First Large Print Edition
published 2011
by arrangement with
Robert Hale Limited
London

British Library CIP Data

Wragg, Sally.
  Playing for keeps.
  1. Families- -Fiction. 2. Soccer teams- -Management- -
Fiction. 3. Soccer teams- -Fiction. 4. Large type books.
I. Title
823.9′2–dc22

ISBN 978–1–44480–601–4

Published by
F. A. Thorpe (Publishing)
Anstey, Leicestershire

Set by Words & Graphics Ltd.
Anstey, Leicestershire
Printed and bound in Great Britain by
T. J. International Ltd., Padstow, Cornwall

This book is printed on acid-free paper

For Richard with love

1

The ball sailed across a sky of cloudless blue, unexpected weather for what had been a late and bitterly cold Easter. A slim leg shot out. Ball and golden-booted foot connected. The net bulged, eighteen-year-old Paris Pryce-Martin turned away, fist raised, and disappeared amid a scrimmage of exuberant black-and-white-shirted bodies. The Rislington Park crowd, starved so long of success, went wild with delight.

From her vantage point on the front row of the director's box, Bobbie Vernon, short for Roberta, leapt to her feet, open-mouthed, arms stretched wide, unmindful of the fact that Paris was her nephew and that somehow he'd so miraculously put the Rogues ahead in front of their home crowd for the first time since Christmas. Her beloved team had scored. There was no feeling like it. Grinning idiotically she flung herself into her father's arms.

No need to look further along the row to her sister Babs and Babs's husband, Taylor. The two deliriously proud parents of Rislington's greatest striking prodigy since his great-grandfather Albert had first pulled on the distinctive black-and-white chequered shirt for which the Rogues were so famed, were similarly wildly embraced.

For one blissful moment a bubbling happiness pushed all thoughts of relegation firmly from Bobbie's mind. This was Rislington Rovers, founder member of the football league, never known to kick a ball in anger outside the rarefied atmosphere of football's highest echelons until last year's relegation to the Championship brought them crashing to the ground.

If only the referee had blown his whistle there and then the crowd would have gone home happy, but twenty minutes and two unstoppable strikes from the visitors' burly centre forward later and Bobbie was left ruing the fact that he hadn't. Her head dropped, all pleasure in the afternoon was gone, the half-time whistle was greeted by the obligatory boos from a disappointed crowd, their clenched fists raised towards the directors' box.

'You're not singing any more!' taunted the gold-shirted Wensley Wanderers fans jammed into the far corner of the Albert Vernon memorial stand.

'Here we go again!' Jimmy Proudfoot, the club's elderly chairman, vacated his seat next to Landon Vernon and stomped off towards the boardroom.

'He'll take it hard if we lose today.' Landon sighed.

The Wensley were relegation rivals. To lose today with only four matches left before the end of the season was unthinkable.

Mindful of Landon's angina, Bobbie laid a comforting hand on her father's arm.

'Let's go and get a cup of tea.'

★ ★ ★

'I can't think what Ronnie's playing at,' Landon grumbled, banging his cup down irritably on the boardroom table. Ronnie Hubberfield, who had for sometime been manager of the Rogues, was an irascible Northerner, a journeyman footballer who'd made a better fist of managing than he had of a playing career forged following a timely escape from a life down the pits. Bobbie didn't have to try hard to imagine the hairdryer treatment he'd be giving the first team at this moment. Ronnie stood no nonsense from anyone, the players least of all.

'It'll be all right, Dad,' she soothed, knowing he took it personally when the Rogues lost. The eldest of three brothers, he'd received the lion's portion of the shares in the club that Albert had left to his sons. He cared about his football more than anything, even, Bobbie sometimes thought, his family.

'There's always another day,' she added brightly.

'Are you kidding, Bobbie?' he snapped.

He wasn't usually so short-tempered. Her mother would be furious if he went home in this mood but there wasn't much Bobbie could do about it. Landon was in a mood. Eleanor Vernon hated football and had never been able to understand the passions it aroused in the rest of her family.

Bobbie finished her tea, aware that her words sprang from nothing other than a desire to cheer them both up. The truth of the matter was, the club was in a mess, relegation a worrying possibility and the boardroom was filled with rumours of the chief executive's resignation amid a police investigation into club finances. Could things be worse?

Her mouth was already forming the question burning inside her since hints of the affair had first appeared in the morning's papers.

'Don't ask!' Landon forestalled her question heavily. 'The Lord alone knows what we'll do if Alan really has gone.'

'He's been under a lot of pressure, Dad,' she sympathized. As club secretary, she worked with Alan Campion on a day-to-day basis and had seen at first hand the normally easy-going and gentle man turned into a shadow of his former self.

'I wouldn't blame him if he'd had enough.' Landon smiled wryly.

Comforting herself with the thought that she'd find out the truth of the matter soon, Bobbie deftly changed subject.

'At least Paris is keeping the family side up,' she hazarded. 'Come on, Dad, admit it . . . you know you're proud of him.'

'Of course I'm proud of Paris!' Landon sighed. The lad was a hugely talented footballer, a rising star of the England U21 squad and, rumour had it, was on the verge of the full England set-up. Scouts from all the major Premiership clubs were sniffing around. He had a golden future in front of him if only they could keep his highly prized feet firmly anchored to the ground. Which, given the obstacle of his mother . . . Landon's eyes slewed sideways towards Babs, who was standing poised, teacup balanced in one hand, a pale facsimile of her mother, slim-hipped, copper-blonde hair braided and fastened to the top of her delicately shaped head, lending her an air of maturity her father wasn't entirely convinced she possessed. He fingered his chin, his eyes brooding and heavy, musing on the enigma of this, his younger daughter. The original footballer's wife, materialistic, caring too much for the appearances of a thing. Someone had made a thriving concern of the country club hotel she ran with Taylor. And having bailed his son-in-law out on numerous occasions Landon doubted that the success of the Cedars was much down to Taylor. Since retiring as a moderately successful Premiership footballer some three years since, his redoubtable son-in-law had appeared too much concerned with the golf course and the chance to while away an idle hour with the guests, leaving Babs to run the business and make of it what she could.

'Babs is OK, Dad. Stop worrying!' Bobbie frowned and put down her cup. The good and worthy of Rislington Rovers were already beginning to filter towards the directors' box to take their seats for the second half, but if she was quick there was still time for a word with Babs.

She cast a nervous glance towards her sister.

'You pair still not made up yet?' Landon mused.

Bobbie shook her head. The atmosphere had been distinctly frosty since Babs had made Bobbie's son Todd resident golf pro at

The Cedars over Bobbie's head. Todd had jumped at the chance, much to Bobbie's dismay.

'She might have asked me first, Dad,' she moaned softly.

'I know, love, but if he's happy — '

'You know I wanted him to go to Uni! Sam's doing well enough!' she protested. As if she had to! Her daughter was a second-year student at Loughborough, studying sports science. It shouldn't be beyond the realms of fantasy for Todd to follow in her footsteps.

'It's Todd's decision and you have to respect it,' Landon answered, stating the obvious and regarding his daughter steadily. Reluctantly she nodded her head.

'I know.' She shrugged, accepting her disappointment, accepting too that she'd get over it. She'd brought her children up to have confidence in their own decision-making; she could hardly grumble now if they were exercising it.

'I'll be up in a minute, Dad . . . '

She threw him a hopeful smile and made her way towards Babs.

'Todd seems happy?' she began, by way of a peace offering, the smile she proffered genuine. Even Bobbie had to admit the appointment had given her dear wayward son some direction in his life, a relief from the

7

succession of part-time jobs he'd taken on since he'd left school. At least he was trying to make a go of this.

Babs's aqua-green eyes swung in her direction, one well-plucked brow raised high. Of the two women, Babs prided herself she was the more immediately attractive. Trained as a make-up artist in her younger days, she made the best of herself, which was more than Bobbie did, she thought smugly, taking note of the jeans and trainers and baggy jumper which were Bobbie's usual weekend wear.

Bobbie's beauty was an inner one, she had to concede. Tall and slender, there the similarity between the sisters ended. Bobbie's hair, which was thick and curly and exactly like Landon's, was of a dark and luxuriant chestnut-brown; some said it was her best feature. Others, more discerning, noticed her eyes, which were of a compelling blue and of a peculiar luminosity, highlighting a gaze that invited confidence. Complete strangers told Bobbie their life stories. It amused Babs that her big sister couldn't go anywhere without returning with some intimate fact about someone she'd never met before in her life.

'I told you he'd be OK,' she murmured easily. 'You worry too much, Sis.'

She worried too much? When Babs was the

one who never slept at night when Paris was playing — at whatever level?

Bobbie swallowed the put-down springing so readily to her lips. She and Babs had never enjoyed an especially close relationship but this nosedive in their sisterly affections had gone on long enough.

'I only wanted to make sure he knew what he was letting himself in for,' she answered doggedly.

'But Todd's a natural!' Babs urged, glancing at her watch and edging herself towards the door. 'He could make golf big-time, Bobbie. You should be proud of him, not stand in his way.'

'Of course I'm proud of him!' Despite all her good intentions a note of bitterness crept into Bobbie's voice. How dare Babs say she was standing in Todd's way? Like any mother she only wanted the best. 'Golf isn't the most stable of occupations,' she went on stubbornly. 'I'd rather he'd got a good education, something to fall back on.'

'Paris hasn't anything to fall back on!' There was no mistaking the icy level to which Babs' voice had descended.

'Babs, Paris is different . . . '

'You mean he's not an intellectual?'

'That's not what I meant!'

It was hopeless. Bobbie regarded her sister

sorrowfully. She'd come to make up and here they were falling out already. She took a deep breath, forcing herself to calm down.

'Paris has such a natural talent; he was never going to be anything other than a footballer.'

At last she'd hit the right note. Babs visibly relaxed.

'I've been on tenterhooks all afternoon,' she confessed.

'There was simply no need.' Bobbie touched her arm gently, a gesture of sisterly solidarity. 'He's the best Rislington player by a country mile. I don't know what we'd do without him, Babs.'

He couldn't carry the team on his own, that was the problem. For once the glances the two women exchanged were sympathetic, giving a hint of how things had once been. Whatever their differences and whatever the root causes — and Bobbie never had got to the root cause of it — they both cared passionately for the future well-being of this football club.

A groan from the largely partisan crowd informed them that the second half was already under way. Babs bolted to her seat, leaving Bobbie to follow more slowly. She sat down to watch in tight-lipped misery as the leaky Rogues defence conceded a further brace. Her mind wandered to the following day and Landon's birthday celebrations, to be held at Cedars and over which Eleanor, in love with Landon if not his love of football, had been in cahoots with Babs for weeks. Much as Eleanor enjoyed the chance of bringing the family together, Bobbie knew full well, that her father was dreading the day. She leaned across and squeezed his arm affectionately, receiving an amused glance for her pains. Landon hated fuss and would have been far happier with a quiet family gathering at home.

Like mother like daughter, Bobbie sighed. Knowing Babs, and even given the fact that it was family, every napkin would be already folded, the champagne flutes polished to gleaming, the cutlery laid out precisely.

Her gaze shifted to the stand below, instantly picking out her daughter Sam's slim figure. As chance would have it, at that moment Sam Vernon looked up, catching Bobbie's eye and shrugging in hopeless resignation. Bobbie waved, smiling encouragement.

At least Sam was giving her no cause for concern, she thought contentedly, remembering how determined she'd been to take on the holiday job that Bobbie had found for her at the club. Her well-meant endeavours weren't

11

strictly necessary. Even if Bobbie hadn't been left so comfortably off following her divorce settlement, Landon would have been only too pleased to step in and support her. Sam wouldn't hear of it.

'How can I make the most of university life if I don't experience it to the full? Part of that's learning how to make ends meet.' How determined she'd looked. How much she reminded Bobbie of herself!

Eventually and to their mutual satisfaction they'd reached a compromise. Sam was to be left peaceably alone to make her own way with the proviso that she was to tell her mother the moment any difficulty, of whatever nature, arose. She was sensible. Bobbie had every confidence that that was precisely what she would do.

'Sam brought her boots?' Landon chuckled, giving up on the match too and angling towards her.

'I wish she had,' Bobbie admitted, surprised he'd made a joke about his granddaughter's starring role in the university football team. As a rule, Landon Vernon didn't agree with girls playing football. But this was Sam, upon whom he doted! She'd won him round eventually even if he'd rather have died than admit it.

The full-time whistle blew, greeted by a

further chorus of boos. An empty coke can flew towards the directors' box, clattering harmlessly into the aisle at Bobbie's feet. Two uniformed constables, positioned against such an eventuality, moved swiftly into the crowd.

'Are you ready, love?' Landon was on his feet.

'Don't worry, Dad! It was just some stupid hot-head . . . '

At least they had the satisfaction of seeing the man, middle-aged and surprisingly respectable-looking, removed from the ground. By the looks on the angry faces turned their way, there were plenty more to take his place.

'Proudfoot out! Proudfoot out!' came the not altogether unexpected response.

'I suppose it had to be me or Ronnie!' Jimmy heaved himself to his feet.

'I wouldn't like to be in Ronnie's shoes when Jimmy gets hold of him,' Landon muttered, seizing Bobbie's arm and marshalling her down the gangway.

They drove home in silence.

★ ★ ★

'Had a good afternoon?'

Eleanor Vernon glanced up briefly before pouring omelette mixture into the pan.

Chopped chives, basil. The kitchen was warm with the aroma of the bread she'd baked earlier.

At thoughts of her practical mother caring one iota what sort of an afternoon her daughter and husband had when she knew perfectly well where they'd spent it, Bobbie's brows rose.

Landon had gone upstairs to change. Eleanor's gaze followed him questioningly.

'Are you staying for supper?'

Bobbie shook her head.

'I'm taking Sam and some friends back to Loughborough to a dance, thanks. I only called to see if you're all set for tomorrow.'

'You do too much running about.' Her mother frowned. 'And yes, of course we're set for tomorrow. Babs has things perfectly organized.'

'As usual!' Bobbie grinned. She leaned forward, dropping a light kiss on her mother's cheek. 'Good job you have at least one reliable daughter.'

'You know that's not what I meant,' Eleanor scolded, musing whether now was the right time to impart what was on her mind. She carried the salad bowl across to the table. There was a conversation she'd been meaning to have for some time if only Bobbie weren't always so absorbed in her

14

blessed football. 'Bobbie, I know you've a lot going on in your life and there's not always time to think about yourself,' she began carefully, smiling to soften the impact of what she was saying. 'It's just I worry about you being on your own so much, especially now that Todd and Sam are off your hands. I wish you'd settle down. Find yourself someone nice?'

A lecture about men or, rather, the lack of them in her life. Bobbie leaned back against the work surface and folded her arms, regarding her mother thoughtfully. 'Don't you think my experience with Gerry was enough?' she answered quietly. Her divorce from Gerald Mansfield had happened years since, reflecting what had become a wretchedly cold and empty marriage. And for now? She had a good social life and occasional men friends and that was as far as it went. As far as she ever meant it to go, and her dear mother knew this perfectly well. 'I couldn't bear marriage again, Mum!' she added, resigned to having to explain things yet again. 'Gerry became so work-orientated. He couldn't have cared less about me or the children.'

'Gerry had too many fingers in too many pies.'

'You can say that again!'

'Don't be so bitter!' Briskly Eleanor cut the

15

omelette in half, easing the pieces out on to two plates. 'One bad experience shouldn't put you off for life,' she murmured. 'It was Gerry's loss darling! Take your dad and me — '

'Not everyone's as lucky as you and dad.'

She was adamant, stubborn as ever and she'd no need to wonder where she'd inherited that particular trait! Eleanor sighed a little wearily and went to the foot of the stairs to call Landon down to his supper.

★   ★   ★

'Are you ready, love?'

Eleanor reached up to give Landon's tie a final tweak. On the polished dining room table, by which they stood enjoying the best of the afternoon sunshine that was pouring through the large bay windows, stood the elegant wine-decanter she'd bought for his birthday. The cards were displayed, bowls of flowers were filling the house with a heady perfume reminiscent of their wedding day. She'd pushed the boat out, but this was a special day and she'd wanted to make sure he enjoyed it.

'Give over fussing,' he grumbled, catching her wrists, his expression enigmatic.

'Grouch,' she retorted, smiling, wondering

how to answer his mood and quickly deciding light-hearted was best. 'You are having a good day, darling?'

'So far . . . ' he admitted begrudgingly, then, thinking better of it, stooping to give this still attractive woman a large and satisfying kiss.

She leaned in against him. The world receded, their troubles with it; Vernon Lodge was settling into the torpor of what was turning into a surprising warm April Sunday afternoon. As if even the sun had come out to celebrate the day.

'I'm surprised you still want a kiss from such an old man,' he teased, lifting her head between his two broad hands and staring down into her face, looking to Eleanor exactly like the earnest young accountant who'd first swept her off her feet. She'd loved him at once. She'd always loved him.

'Of course I still want a kiss, darling! As many as you wish to give me!' She stood back, surveying him critically. 'Landon, you would tell me if there was something wrong? You were so quiet when you got back from the match.'

'We lost, remember?' he retorted, wondering why, after all this time, he still had to point it out.

Eleanor pulled a face. Football! What

exactly was its pull and fascination? If only she could understand!

Landon always insisted his health was fine. He suffered from a little heart trouble, nothing to concern himself with; he left that to the doctors. He had his pills which he used intermittently and as a last resort. He stuck rigidly to the diet advised. Play the whole thing down was his way of dealing with it and who should say him wrong?

She kept an eye on him all the same.

They locked up and went outside to the MG parked outside the double garage. Eleanor drove. Landon's Jag was in the garage for a service and she wanted him to relax. There was little traffic. After a short time they pulled up outside the three storeyed and white-stoned façade of The Cedars and hurried inside to the function room where a sea of familiar faces, cheering loudly, greeted their appearance. Beside her she felt Landon's body tense.

'You'll be OK,' she whispered, reaching for his hand.

He puffed out his cheeks, overcome by the goodwill, raised glasses and birthday greetings flowing his way. There were balloons, a pile of presents, a banner stretching the breadth of the French windows, which were flung invitingly open and offering a view of the rolling greens beyond. He was annoyed now that he hadn't wanted to come, hadn't wanted this day. But why should he wish to be reminded of the fact that he was sixty, his best days behind him?

Looking round the crowded room he wondered how he could be anything other than optimistic! How wonderful that these young people were around to carry on the family name. The family traditions! His face spread into a wide smile. They'd all thought enough of him to give up their time.

★   ★   ★

'I told you you'd enjoy it once you got here.' Eleanor reached up to plant a warm kiss on his cheek, her hand lingering invitingly on his arm. The meal had been eaten and cleared away, the presents opened, the birthday cake cut. The family, enjoying a break from routine, were relaxing, wandering in and out on to the patio to admire the view and watch a round of golf whilst finishing off the last of the champagne.

'Want another, Sis?' Todd Vernon, tall and athletic and looking every inch the golf pro he so desperately wanted to become, waved a bottle of Krug invitingly over Sam's half-empty glass.

19

'Best not!' she cried laughing, quickly covering the elegant flute-shaped glass with her hand. 'They're short-handed in accounts. I've an early start in the morning.' She pulled a face, not knowing whether the dry and dusty accounts office was exactly where she wanted to be. Of late she'd become a maid of all trades. The supporters' shop, the ticket-office, promotions ... It had been a real eye-opener. To Sam's impatiently youthful mind, the whole set-up at Rislington Rovers football club needed dragging into the twenty-first century. No wonder things were so wrong on the pitch when they were so patently wrong everywhere else. Her gaze wandered across the crowded room to the good-looking figure of her cousin Paris, an expression of glee flitting across her face.

'I see Paris is enjoying himself as usual,' she laughed. They'd both been surprised that he'd deigned to attend what, after all, was a quiet family occasion. Hardly Paris's scene! True to form he'd turned up with a pretty girl on either arm, causing general murmurs of condemnation. Aunty Babs was spitting bricks. Sam guessed he'd be in trouble the moment she managed to prise him away from his entourage. No wonder he was in the process of buying a penthouse suite in nearby Nottingham. No wonder he couldn't wait to branch out on his own! Sam wouldn't want her Aunty Babs watching her every move either. Sometimes she almost felt sorry for Paris.

'Do you think mum's all right?' Her face softened. Bobbie was flitting amongst the guests with more champagne, filling glasses and chatting and seeing everyone was all right. A role she usually played in family get-togethers. She ought to think about herself more. 'She must get lonely,' she mused thoughtfully. 'I wish she'd find someone else, Todd. A man to put a little happiness back into her life.'

'I guess she would if she wanted.' Todd frowned, not altogether sure that that was what he wanted for her.

'I always hoped she'd get back with Dad!' Sam blurted out, sounding defiant.

She'd never understood why her father had high-tailed it to Spain leaving his family high and dry. A venture into the Spanish property market was the official explanation but there'd been far more to it than that. She and Todd had been young children, barely starting primary school at the time. She remembered her mother, increasingly isolated and left to bring them up alone. Even now Sam could remember the rows — or more often the silences, which had been even worse.

She'd asked her father, on one of their increasingly infrequent visits to south-western Spain. He'd been his usual evasive self, typically muttering something about how they'd been simply incompatible. No one's fault, Sam was to understand, just one of those painful things.

They hadn't seen him for months. He was busy. They were busy. It seemed to Sam that it was the unhappy end to a relationship going nowhere.

'I just want her to be happy,' she murmured. 'She's capable of so much more than a tin-pot little job and worrying herself silly over us.'

'Grandad's always extolling her virtues,' Todd prompted.

'She's taken advantage of!' Sam retorted fiercely, tossing back her thick dark hair in an action so reminiscent of their mother, that he couldn't help but smile.

'OK Sis! Our mother's wonder woman.'

'Wonder woman, indeed,' Babs Pryce-Martin muttered mutinously, turning her back so she wouldn't hear more of a conversation she'd never intended to listen in on in the first place. Taylor was unnaturally quiet and, inadvertently, she'd caught the tail end of Sam's words. They'd discomfited her, that much was obvious. Taylor lodged his glass on the fine mock-Adam stone fireplace and put his arms around her waist.

'Babs, when exactly are you going to grow up? You and Bobbie are chalk and cheese. Be proud of the success you've made of your life. Gracious, woman, you married me!'

'That's just it . . . This place is based on your success!' Babs frowned, glancing around, her lips pouting into a familiar expression of discontent. The Cedars had been built on Taylor's money when he'd retired, enough to set them both up for life.

He grinned and Babs's heart flipped over. He was still a good-looking man, retaining the power to attract admiring glances wherever they went. So far she'd managed to keep his gaze from wandering.

She sighed, acknowledging she ought not to feel this way. He'd never given her cause to feel so insecure . . . yet. Taylor loved her, but when they'd first got together he'd had a string of beautiful and successful girlfriends. She'd never convinced herself she was quite good enough.

'We both know the driving force round this place, much as you try to hide your light under a bushel!' Taylor's keen blue eyes narrowed at the familiar sulky expression settling over his wife's face. 'Spit it out,' he coaxed.

23

'Oh, it's nothing!' she burst out petulantly. His brows rose.

'OK.' She laughed, holding up her hands, accepting the truth of what he'd been trying so hard to tell her. 'Of course it's something . . . '

'Babs . . . ' He was beginning to lose interest, the last thing she wanted.

'All my life Dad's thought more of Bobbie,' she blurted out, speaking in a rush, whilst she still had the courage. It was nothing new. Taylor knew exactly how envious she felt towards Bobbie.

'Haven't we been here before?' he groaned.

'It doesn't make it easier!' she snapped, frustrated. 'Trust Bobbie! Perfect life, perfect children — '

'That's not exactly fair,' Taylor pointed out, his gaze settling on Paris and the coterie of females by whom he was surrounded. A smile illuminated Taylor's face. 'Your son has the talent to become England's next centre-forward for the next ten years if only he doesn't get sidetracked.'

'He won't be sidetracked!' A doting smile flitted across Babs's face. Paris had more talent than Sam and Todd put together. He was bound for fame, for the sporting history books if his mother had anything to do with it.

'Would you like more champagne, Dad?' Bobbie angled her tray, bearing the one solitary glass, under her father's nose. Landon Vernon grinned.

'Best not love . . . Two glasses only, the doctor said. I don't want your mother breathing down my neck.'

Disengaging herself from one of her numerous god-children, with whose life she'd been bringing herself up to date, Eleanor swung round. Her husband threw up his hands in submission.

'Don't worry! I'm doing exactly as I'm told.' He had no other option. He grinned, looking instantly boyish, turning away and, in one swift movement unburdening Bobbie of her tray and seizing her arm. 'Now's not exactly the time to be talking business but . . . as I said, Jimmy rang me this morning to confirm Alan's resignation.'

'Landon!' Eleanor warned.

'The chief executive's resigning has really left us in a hole,' he went on, regardless of the interruption. Sometimes the way to deal with Eleanor, the only way to deal with Eleanor, was simply to ignore her. 'I've half a mind to take on the role myself.'

This time she wouldn't be ignored. She reached for his arm and pulled him round, incensed to discover he was laughing. She could have shaken him.

'Landon Vernon, you'll do no such thing! What do you imagine Eric Wright would have to say?'

'He's my doctor, love. He wouldn't say I had to give up on life altogether.'

'He wouldn't agree with you taking on more than ever, either,' she scolded. 'You're meant to be winding down, or have you forgotten?'

Landon cast a beseeching glance towards Bobbie, but if he was expecting support he was sadly disappointed. For once Bobbie looked the image of her mother. Landon's heart sank.

'What a crazy idea, Dad!' she exploded, unable to believe what she'd just heard.

Alan Campion's position had been the most stressful in the club. If her dear stubborn father thought for one moment she was going to agree to him stepping into such a situation . . .

★   ★   ★

'Have you any comment to make about the position of Alan Campion at the club, Mr Vernon? Our readers would like to know if there's truth in the rumour he's resigned . . .'

The reporter was young, brash and out to

get his story. Biting down the retort that their readers could go think what they liked; Landon placed firm hands on Bobbie's shoulders and propelled her through the throng of assorted reporters, photographers and various hangers-on positioned outside the entrance to the club. Flashlights exploded. 'There'll be a statement after this morning's board meeting,' he called over his shoulder. Freddie Vinter, the door man, smart in his burgundy and gold-braided uniform, ushered them quickly inside the glass-fronted foyer and shoved the door shut.

'I see you've met the welcoming committee,' he commented drily, turning to stand, arms folded, guarding their retreat. He had been an ex-player down on his luck and Landon had secured him a job at the club for life. Once a Rogue, always a Rogue, according to Landon. Freddie was eternally grateful.

'I didn't know Alan's resignation was going to cause this furore,' Bobbie groaned, crossing the marble foyer slightly in front of her father. 'He wouldn't have guessed what he was letting himself in for.' Poor Alan! Press interest outside his home on the outskirts of Rislington would be equally intense and she was sorry for it. She didn't blame him for what had happened but she had to agree with Landon, his abrupt exit had left them high

27

and dry. The job of chief executive involved every aspect of the football club. It needed sorting and quickly.

Jimmy Proudfoot was already in the boardroom, in conversation with Ray Lovett, a self-made millionaire who'd been co-opted on to the board when the club was relegated, his injection of cash a desperately needed lifeline. The other directors, making up the complement of eight, began to filter in, looking variously harassed.

'Can we call this meeting to order?' Jimmy thumped a large fist down on the table.

Bobbie read the minutes to which she was aware no one was paying particular attention. Everyone was too strung up; the air was thick with cigar smoke and a barely suppressed excitement. As she glanced up quickly her gaze fell on the framed sepia print of Grandad Albert captured in full flight, scoring the winning goal in the Rogues' one and only Cup Final success. Once he'd retired from football Albert had gone on to make a fortune in scrap metal, enough to buy shares in his beloved football club. He'd been a character, by all accounts, one of the original Rogues, four members of the first team who'd celebrated their cup win in an over-exuberant style, resulting in a sobering night spent in a London nick. The local paper welcomed them home with the headlines, 'Rislington Rogues Released for Cup Parade'. The name had stuck. Grandad never had lived that one down, though, to be fair, he'd never touched a drop of drink after it.

'I suppose you've all seen the headlines?' Scowling, Jimmy Proudfoot lifted the local paper from the table. Grandad faded back to his photograph.

'That rubbish?' Landon hooked his thumbs in his braces and rocked back in his chair. 'Papers like to kick you when you're down, Jimmy. Take it with a pinch of salt, lad.'

There was a general murmur of agreement.

Jimmy fingered his chin, glancing shrewdly round the faces turned so expectantly in his direction.

'There's no denying the truth,' he stated. 'It's bound to affect our finances if we're relegated into division one. Gates are down, the fans up in arms and forming protest groups. There's scarcely enough in the coffers to pay the players' wages. No wonder folk are wondering where the money's gone. No wonder the police are sniffing round — '

'They'll not find a thing Mr Chairman!' Brendon Mills, Director of Finance bridled instantly. 'I've been through those books with a fine-tooth comb.'

'Calm down, lad,' Jimmy butted in

smoothly. 'No one's accusing you. I'm just sorry Alan's chosen now to jump ship. It doesn't look good, that's all I'm meaning.' His voice rose a decibel, commanding attention. 'We need to rectify the situation and quickly. Any suggestions?'

There was a brief but pregnant pause. Everyone was on the ball this morning, riveted by the nosedive in their collective fortunes. There was nothing like hard times to bring the board together.

'Alan won't be coming back,' Landon pointed out. 'It isn't fair to ask him. The investigation's left him a broken man.'

'New blood then?' Brendon suggested.

'How could we possibly attract new blood? We haven't the money . . . '

'It would have to be in-house,' Layton Thomas, director of football growled.

'Whoever would want to take this mess on?'

'Have you taken all this down, Bobbie?'

'Yes, of course I have, Mr — '

'Good girl! Knew I could depend on you! It's great to have someone who'll do exactly as they're told!'

Jimmy thumped his fist on the table, making Bobbie jump.

'I've heard enough!' he bawled. 'I'll sum it up, shall I? We need someone bright, someone with fresh ideas who knows this club enough to want to roll up their sleeves and get stuck in!'

'A paragon, you mean?' Landon laughed drily and without the slightest trace of humour.

Jimmy ploughed on, ignoring the interruption. He glanced round the table, a broad smile springing to his lips.

'We need something to make the press jump! I'll give 'em a story to fill the papers if that's what they're after.' He rocked back in his chair, his expression hardening. 'I'll tell you exactly what we're going to do.'

★ ★ ★

'What news on the Chief Executive front, Mr Chairman . . . this way if you please Mr Chairman . . . would you care to expand on the difficulties at the club . . . any message for the fans . . . ' This last from Corby Henderson, sports reporter for the *Green 'Un* and the *Rislington Evening Telegraph*, shouldering his way through what was fast developing into a rugby scrum.

Jimmy Proudfoot stood at the head of the steps outside the entrance, blinking heavily under the glare of the camera lights from both Sky Television and the BBC. The commentator from Radio 5 Live jammed a microphone under his nose. Jimmy threw up his hands in resignation.

'Gentlemen, please! The club has prepared a statement . . . '

Landon stood glowering by his side, one arm pressed protectively in the small of Bobbie's back. Brendan Mills and Sam Lovett brought up the rear, representative of a united board. The thought made Landon want to laugh out loud! His head was still reeling from the shock of the last two hours. He glanced down at Bobbie, registering that she was as pale as a sheet. Jimmy thrust his hands easily into his pockets and smiled broadly, savouring every moment.

'I'd like to confirm that Alan Campion offered his resignation to me here, yesterday,' he began, 'and that I accepted on behalf of the board. Gentlemen, I'm sure you'll join the board in thanking him for all his efforts on behalf of the club.'

'Have you a replacement in mind yet, Mr Chairman . . . does Alan Campion leave under any kind of a cloud . . . Mr Chairman, how can the club possibly attract new blood given the precarious nature of your financial affairs . . . ?'

The clamour broke out anew and this time

was seemingly unstoppable. Jimmy held up his hands again, his smile this time only a little more fixed.

'Come on, lads! You know better than this!' he commanded. 'Alan Campion leaves under no kind of a cloud whatsoever and only with the club's good wishes. And as to a replacement . . . ' He halted, brows raised, as ever the consummate showman, leaving the pause only long enough to maximize dramatic effect. His gaze swept theatrically to his right. 'You tell 'em!' he crowed to no one in particular. 'You might as well get used to it . . . '

Eyes swung amazed towards Landon who only shook his head. To a collective gasp of astonishment, Bobbie stepped forward to stand, blinking nervously in the glare of camera lights. For one long and terrible moment the panic that had been hovering since Jimmy Proudfoot had first mooted the idea of her taking over the role of chief executive threatened to overwhelm her completely.

'Gentlemen . . . ' Her voice emerged as a croak, nothing like her own.

She stopped and took a deep breath, trying desperately to still the trembling that had started somewhere in her legs and was now in the process of working its way up the whole length of her body.

'Gentlemen, I'm as surprised as you so obviously are that this morning the board has offered me the appointment of chief executive . . . '

'And you've accepted?' Someone laughed, his incredulity patently obvious.

A barrage of guffaws followed. These largely hard-nosed reporters were only too ready to see her fall flat on her face. She could see the headlines already.

The pressure of Landon's hand behind her back gently increased, offering her whatever strength he could. Where was her family pride — her belief in family tradition? In the silence that followed came the sound of Ronnie Hubberfield taking the first team for training on the Rislington Park pitch. His voice sounded as though he were harassed, at the end of his tether.

Some kind of a resolve came to her rescue. The team depended on her. This football club depended on her!

'Of course I've accepted,' she retorted angrily. 'I hail from a background of proud family tradition in the service of Rislington Rovers and I shall do everything in my power to ensure the future stability and well-being of this football club . . . Survival's the aim! Next season we mean to press on . . . a top ten finish . . . the play-off's the season after.' In other words, Premiership here we come! She paused, her voice shaking with emotion. 'Gentlemen! As from now, this club is on the way up!'

A barrage of camera flashes erupted over a cacophony of voices as the press advanced and surrounded her. She gasped, the panic she'd somehow kept at bay returning with renewed vigour. What moment of madness could possibly have encouraged her to agree to one iota of this? She'd be a laughing-stock . . . she'd merely prove every man jack of them only too right in their chauvinistic posturing . . .

She found a smile from somewhere. However she felt, whatever the media happened to think of it, she'd meant every word she said.

2

'I'd given you up, Landon!' Eleanor Vernon slid her hands into oven gloves and carried the casserole dish carefully across the kitchen to the table. Boeuf Bourguignon, Landon's favourite. Wine, candlelight. He whistled appreciatively.

'We deserve a treat,' she asserted, answering the question before it was asked. Briskly, she spooned it out on to plates, her cheeks glowing, a phenomenon not just down to the warmth of the kitchen. She had something to discuss, a growing excitement which had seen her running to the door several times already, imagining the sound of his car. Sensing it, Landon poured the wine, threw off his jacket and pulled out a chair. A fine spring evening spilled through the kitchen door, which was propped open, allowing the scent of the daphnes and hyacinth to drift in from the garden, mingling with the warm candlelight flickering on the walls of this, the kitchen, the core of Eleanor's life. Landon's hands were curled around his glass, acknowledging how much he always looked forward to this moment. He loved the effort Eleanor put into the domestic side of their lives. He was a lucky man and told himself so constantly.

'Busy day?' she asked, putting his plate in front of him, not taking her own until she was assured he was starting to eat.

'Mmm, something like that,' he agreed through a mouthful of the casserole, which was delicious, as usual. 'The police investigation's riling everyone. It hardly makes for a good atmosphere about the place.' The inquiry was ongoing and complicated and he was beginning to wonder where it was heading.

Eleanor frowned, not wanting this conversation, not sure how to deflect it, discontent surfacing as to why their lives were so firmly linked to football which, as a subject, failed to capture her interest.

'Do you want to tell me what this is about?' Landon teased, reading her exactly, flapping one broad hand at the table with which she'd obviously taken so much care.

Eleanor smiled, at last letting her excitement bubble over.

'I went to Susie's for coffee this morning,' she began eagerly.

Susie Lamoure's husband, Eddie, was an entrepreneur who'd made his fortune through computer software and Lamoure Logistics into a world-famous brand. The two women had met through Eleanor's work for a local children's charity. Eleanor had needed space for a projected fête — the grounds to Susie's manor house had provided it, leading to an unlikely friendship. Even Landon was impressed by Eleanor's moving in such highflying circles nowadays. She took a deep breath, hoping he was in a good mood.

'She was wondering if we'd like to spend some time on their yacht in the Mediterranean. A house party. Nothing too grand, of course . . . ' She spoke too fast, her hands folding around her wineglass, allowing her gaze to drop resolutely into its depths.

The silence lengthened. Why wouldn't he speak — say something at least?

'A business associate of Eddie's dropped out,' she murmured, frowning, deciding she might as well tell him the whole of it. 'Susie asked if we'd like to fill in, that's all. It seems a shame if the places are going begging? I said I'd discuss it with you . . . see what you thought?'

Landon put down his glass, trying not to show he was thinking furiously how he could get out of it. Eleanor's excitement crashed over him in waves. But she knew how he felt about sailing! And yet . . . His gaze softened. It wasn't so much to ask. He could surely put up with so much, if only for her sake.

'Is there anything to discuss?' he teased, partly wondering if there was more and hoping vainly that that was all.

'It is rather short notice,' she went on quietly.

'How short?' he returned, equally quietly.

Eleanor's gaze fixed on his.

'They're flying out to Le Havre Friday. Eddie's private jet.'

Landon took a steadying swallow of wine. So that was it! That was the reason for the wine, the special effort.

'Have you forgotten about the match on Saturday?' His blunt features darkened, any chance of their taking the Lamoures up on their offer disappearing instantly.

'Oh, the match!' Perceiving her plans so easily dismissed, Eleanor's voice was heavy with sarcasm. 'Landon, please don't tell me you're going to throw up this chance because of the blasted football?' she pleaded.

'It's the last match of the season. We've got to win it. Of course I've got to be there!' Surely she understood?

'They'll win or lose whether you're there or not, Landon!' she retorted, proving she patently didn't understand. She put down her knife and fork, all pleasure in the occasion vanished. Football! The thorn in their married lives. Landon ran a hand through

39

hair which, if threaded with grey, was still as thick as ever.

'Eleanor, I'm a director,' he explained tiredly, not understanding why he still had to. 'I can't go swanning around the Mediterranean and miss a match of such importance. I simply can't.'

'That's it then, we won't go!' She sprang to her feet, gathering the plates, stalking across the kitchen and tumbling them into the sink, her back rigid with disappointment. She ran the tap, then returned to blow out the candles. 'I hate football.'

'I know you do.'

'Look what it's . . . you've done to Bobbie!'

'What's Bobbie to do with this?' He frowned, losing her thought process. As so often happened, the argument was broadening, moving away from its central theme. All the little resentments she'd been harbouring tumbled out together.

'I mean landing her with the chief executive's job, Landon. How could you!' Her voice was full of accusation.

'I didn't land her with it! Besides . . . it's good, isn't it?' He hooked his thumbs in his braces, rocking back in his chair. She'd been so quiet about Bobbie's new appointment. He could see why now.

Eleanor folded her arms, unable to believe

40

he was being so obtuse when he knew how badly she'd been affected by the break-up of Bobbie's marriage. How she longed for her to settle down! 'This job will be the finish of her,' she concluded sadly.

'You're wrong! Bobbie's thrilled to — '

'Bobbie doesn't know what's good for her.'

'And you do?'

'I'm her mother.'

There was no answer to that, other than that he was her father and that gave him rights too. He was also a diplomat, and Eleanor had a temper when riled. He took a deep and calming breath. They were coming at this from too obtuse an angle. Eleanor was desperately keen to go on this cruise. He felt guilty for inadvertently spoiling her plans. There should be a way round it somewhere. He reached for the wine and refilled their glasses.

'I'm really sorry I can't go,' he said cautiously. 'But there's nothing to stop you. Why don't you go on your own?'

'Go without you?' Eleanor's voice had descended to a whisper.

He should have taken the hint but he was too taken up with the idea, the obvious solution. He beamed happily, his belief in the evening thoroughly restored. 'There'll be some loose ends to tie up at the club. You know what it's like, the end of the season. I should be free by . . . let's see . . . Wednesday? Thursday at the latest! If you can get an itinerary from Susie, I could fly out and join you then.'

His smile was expressive of his general contentment. There'd been a disagreement. Here was the perfect solution! Eleanor's lips tightened perceptibly.

'I might just do that,' she answered quietly. The atmosphere dropped even further until even Landon was aware of it. His smile faded.

'You'll have a wonderful time, love.'

'Of course I will,' she replied. 'I can see you'll be far too busy to join us. Don't worry. I'll be quite all right on my own.'

Reining in her dignity, smarting with pain, she stalked from the room, only just resisting the impulse to slam the door. She wouldn't give him satisfaction!

Listening to her heavy tread upstairs, her indignation ringing in every step, Landon swallowed the rest of his wine in one gulp, comprehension dawning that he'd dropped himself in it — again, something he'd been doing far too much lately.

★   ★   ★

'Ready yet?' Sam poked her head round the office door, eyes widening at sight of her mother's plush new working environment; it was the first time she'd seen it. Following Alan Campion's resignation the decorators had been in; the room now boasted several shades of pastel. A deep leather sofa and vases of fresh spring flowers completed the picture. It beat the dingy ticket-office where Sam had spent the first day of her spring break from university. She stood, watching Bobbie fondly, aware considerable strings had already been pulled to ensure she would have a job here for the summer vacation, too.

From under the welter of paperwork scattered over the desk came a deep sigh.

'Sorry, love. It looks like I'll be working late.'

'I ought to be used to being a latchkey kid by now!' Sam's voice was high on irony, the glances the two women exchanged acknowledging the truth in her teasing. It was her first day and here was Bobbie, already too busy to exchange pleasantries.

'Love, I'm sorry,' Bobbie muttered. 'But I've already said that, haven't I?'

'I'll see you later!' Sam grinned before withdrawing her head and retreating down the corridor, aware, despite her assurances to the contrary, of a growing concern. Even Todd, living in at The Cedars, worried over the effect this so shocking new appointment was having on their mother's life. Late nights, skipped meals, up to her eyes in all things football. Everything her brother had warned Sam about was coming true.

She called a cheery goodnight to Fred, and made her way across the car park. If only her granddad Landon had thought properly before agreeing to such a crazy appointment. Bobbie had scarcely had time to surface. And at her age too!

The thought made Sam smile. According to Gran, her mother was still young enough to settle down and find herself a new man!

As she was fumbling in her bag for the keys to her Nissan, a present from Landon, out of place amongst the general assemblage of Porsches, Jags and sports cars littering the car park, she was joined by Paris, who had detached himself with difficulty from a crowd of teenage girls demanding autographs.

'How's life treating my favourite cousin?' he teased, swinging the keys to his BMW nonchalantly round one finger. Life was too good for Paris, Sam considered, thinking of some of her university friends and how they struggled simply to get by. Paris, on the other hand, had the sort of good looks that made teenage girls swoon and a job most young men would die for, paying more money than he knew what to do with. How was that fair?

She worried about Paris.

'No need to ask how life's treating you?' She smiled, reserving the best of it for George Carter, the young reserve team player who'd followed Paris out through the foyer, remembering, shyly, the last time she'd seen him had been at the players' official Christmas party. He'd asked her to dance. She'd accepted, not knowing how to get out of it, staying with him for a few moments only before excusing herself. She really had promised to help out with the refreshments but she could tell he'd been disappointed at the time. He was a nice guy but a footballer too, she reminded herself. Coming from such a football-orientated family she had no intention of embroiling herself with anyone to the remotest degree attached to the sport.

'It's good to see you again, Sam,' George uttered warmly.

She hadn't imagined his reaction at the party. He *was* blushing.

'Good to see you too, George,' she admitted, surprised to see him in Paris's company. George was the steady sort, keen to work hard in training and seize his chance when it came along. Unlike Paris, who had so much natural talent he hardly had to lift a little finger. Perhaps her wayward cousin was seeing sense at last. She could always hope!

'No time to stand here chatting, children' Paris interrupted, throwing an arm round his teammate's shoulder. 'We've a hot date. Several hot dates if our luck's in!'

George frowned.

'We're only going for a drink. Sam can join us if she likes?'

The invitation was plain in his eyes and momentarily she was tempted.

'I'm whacked actually, George,' she murmured reluctantly, trying to let him down gently. 'I've had a really busy day. Best get an early night.' It was an untruth and they both knew it, the ticket-office had been pretty quiet.

'It isn't as if we need any woman cramping our style. We're off to the new nightclub down town . . . ' Paris interjected, good-naturedly. The prospect was evidently news to George.

'You do know there's a match, Satur-day . . . ?' He frowned.

'And Ronnie likes you tucked up in bed early,' Sam added swiftly; feeling she had to, even if, knowing Paris, she was aware it wouldn't do the slightest good. Spoilt, egoistical, selfish sprang too easily to mind.

'Tucked up's exactly where I mean to be!' Paris's too handsome face creased, the ready grin exploding in a paroxysm of mirth before he dragged George off across the car park towards his car. Immediately, the gaggle of teenage girls who'd been hovering nearby ran after them.

'I'll look after him!' George called over his shoulder, shrugging helplessly but laughing now too.

She hoped Paris wasn't leading George astray. Her cousin was incorrigible and it was about time he grew up.

She drove home thinking about George and the white lie she'd told him, even if it was true she was feeling tired. Home, she had a shower and fixed herself a light supper before retiring straight to bed, leaving Bobbie a ham salad on a plate and the remains of the bottle of wine they'd shared the previous evening. Her head had no sooner hit the pillow than she dropped into a deep slumber, dead to the world, dead to Bobbie's return and the contented supper sounds emanating from the kitchen. Oblivious, she slumbered on, immersed in a dream in which she was trapped in the ticket-office by an unending queue of fans demanding tickets at a rate she couldn't possibly supply. They were becoming angry, hammering at the serving hatch. She was hot, bothered, with a growing feeling the walls were pressing in.

'I'm working as fast as I can!' she cried,

sitting upright in bed, the centre of her being still clinging remorselessly to her dream world. The knocking increased in intensity. Somewhere it registered, dawn was creeping through the curtains, the luminous hands of her alarm clock were pointing to the ungodly hour of 5.35 and there really was someone knocking — at the front door.

Half-asleep still, she stumbled out of bed, reaching for her dressing-gown.

'Paris?' She stared at him groggily, only partly registering his dishevelled state and that he was still wearing the suit he'd worn the previous evening, albeit now crumpled. He'd been drinking too. She wrinkled her nose as he bundled the early edition of the morning's papers into her arms and marched past her, through the hall and into the kitchen.

'Haven't you been to bed yet?' she cried, rushing after him.

'I wish I had!' he wailed, deathly pale and spinning round to face her. She had no idea what could have happened. 'I wish I had listened to you and gone home,' he muttered more calmly, running a hand through his hair as Sam dropped the papers on to the table and began to read the headline on the top copy.

It didn't take much understanding. 'Rogues

star in fracas outside nightclub!' The words jumped from the page. There was the picture to prove it too, though what canny bystander had been quick-witted enough to snap a distinctly the-worse-for-wear Paris, aiming a misguided punch at a burly nightclub bouncer, beggared comprehension. The worried face of George Carter looked on: a man astonished by what he was witnessing and had no idea what to do. So much for his promise to look after his teammate!

'I wouldn't like to be in your shoes when Jimmy sees this,' she observed.

'Does he have to?' he cried. 'Can't Auntie Bobbie get it stopped?'

What did he think? That they could paper over the cracks of something as big as this? Cursing the snap-happy use of mobile phone cameras, Sam shook her head.

'Can't Auntie Bobbie do what?' Bobbie appeared, her face still closed with sleep, fastening the ties of her dressing-gown. Wordlessly, Sam thrust the top paper towards her and turned to the next, which was just as bad. He really had done it this time.

'Sorry, Auntie Bobbie,' he muttered sheepishly, hanging his head. A small boy who'd been found out, expecting the grownups to make things right.

Bobbie removed her disbelieving gaze from

the impossible headline and glared, accepting that she shouldn't be surprised. He was an accident waiting to happen, the wonder was that it hadn't happened long before now.

'Sorry's all very well and good, young man, but it won't get us far!' she cautioned. 'Whatever did you imagine Jimmy was going to say?'

'My sentiments entirely,' Sam agreed cheerfully, wondering if this would knock some sense into Paris's head at last. Misdemeanours. Repercussions. It was the way she'd been brought up; sensibly too, she had to admit, even if she and Bobbie had had their arguments about it over the years. She and Todd had never got into this kind of trouble. It was beginning to make her feel smug. 'Whatever will Babs say?' she added, unable to suppress a bubble of glee at the thought. Oh, she did feel sorry for him but there was a funny side to this, surely? Watching Bobbie's frowning countenance, she quickly decided there wasn't. 'I'll put the kettle on,' she murmured, diplomatically.

'I'll phone Ronnie,' Bobbie asserted, taking charge, her voice tight with anger. She could box Paris's ears! It was too early, but better Ronnie should know now and from her lips rather than from some enterprising hack out to make a quick profit for a quote.

She went through into the hall to the phone. For this to happen now was unbelievable. She'd known accepting the chief executive's job had been bound to cause difficulties but the reality, of course, was she'd simply had no idea of the havoc it would wreak on her life. She'd been crazy to take it on, caught in a moment of weakness into helping a club that was her lifeblood. Everyone had told her at the time and she should have paid attention.

She emerged several minutes later and after a long tirade from Ronnie Hubberfield to discover that Sam had packed Paris off to bed in the spare room and had begun to prepare the breakfast.

'It hardly seems worth going back to bed,' Sam remarked, dropping two lightly boiled eggs into eggcups and motioning Bobbie to sit down. Bobbie did so gratefully, plunged instantly into earlier less frenetic times, Todd on his paper-round and the two of them sharing a happy breakfast together before school. Had things changed so very much? They'd always been close. She'd always been able to talk to Sam about things.

Because she lacked a partner Sam, perhaps unfairly, had often been Bobbie's first port of call when she'd needed to talk a problem through. It had been unfair to burden her so young, Bobbie realized now.

At least she'd made a better job of raising her offspring than Babs had. Or was that being unfair too? Her eyes rose ceiling-ward, her hands curling round a comforting mug of tea as she settled back in her chair, relaxing at last.

'A good job he's getting some rest,' she observed. 'He'll need it, given that the heavens are about to open over his head.'

'Ronnie that bad, huh?' Sam sympathized.

Her mother nodded, rolling her eyes, unable to describe the tirade the Rogues' manager, disturbed from a night's slumber, had lashed himself into.

'He's banned training, fined a fortnight's wages and consigned to youth team fatigues! And that's just the start of it. I'm meeting Ronnie at the ground after training to discuss it. Oh, and believe it or not, he's under house arrest here, too. It never seemed to cross Ronnie's mind that I might not agree. What are we going to do, Paris twiddling his thumbs here?'

Sam nearly choked over her toast, her lips curling upwards gleefully.

'Looks like you've swopped sons, Mum!' she chortled. 'Todd living at Cedars, Paris here. What a hoot! Aunt Babs'll be simply furious!'

'I'm glad you find it funny, young lady!'

Abruptly, surprisingly, Bobbie started to laugh too, though it wasn't funny. She cracked the top off her egg and spooned up yolk, spread marmite on toast. It was comfort food and just what she needed. Sam watched her affectionately.

'You know, Mum, I've not seen you laugh for a long while.'

'Haven't you?' Bobbie put down her spoon, surprised to realize that it was true. But in her own defence, she hadn't had much to laugh about of late.

'Don't let this job take over,' Sam blurted out, not meaning to.

Bobbie frowned.

'Of course it isn't taking over . . . ' she hazarded, sounding uncertain.

Silently, she acknowledged that that wasn't exactly the truth. She had become immersed in her work, inadvertently of course, swamped by the sheer volume of the task. But to the detriment of everything — and everyone else?

'There are other things in life,' Sam concluded softly.

'You've been talking to your gran,' Bobbie retorted swiftly, instantly on her guard, too aware of the way Eleanor's mind had been running of late. Find a man and settle down. Get some kind of normality into her life

— away from football. It was obvious that the pair had been colluding. Sam grinned sheepishly, confirming her suspicions.

'She might have mentioned something or other along those lines,' she agreed cheerfully.

'Oh love; it's not me, is it?' Bobbie groaned, spooning up the last of the egg. 'It's not the path my life's taken — difficult as your gran finds it to accept. And as you might well find out yourself one day! Things happen and not always as you want them!'

'You mean Dad, don't you?' Sam frowned, not sure how to continue, guessing Bobbie felt guilty over the break-up of her marriage even now. As if she should have hung on to it, in what ever state, if only for her children's sake. 'I always hoped you and Dad might get back together some day,' she concluded wistfully, wise enough to know now that it was just wishful thinking.

'Did you, love?' Bobbie crumbled toast, aware it was too early in the morning for painful truths and her mind already wandering to the day ahead. She looked up guiltily, suddenly all too conscious that Sam was talking to her about something important and she'd allowed her mind to drift. Her dear daughter was right! She was letting the job take over. She smiled ruefully, her eyes holding a plea that the young woman would at least try to understand.

* * *

'There's no time for breakfast!' Babs snapped, stalking across the terrace to drop the morning's papers on to the table and waiting whilst Taylor casually picked the top one from the pile, quickly scanning the headlines. He whistled appreciatively.

'He's excelled himself this time,' he hazarded, shooting her a curious glance. He was too often unsure how to respond to Babs nowadays. She seemed so defensive, so unsure of herself, despite the success she was making of Cedars.

He sighed, letting the paper fall; one of the tabloids, naturally, refusing to give the rest a second glance. Paper talk. Why listen? Beyond, the greens of Cedars rolled in splendid solitude. Taylor normally liked this time of morning, the day stretching ahead invitingly, to fill exactly as he desired. Chatting to the guests, a round of golf or a drink at the bar, if he had the inclination, or could find the time. The mess Paris had apparently got himself into threatened what had promised a peaceful day.

'Don't worry,' he placated. 'Paris is fine.'

He was unsure what the fuss was about. Babs was surely used to the depths the tabloids would sink to nowadays. She sat down and poured coffee into an empty cup, running a weary hand through her hair. She looked tired.

'He's disappeared. I've rung simply everyone I can think of!' she complained bitterly. So many people had attached themselves to Paris's bright star. The list was endless and she'd been on the phone too long. Was he ashamed to confront her?

Her face clouded in frustration.

'What's he playing at, Taylor? Where's he gone?' She took a quick gulp of the coffee which was scalding hot, looking to her husband for some kind of reassurance, unsurprised when, as usual, none was forthcoming.

Taylor only shook his head, rocking back in his chair, his eyes puzzled and uncertain, still trying to gauge what ought to be his response.

'Babs, try and calm down,' he advised, tactlessly. 'He's eighteen and enjoying himself. What do you expect?'

'I might have known you'd stick up for him!' she fumed, instantly affronted.

Taylor's chair snapped down abruptly, rattling the tiles.

'Do you think I want our son to throw away his talent too?' Babs's colour was high, her frustration at the unexpected events spilling over. Her words were unforgivable and she should have kept them to herself.

'I suppose that's a dig at me?' Taylor's voice was light and anyone who didn't know him would have said the barb had blown harmlessly over his head. An expression, albeit fleeting, said otherwise. She'd done it; hit the one spot that could hurt him even now. His features darkened.

'Think what you could have done, Taylor — ' she moaned softly.

'If only I hadn't thrown my talent away too?' he interjected swiftly, rising to his feet. He dropped his serviette on to the empty plate, so many words bursting for air space. Hating arguments, he took a deep breath and somehow battened them down.

'I didn't mean it,' she muttered, watching him awkwardly, aware that both of them knew what she'd said was true. Taylor had been a remarkably promising footballer in his youth, a time when he'd thought his talent would be never-ending, no matter how he abused it. Late nights burning the candle at both ends on too many girls and a fast-developing taste for champagne. Too late he discovered that a talent left unnurtured shrivelled for lack of light. The offers had dried up. There'd followed a stream of small clubs, none of which had managed to bring out the talent he'd once so obviously displayed.

'If only I had my time again . . . '

And how many times had he said that over the course of their married life?

This time, ominously, he said it to himself, a note of yearning in his voice that Babs could hardly bear. He hardly ever said anything of importance to Babs nowadays — as if he'd shut her out of his life.

'Don't you see now, why I'm worried about Paris?' she murmured, aware he wasn't listening. She picked up a piece of toast, chewed it listlessly. Taylor was stuck in the past; she was obsessed with the future. She acknowledged it and still couldn't stop. They were poles apart and it was happening increasingly nowadays.

'Why worry?' The smile didn't quite reach his eyes, which at that moment were following the line of a slim young woman who'd just emerged from the foyer of the hotel and stood, shading her eyes and looking around her help-lessly. 'Isn't that the new wine rep?' he murmured, brightening instantly. 'I'd forgotten she was coming.' Even Babs couldn't fail to see the gleam in his eye. She was already rising to her feet but, dismissively, Taylor flapped a hand.

'It's about time I earned my keep, isn't it?' he cried, jumping up quickly.

Not giving her a second glance, he stalked away. She sat, watching his face light up and the woman smile in return, his hand sneaking around her waist as he ushered her back inside.

Babs frowned heavily. She was pushing him away and no wonder his gaze was wandering!

Her heart contracted in pain. She'd seen the way he looked at the wine rep. When did he ever look at her like that nowadays?

★   ★   ★

'Paris Pryce-Martin's nowt but a stupid young fool!'

Ronnie Hubberfield perched his large and robust frame precariously on the corner of his desk, regarding Bobbie through small and hostile eyes, as if he considered the whole wretched episode was all her fault. She frowned, already on the defensive, intuiting that this was about more than her nephew and accepting it was more likely that Ronnie was still unhappy about the appointment of the new chief executive.

The Rogues' manager was a man of his time, very much of the old school. A woman's place was in the home and certainly nowhere near a football ground. He was using this affair as a stick to beat her with. He'd been waiting his chance long enough.

'He hasn't been entirely sensible,' she hazarded carefully.

Ronnie snorted, thumping his mug down on a desk already littered with the morning's papers. 'We'll see how he feels when I drop him,' he warned smugly.

One glance at his face told Bobbie that, unfortunately, he wasn't joking.

'Ron, you can't drop him!' she protested forcefully.

'Try me . . . '

He lumbered up, towering over her, putting her at a disadvantage. Somehow she stood her ground, resisting the temptation to turn this into the battle he so obviously desired.

'I know you'll do whatever's needed, Ronnie. You are the boss, after all,' she murmured, gazing up at him provokingly, part of her inwardly cringing at her so obvious use of feminine guile. Grimly, she pressed on, hating herself for the artifices this job was urging her to. 'I'll back you fully.' She smiled. 'I'm only worried what Jimmy will have to say. He'll hardly be enamoured if you drop our star striker.'

She watched the truth of her words penetrate the bluff old Northerner's blustering façade. He blew out his cheeks, pulling at his lower lip with a large hand.

'Jimmy's not always in the right,' he argued.

'Jimmy's the chairman.' And pays your wages. Did she have to remind him?

Some of Ronnie's righteous indignation dissolved.

'That boy's going off the rails.'

'I agree!' She smiled, naturally this time, pleased to find something they could agree on. 'Isn't there anything else you can do, Ron? I mean give him the mother of all dressing-downs?'

'He'll be getting one, don't you worry,' he answered, gazing at her thoughtfully, then moving on to what had been on his mind for some time. 'All being well, I'll be asking Davie Mackenzie to keep young Paris under his wing next season.'

'Davie Mackenzie?' A sudden and unexpected note of caution entered Bobbie's voice. The smile froze on her face; she was glad Ronnie couldn't hear the way her heart banged against her ribcage. 'Davie Mackenzie, the Premiership forward?' Her voice wavered, her hand reaching to rest on the table edge and steady her weight.

'Is there another?' Ronnie smiled happily, enjoying the fact that their curmudgeonly old chairman so obviously hadn't told the new executive as much as she liked to think he had. He sat down again and became positively garrulous. 'So Jimmy's not told you! Davie's agent phoned last week. Providing we stay up, he reckons Davie will give the Premiership a miss next season and come to us. He's at the end of his career, he fancies putting something back into football. He started off here, remember?'

Remember? How could she ever forget? Some of Bobbie's distress must have registered on her face.

'You've nothing against the move or Davie Mackenzie, I take it?' Ronnie was watching her curiously.

Ronnie hadn't been manager when Mackenzie had been the up-and-coming young striker, and Bobbie had been attached to the club in a minor capacity only.

'Of course I haven't,' she lied bravely.

Somehow she escaped from Ronnie's office, her face hot with colour, her every nerve vibrating with shock. The years, her marriage to Gerry, even the children, simply faded away and she was a young woman again, fresh from university, not sure what she wanted to do with the rest of her life.

'I've fallen in love with you . . . ' Davie had sounded shocked, even angry, as if it were her fault, so she didn't know now how she'd managed to hold back. She'd managed it by reminding herself of the difference in their ages and the fact that Davie was so young he couldn't possibly understand the implications of what he was saying. It had been true too, at the time; settling down had been the furthest thing from her mind.

'I . . . I do like you,' she'd mumbled miserably, aware that it was so much more and not wanting to raise his hopes.

They'd been walking by the meadows, she remembered, recollecting too the rippling song of bright water coursing along over the riverbed, the sun shining on the wild flowers of which there'd been a profusion that year. Davie's face had been bright with love. Why did that image hurt even now?

How she'd hated hurting him, doing it anyway, unable to stop.

'Only like?' He'd nearly exploded, knowing, as she did too, that it simply wasn't true. It was only that she couldn't admit to feelings that sent her pulses racing every time they met.

They'd broken up, got back together, only to break up again. He'd had too much else to cope with, Premiership scouts had been taking an interest, the club haggling to get as much from any deal as they could. Eventually, exasperated, Davie had got himself a transfer and put her resolutely from his life. He'd been ridiculously proud even then; she expected now that he'd grown into a proud man. Somehow she'd become embroiled with Gerry, the mature man she'd thought she wanted at the time, who'd swept her off her feet. She hadn't seen Davie since. She doubted he ever gave her a thought nowadays; he couldn't conceivably guess that she'd seemed to spend the biggest part of her life wondering what would have happened if she'd settled down with him instead of Gerry. How different her life would have been!

She'd reached the sanctuary of her office, where she swiftly crossed to the window and stood staring moodily down at the pitch beyond, the glass soothing her cheek which was burning-hot.

Did she want their paths to recross? That was the question.

Her heart was hammering, sounding like a cloudburst in her ears. He must know she was still around. Was his proposed move back deliberate, a chance to look her up? How would he feel, given how angry he'd been at their break-up, to find the pair of them forced into such close proximity again . . . ?

3

Eleanor had something on her mind, by the looks of it. Bobbie dropped her bag on the kitchen table, stifling a rising guilt at the thought that she'd been so busy they'd had no chance to talk of late.

The last two long and painful hours had been spent holed up in the office, in the too close proximity of Davie Mackenzie and his agent, whilst the various parties went over Davie's contract for the coming season with a fine-tooth comb. It had been difficult, to say the least, and Bobbie had been only too glad to get it out of the way.

'Dad not here?' she smiled encouragingly.

Her mother released the dough she'd been pummelling and dusted the flour from her fingers.

'You must have missed him. He's just driven over to see you,' she answered, surprisingly. Then with a touch of waspishness, which told Bobbie something was up: 'Don't ask why! You'll find out soon enough!'

She was in a mood, stalking across the kitchen to wash her hands at the sink, drying them with a preoccupied air. Bobbie shot her an amused glance.

'Haven't you and Dad made up yet?' she probed, waiting until they were comfortably seated at the kitchen table with a mug of tea apiece, before asking. She was fishing; aware that the atmosphere between her parents had taken a nosedive since Landon had failed to accompany Eleanor on the Lamoure's cruise in the Mediterranean. It wasn't like them still to be at loggerheads. They never let things fester.

She sat back, hands cupped around her mug, sipping the tea meditatively; she was aware that, despite her parents loving each other desperately, they'd always had a stormy relationship. Eleanor's eruptions were a family joke and fortunately something that neither of the girls had inherited. Bobbie was too like Landon; Babs too much her own person, bottling things up so that no one knew what she thought.

'You might as well tell me,' she coaxed.

Eleanor stared hard into her mug.

'I expect I'm still fuming about the cruise,' she admitted reluctantly.

'Dad was extraordinarily busy at the time.' She'd mentioned this before, surely?

'So he said,' Eleanor retorted drily. She glanced up and treated Bobbie to such a pained look that Bobbie had no idea what to say to it. Landon really had landed himself in it this time.

'Mum, Alan was arrested last week.'

'I know that!' Eleanor, frowning at the change of subject, remembered Landon, white-faced when he'd got home from the club. She'd been shocked too when he'd blurted it out, relieved to get it off his chest. Following weeks of police investigation, Alan Campion was in police custody and charged with embezzlement. The following day, he'd been released on bail. The last person anyone would have imagined helping himself to club funds.

'Love, what's it to do with . . . '

'Everything, don't you see?' Bobbie continued steadily. 'He and dad were at university together. Think how he must feel! He's so upset.'

'Of course he is, but I still don't see what it has to do with this.'

'You don't, do you?'

Eleanor took a swallow of tea, feeling she was being got at and doggedly returning the conversation to the subject of her marriage, surely beyond any external pressures, no matter how upsetting. 'Don't I matter too, Bobbie?' she cried, 'I'm the one who's kept this marriage together. This place, you and Babs . . . It doesn't seem to have crossed your father's mind; I might have had difficulties too, over the years.'

'Of course you have . . . Dad knows that! You know how much he loves you.'

She might as well have tried to stem a tidal wave. Eleanor shook her head, building up a head of steam.

'The cruise at least gave me chance to think things through and realize how lopsided my marriage has become. I swear your father believes there's only one person in it who counts!' She sat back, cradling her mug, her expression one of bewilderment. Since her return from the cruise — which Landon had failed to join, his indifference to her feelings which was in such contrast to his passion for things she couldn't begin to understand, caused all her worst nightmares to roll into one, hurtfully revealing the gloss she'd put on his behaviour over the years.

She was relieved at the chance to unburden herself and to whom better than Bobbie?

'We've lost sight of each other and I've never even realized,' she admitted quietly, a hint of desperation in her voice. 'How could he do this to me, Bobbie? Doesn't he realize I've feelings too . . . ' Her voice wavered, rising in a crescendo of hurt. 'Just because we're getting older it doesn't mean our relationship isn't still important. Giles says — '

'Giles?' Bobbie was clearly bewildered.

'Giles Barnard . . . One of Eddie's business associates. We met on the cruise.' A tell-tale blush rose to Eleanor's cheeks. A man who misinterpreted the fact that Eleanor was alone had taken no trouble to hide his finding her attractive. This had been balm to her fractured nerves, she had to admit it. She still blamed Landon for that, and if only he'd been there they'd surely have shared a joke about the attractive widower with the silver hair and would have found ways of dissuading him gently, together. As it was she'd had to cope with that on her own too. She rejected the thought of how long it had been since a man had found her desirable.

'He was very nice-looking,' she mused.

'Mother!' Bobbie, unsure whether to laugh it off, sounded scandalized.

'I don't mean anything happened!' Eleanor retorted quickly. She stood up to stack the tea things and carried them over to the sink. She leaned back against the unit, her brow furrowed in thought.

'I just meant Giles and I spent a lot of time talking. You know what cruises are like . . . There's not much else to do! He had a knack of hitting the nail on the head. He said . . . you don't know what you have, until you've lost it . . . That's so true, love! Your dad and I . . . I don't want things getting to that stage.'

Giles had been talking about his marriage and somehow it had seemed to include her marriage too, or at least the state it had fallen into. Her arms folded defensively as she thought of the last night on board: the stars reflected in the warm glow of the Mediterranean, the soft and insistent lap of waves against the boat, which seemed becalmed, when inside Eleanor had felt anything but. She thought of Giles standing too close, his eyes full of an emotion she couldn't fail to interpret.

In the end — and thankfully — common sense had prevailed. Eleanor was too mature, too long in the tooth to allow a momentary fancy for another man, no matter how attractive, to stand in the way of her marriage and the man she truly and deeply loved. Still. Even after the way he'd treated her.

'You know Dad loves you,' Bobbie muttered awkwardly, not sure if this was the kind of conversation she should be having with a parent. Her dear father was selfish and thoughtless, she conceded while still loving him for it. She sprang up quickly to give her mother a hug. 'You two need to talk.'

'I expect I'm just being foolish.' Eleanor busied herself running the water into the

70

bowl, handing Bobbie the tea-towel. The crisis appeared to be over.

Bobbie heaved an inward sigh of relief. 'At least you had a good holiday, Mum.'

'I had the feeling that Eddie was sorry your dad didn't manage to join us,' Eleanor replied, glad that at last she'd managed to get her feelings under control.

'Football stuff?' Bobbie queried, picking up a mug and shaking off the bubbles. 'But I thought Eddie wasn't into that kind of thing?' Eddie Lamoure was first and foremost a businessman. A run-down championship side like the Rogues was hardly likely to be near the top of his list of interests.

'It was only a feeling. I might be wrong of course,' Eleanor conceded.

'Come off it, Mum! When are you ever wrong?' The atmosphere lifted. Bobbie grinned. 'Now if you could only sort out this problem between me and Babs?'

'She's still got the hump?' Eleanor was surprised. 'She can't still be blaming you for Paris, surely?'

She could and was. Relations between the two sisters had sunk to an all-time low, consisting of barbed comments on Babs's part and half-hearted efforts of reconciliation from Bobbie. Bobbie couldn't for the life of her see what she'd done wrong. She lifted pained eyes heavenward.

'It's hardly my fault Ronnie put Paris under house arrest. It was no more than he deserved. It's about time Babs realized Paris is grown up, Mum! He has commitments . . . ' One of which had been scoring the winning goal in the last match of the season, thereby ensuring the Rogues's Championship safety. Even hard-nosed Ronnie Hubberfield, dour Yorkshireman that he was, had been hard-pressed to maintain disapproval in the face of his protégé's brilliance. As it was he'd softened enough to allow the young man the luxury of two weeks' bonus-paid holiday in St Tropez before the players resumed training on Monday. That was two days since and still he hadn't returned.

Bobbie's heart skipped a beat at the thought of what Ronnie would have to say about it.

'I wonder what he's doing at this moment?' Eleanor mused, her face bubbling up with laughter.

Paris let loose in St Tropez? Was St Tropez ready for it? Bobbie laughed out loud, guessing they'd both just love to know.

★ ★ ★

He woke to the sound of bees, a whole hiveful, astonishingly airborne at one and the

72

same time, filling his head with their collective humming. Paris fought his way out from the quilt under which he'd been comatose since first he'd tumbled into bed, sometime in the early hours of the morning, and lifted his head. Immediately he wished he hadn't. Too many nightclubs. Too many girls.

His eyes came ungummed, ascertaining that the bees weren't, after all, inside his head, weren't in fact bees at all, but the droning of a vacuum-cleaner in irritating proximity. He sat up gingerly, hand clamped to forehead, waiting for the world to stop spinning. Beyond the bowed window of the luxury Côte d' Azur Hotels complex, the bay of St Tropez glittered invitingly in the midday heat. Abruptly, deliciously, the droning stopped and the slim figure of the girl who'd been trundling the machine up and along the white-tiled floor swung swiftly, giddyingly towards him, her face registering surprise. Maid? Guest who'd lost her way? One of his legion of astute and beguiling admirers?

Ignoring the beginnings of a hangover of prize-winning proportions, Paris snapped to attention. She wasn't exactly pretty but something made him take a second glance and then look again.

Strictly speaking her features were irregular. A turned-up nose, a wide mouth, thick copper hair pinned up to the top of her head, curling strands of which were escaping their confines. Her eyes were large and green and set wide apart and seemed to look right through him. Worse, they didn't appear to like what they saw.

Paris's smile, the one more usually knocking the girls for six, died instantly.

'Sorry, I didn't mean to startle you.'

'You didn't!' She bent down and yanked the vacuum cleaner's plug out of the socket, treating him to another hard stare. 'Guests normally vacate rooms by eleven on the day of departure,' she muttered accusingly.

'I haven't made my mind up whether I am departing yet.'

'I'll come back later. You've really messed my schedule up!'

'Are you always this rude?' he demanded peevishly, feeling ridiculously hurt. He was a guest after all. He could lie in bed until whatever time he wanted. It was on the tip of his tongue to tell her he was a famous footballer. Normally nothing would have restrained him, though usually he didn't have to say anyway. Normally, he was recognized instantly.

Some innate common sense made him keep the sentiment to himself. This girl, he sensed, wouldn't be impressed. Vainly, he racked his brain for something else he'd done of late to impress her with, but it was no good. All he was good for was kicking a football about.

For the first time in his life, the thought crossed Paris's mind that perhaps he ought to have more to say for himself. He looked away quickly, out of the window to the blue and glistening sea beyond.

'I'll get on then,' she muttered, frowning.

'Perhaps I'll see you later?' he enquired, remembering then, too late, that he'd already arranged to meet a girl in the bar downstairs. He wished it was this girl.

'I doubt it. Today's my last day. I'm back home again tomorrow.' The words, delivered in such an offhand way, told him that whether she saw him again or not was a matter of complete indifference to her.

That irked him.

'Back home in England?' he demanded far too quickly, for the first time registering she was English. Something in his heart lifted at the thought. At that moment he decided to catch the return flight home he'd booked some days before, uncertain then whether he'd be on it or not. 'Perhaps we could meet up back home?'

'Oh . . . um . . . no, I'm sorry!'

She was backing towards the door. In

desperation Paris made to throw the covers back, remembering only just in time that his clothes were scattered over the floor where he'd dropped them. He was horrified to find himself blushing. Worse, it appeared she'd realized his predicament.

'I've seen quite as much of you as I'd like . . . ' Her face broke into a wide, impish smile of glee, a wonderful gorgeous smile that instantly made Paris's heart turn delicious somersaults. Just when he wanted to tell her as much, maddeningly, exasperatingly she'd backed towards the open doorway and, laughing, shot through it, leaving him ruing the fact he knew so little about her. Nothing, in fact.

Who was she? Where had she come from? The questions tipped somersaults in his head. More important, even more tantalizing to Paris in that moment, when was he going to get to see her again?

★ ★ ★

'Here you are, grandad . . . ' Sam walked down the thin ribbon of path, balancing a tray bearing three glasses of orange squash. Carefully she passed one to Landon, sprawled on the bench enjoying the midday sun. Beyond his gaze, George Carter and Stephanio Rivera,

76

the two young reserve team players who'd accompanied him, made a start on the jungle that was Bobbie's back garden.

'Thanks love . . . ' Landon sat up, easing himself back against the wooden struts of the bench, watching his protégés hard at work, the best idea he could come up with to get himself back into Eleanor's good books after coaxing Bobbie into the chief executive's job. According to Eleanor, the mess that was his daughter's life was all her father's fault. It was hardly his fault that he didn't agree with a word of it.

'Your mother will be pleased,' he commented.

'And Gran too,' Sam replied, astutely.

Landon laughed. Not much got past Sam, he mused, watching as she continued her progress, handing their drinks to the two young men, who stopped work immediately, only too eager to take a break and talk to Sam whilst they'd a chance. They were falling over themselves, vying for attention, conceited young popinjays!

It was hardly surprising; Sam had grown into an attractive young woman of late. College, the chance to spread her wings had given her confidence. Landon pressed his head back against the bench, enjoying the feel of the sun on his face and thinking too, for the first time in his life, that he was beginning to feel his age. Life was too short for arguments and Eleanor throwing one of her tantrums. He rubbed his chest, closed his eyes, content to take a rest and let the world go by.

'Grandad will be asleep in a minute,' Sam murmured, shielding her eyes and watching him fondly. Stephanio, on the other hand, was watching her in undisguised admiration. She shot him an amused glance, instantly aware too, of George's quick frown of disapproval. Her smile cooled. Her relationship with Stephanio was none of his business.

She hadn't given either player the slightest encouragement. Everyone knew what Sam thought of footballers — good-looking or not!

'Is a good man, your grandfather, Sam,' Stephanio proffered. 'Family is good, yes?'

'You must miss yours, being so far from home,' she answered quickly, guessing instinctively how hard it must be to leave everything familiar to chase a dream in a foreign country. 'Is it worth it?' she asked quietly, ignoring her instinct that it was none of her business.

'My family are poor,' he replied, not minding the intrusion and nodding his head rapidly. 'When I make it . . . how you say . . . big time? I buy house, a little land. I set them up good, huh?' The shy, diffident smile she'd so taken to illuminated his face. A nice face, she decided quickly and one, she guessed instinctively, that she could trust. Watching them sourly, George snorted, an unattractive sound midway between ill-humour and sarcasm. Sam frowned, ignoring it and retaining her attention firmly on Stephanio, if only to pay George back for being so annoyingly possessive when she'd never given him cause.

'Looks as if Sam has her hands full!' Bobbie had come hurrying down the path, coming to a halt by Landon. Her gaze encompassed the garden before returning to her father. She smiled fondly. There was no doubting where her sympathies lay. 'So this is what Mum meant! But it's wonderful, Dad.'

'I thought you'd be pleased!' Landon relaxed, basking in an admiration he considered had been severely lacking in his life of late. 'I've not exactly been fair, love,' he admitted reluctantly. 'Landing you with all the extra work at the club. No wonder you've had no time for anything that needed doing here. Your mother's been worried.'

Another allusion to the atmosphere back home and Landon's subsequent reaction to it. Bobbie frowned. Now was an ideal opportunity to tackle him.

'I see you and Mum haven't made up

yet . . . ' she began, wondering how to go on and plunging straight in. Landon looked blank. 'The cruise?' she prompted, crossly.

'A temporary blip!' He flapped his hand vaguely. 'I've already explained all that. Of course I couldn't get away.'

Bobbie took a deep breath. She believed that if a thing needed saying, it should be said. It was the way she'd been brought up and how she'd tried to bring her children up too. She couldn't bear to see Eleanor so upset and her father apparently unaware of it. Unless he was putting a gloss over things? One look at his face told her he wasn't, he genuinely did think there was nothing to worry about. He needed putting right.

She laid a firm hand on his arm.

'I wouldn't be so sure things are all right, Dad. According to Mum they're not. Of course she's still upset! She's had a lot to put up with and just at a time of life when — '

'Oh, you mean it's an age thing? I had wondered.' Landon sat back, nodding his head rapidly in agreement. 'Precisely what I told her! Hormones all over the place . . . '

Women of a certain age? Bobbie rolled her eyes. No wonder her poor mother was so fired up.

'I think it goes a little deeper than hormones, Dad! This needs love and lots of it.' She shook her head in disbelief that he didn't know all this already.

Sam extracted herself from her admirers and rejoined them. The little party made its way back inside. Bobbie wondered whether she'd said enough or did she need to labour the point. 'Remember what I said,' she warned, deciding she had and reaching up to drop a light kiss on his cheek.

★ ★ ★

'Grandad looks well,' Sam remarked, switching on the kettle. Landon had already departed, in haste to get back to Eleanor and sort things out. She reached down the cups, her mind annoyingly still on Stephanio when there was something of greater importance that she needed to talk to her mother about.

'What is it now?' Bobbie asked wearily, a hint of resignation in her voice. One problem solved and another presented itself. It had been that sort of a day.

'I'm worried about Dad,' Sam blurted out, catching her mother by surprise.

Instantly, Bobbie's whole demeanour changed. It would have been far neater and cleaner if only the separation between her and Gerald Mansfield had been permanent but how could it be when the children were involved? Gerry's children. Given the way he behaved, it was sometimes something she chose to forget.

'What's he done now?' she asked wearily.

'He hasn't done anything,' Sam answered, not exactly making sense. She frowned; aware that Bobbie hated talking about Gerry but her own need overriding it. 'It's been ages since I've heard anything from him, Mum.' She frowned. 'I've written, phoned . . . Even his mobile's switched off.'

'Have you tried the office?'

The young woman nodded miserably.

'The staff will only say he's out. They're either being deliberately obtuse or there's something else.' She had only a smattering of Spanish and no one there spoke English. Or wouldn't admit it! She watched Bobbie fretfully, waiting to be told what she ought to do.

'It'll be something and nothing darling.' There was Bobbie, right on cue with the reassurance. Suddenly Sam wasn't so sure.

'He's disappeared.'

'Of course he hasn't.'

'Where is he then? I can't get hold of him at his flat either!'

'You know your dad!' Bobbie urged. 'He's probably up to his eyes in some new business venture. Something hush hush, over which he's sworn the staff to secrecy.'

'Do you think I ought to go over there? There's plenty of time before term . . . '

Bobbie shook her head, annoyed with Gerry because he was causing the poor girl so much worry. 'He'll be in touch soon, love, you see. I really don't know what you're worrying about . . . ' Cursing his lack of thought, the pain he'd caused his children all their young lives, she gave Sam a reassuring hug, hoping vainly that that would be an end to it.

★ ★ ★

The promise of morning had disappeared and, as more usual for August and what passed for summer, grey clouds came scudding across the horizon, delivering a short sharp shock of rain, sending the more energetic of Cedars residents scurrying across the greens towards the welcoming shelter of the hotel complex.

Annoyed at the end to what had promised a good afternoon's golf, Todd Vernon shook the rain from his hair and headed across the foyer towards the Green Leaves café and his Aunty Babs, who sat at a table by the window, enjoying her afternoon tea-break. Immediately, Todd's spirits lifted. He'd been looking for the chance of finding her alone. It was too good an opportunity to miss.

Babs beckoned the waitress to bring another cup.

'And how's my favourite nephew?' she demanded, waving the teapot in his general direction.

'Have you any other?' he asked, grinning widely. He sat down, helping himself to the scone uneaten on her plate. 'I've been wanting a chat, Aunty Babs,' he announced cheerfully.

'Something important?' she murmured, astutely, pouring the tea and not taken in for a moment.

He smiled sheepishly, acknowledging that the slim, elegant woman sitting across the table might have been many things but never a fool. Todd had only admiration for the way Babs had taken Cedars by the scruff of the neck and made a going concern of it. He took a steadying swallow of tea, too aware of everything he had to thank her for.

'Aunty Babs, I've really enjoyed working here . . . ' he deliberated for a moment not sure how best to proceed. 'It's been a great experience being the golfing pro, but . . . '

'But?' she smiled, looking as if she might have guessed already what was coming next.

'But I reckon it's time to move on!' he

concluded hastily, before his courage deserted him. 'You know I've always wanted to become a professional and enter the big tournaments. There's opportunity to get on the circuit if I can only apply hard work to whatever talent I have.' He sat back helplessly, longing for her to agree that his talent, if he even had any, would be enough to get him where he wanted. 'I reckon now's the time to do it, that's all,' he finished quietly, running out of steam.

Babs sipped her tea, regarding the earnest young man, so eagerly spilling his every dream, with an affection that was surprisingly genuine. Dreams and the young. They were made for each other. Her gaze softened, remembering a time when she'd been young too. A time when she'd had dreams, crazy as that seemed now. Who was she to spoil things for this young man, when he looked so excited at the prospects opening up so tantalizingly? There was no need to point out the pitfalls; he'd surely find them out soon enough.

'And what's your mother had to say?' she asked quietly, introducing a note of caution. One of them had to remember Bobbie. Bobbie who hated Todd's having come to work for Babs.

'Oh . . . um . . . Mum doesn't know yet.'

He flushed, betraying only his youth. Babs's heart contracted in pity. She'd been behind Paris every step of the way, encouraging, cajoling, demanding that he should use every scrap of his considerable talent. She couldn't understand Bobbie sometimes. Not being proud of Todd. Not realizing he needed encouragement too. Look where Paris was now and whom he had to thank for it! Even if sometimes he didn't remember, she certainly did.

Todd would never have shown such ingratitude. She caught herself wishing her own son could be more like this young man.

'Do you want me to have a word?' she asked quietly, quickly dismissing the thought that she was siding with Todd to get back at Bobbie for her response to the silly nightclub business, which had got into all the papers.

'Would you?' Relief sprang into his eyes, all too quickly followed by his more usual air of thoughtful bewilderment. It was an anxious air, that would make him appealing to some good woman looking for a decent man with whom to share her life, Babs mused, wishing suddenly that Paris would leave off embarking on so many shallow affairs and find someone level-headed to settle down with too. She was beginning to wonder if such a paragon existed.

'Um . . . I suppose it'd be better coming

from me?' he ventured.

Given the dismal relationship that she and Bobbie currently shared, she knew it would. She nodded, smiling, not needing to put it into words. Everyone knew the state of her relationship with Bobbie.

'I'll see if I can catch her in a good mood.' He grinned, relieved that at last the whole tricky business was out in the open.

Rain slashed against the window. If there was no prospect of more golf, there was still time for a work-out in the gym. He swallowed the last of his tea, made his excuses and hurried away, leaving Babs's mind free to wander to Taylor and how little she'd seen of him of late. She had, she realized, been lingering here over her tea, hoping against hope, that he might join her.

A quick check on the terrace and bars proved fruitless, ditto the office, though she'd hardly expected success there. Taylor hated office work! Rosie, on reception, nodded in resignation towards the restaurant, causing Babs's elegantly plucked brows to rise sharply upwards. Most likely he'd be chatting up one of the guests, taking the chance to slack off, which he did at every opportunity. Anything other than help with the running of the hotel, she mused, indignation rising.

At last she found him, in one of the more

intimate little alcoves that the restaurant boasted. That he was in the company of the new and too-attractive wine rep did nothing to improve her humour. The woman had visited Cedars already, the previous week. They had no need of more wine, the cellar was already full. Young. Pretty. Babs's high heels struck sparks against the tiles.

'There you are, Taylor . . . ' Her voice was as cool and contained as she could make it, given the circumstances, given that her whole system had instantly gone on red alert. She knew how to handle Taylor . . . usually. A sinking feeling told her she wasn't so sure of anything nowadays.

The woman was smiling across at Taylor, who was returning her doting gaze in full. Babs bit down hard on her lip, pretending not to see.

'There you are,' she repeated icily.

Taylor frowned. 'You'll join us for a glass?' He reached for the bottle of wine, waving it in her direction, giving the impression that he rather hoped she wouldn't.

'What could be nicer?' Somewhere she found a smile and sat down, wishing she could convince herself that he was, in any way, pleased to see her.

★　★　★

It was a relief to Bobbie to have the house to herself. A hot bath, a good book, the evening stretched before her to fill as she pleased. Silence enveloped her, soothing like balm, all the more precious since the young people had gone out for a pizza, their plans for more gardening spoiled by the rain which had come down so unexpectedly.

Quickly she scanned the day's papers and washed up the few tea things, thinking in amusement of Sam's self-conscious efforts at denying the effect Stephanio had so obviously had on her, whilst doing her valiant best to placate his increasingly irritated teammate. George liked her too, that much was obvious and was annoyed at his young Italian teammate. There was the prospect of romance on the horizon, no matter which of them Sam plumped for . . . if she plumped for either!

She was on her way upstairs to run a bath when the front doorbell rang. It couldn't be Sam back already. Screwing a firm lid on patience already frayed by the day's events, she returned downstairs and opened the door.

The colour fled from her face. Suddenly her heart was hammering, her every thought extinguished as if the world — her world — had crashed to a grinding halt.

'Bobbie . . . ' Davie Mackenzie straightened up from the door-jamb against which he'd been leaning, watching her warily.

The last person she'd expected. He had no right to come here and he knew it.

'Jimmy gave me your address. I hope you don't mind?' he muttered, already on the defensive. 'I told him there were a couple of points on the contract I still needed to have explained to me.'

Dumbly she nodded, taking in his appearance, which was dishevelled: jeans, a crumpled T-shirt. Nothing like the smart and reserved man with whom she'd spent the morning. She stepped back as he brushed past her and into the hall.

'You'd best come through.' Thankful that her voice sounded steady, giving no hint of the turmoil within, she led the way into her tiny sitting room, standing by awkwardly as he settled his long frame into a chair.

'You're looking good, Bobbie . . . ' he proffered, unexpectedly.

'You've come all this way to tell me that?'

She couldn't work out yet why he'd come. She perched herself on the arm of the chair opposite, aware only of the fact he was here, invading her space, filling her with feelings she'd rather not examine too closely. They were painful feelings, raking over something that hadn't quite died. Too much unfinished business. It lay between them, filling the room with a crackling intensity.

He sprang up and began to pace the carpet.

'There are one or two things that need saying Bobbie. You must know that. If only to clear the air,' he muttered, coming to a halt. He thrust his hands in his pockets, watching her broodingly.

'Nothing you couldn't have told me this morning.'

'Are you kidding?' he demanded, clearly irate at even thoughts of what had happened this morning. The meeting had been carried out under the hardened gaze of Davie's agent, Eric Byers, and Jimmy Proudfoot, the Rogues' chairman, who'd turned up determined to see things ran smoothly. Between them, they'd managed a lofty silence, the best they could come up with in awkward circumstances.

'I thought long and hard before coming back to Rislington,' he volunteered abruptly. 'And just in case you were wondering . . . Where you and I are concerned, I have no intention of starting anything up again.'

His arrogance hit her with the force of a blow. She sprang up quickly, realizing too late that what she'd been expecting was something along the lines of their putting their shared past behind them. Two people with a job to do. To think he imagined he'd only to crook his little finger and she'd hot-tail straight back to him was intolerable.

'You and I were a long time ago, Davie,' she answered, icily, hanging on to her temper.

Some of her anger must have got through. Immediately, his stance softened.

'You never forget some things, Bobbie. No matter how much time passes.' The toe of his trainer traced a circle in the pile of the carpet. He looked up, frowning. Just as it always had done when he was worried about anything, the space between his eyebrows crinkled. Once, she'd have smoothed it away without a second thought.

The knowledge stirred feelings she didn't want to reacquaint herself with.

Davie's frown deepened.

'Did you really have to marry Gerry so quickly after we'd split up?' he demanded, jolting her rudely out of her reverie. Her temper rose.

'That's hardly any of your business — '

'You said marriage was the last thing on your mind!'

'And so it was!' she cried, put on the defensive, unsure how it was that they were having this conversation when he'd apparently only come to tell her there was no way back. 'Things . . . just happened.' She floundered. It was no explanation, and yet there was no need for her to give him one anyway. She owed him nothing. Her voice trailed away, her emotions finding no outlet in her words. The truth was, even now, that she had no real idea why she'd married Gerry Mansfield. Because he was so much older and appeared sophisticated to her youthful eyes, making her feel grown-up when she so patently wasn't? He'd acquainted her with a side of life she'd never yet seen. The early stages of their relationship had been heady times, a way of forgetting this man here and everything that had gone wrong between them.

'You never gave us a chance, Bobbie,' he murmured softly, the look accompanying his words causing her to jump up quickly, to occupy her restless fingers by straightening the magazines on the coffee table.

He'd come to warn her off. So why was he talking like this, stirring up things they both must know were better left to the past, where they belonged, if they were to maintain any kind of a professional relationship?

Tears pricked the back of her eyes, which she blinked away fiercely; her swimming gaze perceiving too late Davie crossing the room to stand beside her. His hands stole upwards, turning her gently towards him; he gazed down into her face, his own expression one she couldn't fathom. Did he too, have his own battles? Feelings he didn't want to own, too?

Her heart was beating way too fast.

'Bobbie, you are OK?'

There was a tender note in his voice which undid her completely. She nodded dumbly, knowing she was anything but. Her gaze stole upwards, horrified to read the emotion springing into his eyes. He still had feelings for her too, feelings he was trying to deny because, like her, he knew it wouldn't work. Too much had happened and you couldn't go back. His grip on her shoulders tightened. Long moments passed, moments in which she realized, crazily, that she was fighting a losing battle not to fall forward and into his arms.

'Just so long as we both know where we are.' Just when she was so nearly undone, he released her abruptly, the tension in his whip-cord frame falling away, bringing her crashing back to normality.

So he'd come back. So what! She did have other, more pressing difficulties to deal with and none would be solved by her standing here, a mass of quivering uncertainty. There was too much at stake, too many people waiting for her to fail and she wasn't going to give them the satisfaction. Ronnie Hubberfield, using Paris's indiscretion as a stick to berate her with, the steadily growing feeling that Jimmy Proudfoot had appointed her merely because he thought her someone who'd jump at his slightest command. She'd heard the fans on the Saturday-night phone-in, bemoaning the club's poor showing and laying it firmly at the door of the club's new chief executive!

She straightened up, regarding Davie coolly. Did Davie want her to fail, that was the question? Did he perceive running a football club to be beyond the capabilities of a woman — and this woman in particular?

'I'll see you at work Monday morning, Davie Mackenzie!' she dismissed him crisply, a challenge in the words, expressive of her burgeoning desire to succeed, to be the best at what she did. The chief executive of Rislington Rovers football club and proud of the fact. Proud too of her family's associations with this wonderful old football club.

A woman in a man's world. She'd show them, this man included. Somehow, whatever it took. Bobbie Vernon was on the up and, like it or not, she was taking this football club with her.

4

'Staying late, Paris?'

It was well after training. Sam Vernon breezed into the players' lounge, surprised to discover her famous cousin leaning against the bar, alone. It appeared that everyone else had gone home already. Looking at the few gaudy baubles and tired tinsel hanging limply over the fittings, it wasn't hard to see why. Not many would choose to spend a chilly mid-December evening here, Paris least of all.

'Sam! Have a drink with me?' he demanded eagerly.

She shook her head but pulled out a stool and sat down. 'I'm meeting Steph . . . We're going to the charity do at the Lamoures. Grandad's roped us in,' she volunteered happily. She'd been home already to change and had only just returned. Under her coat was a little black dress, hugging her figure exactly. She looked good and felt it.

'You two are becoming quite an item.' A tight smile flickered across Paris's face. Sam was annoyed, unaware that she and Steph were already the subject of gossip. They'd been out for meals together, the odd drink and trip to the cinema, mostly to help Steph with his English which was coming on wonderfully. Sam had assured herself it was only because she'd felt sorry for him, living so far away from home, and everything he loved. An act of common kindness, surely, anyone would have offered.

It didn't explain her eagerness to see him and the fact that he was never far from her thoughts. Oh, she did like him, and just how much she had no intention of telling Paris, or anyone else, come to that, not even Stephanio. College took up so much of her life. Exams were looming, a vast and exciting future beckoned; becoming serious over anyone shouldn't, couldn't come into the equation.

'Don't get the wrong idea,' she warned the young man who was staring so morosely into his orange juice, making a mental note to herself too, determining to put the brakes on feelings that, she sensed, were on the verge of spiralling out of control.

Whoever his cousin chose to spend her time with was apparently irrelevant to Paris. Something was wrong and his being so quiet of late should have warned her.

'Paris, what's the matter?' she asked bluntly.

He shrugged. 'I've met someone,' he answered, looking surprisingly miserable about it, whoever she was. Listlessly, his thumb circled the rim of his glass, his expression wonderfully one of hurt and confusion.

So that was all, some girl. Sam relaxed. There was no need for such a fuss. Girls were constantly throwing themselves at Paris's feet and she doubted there was much that was different about this one.

'Paris Pryce-Martyn! I do believe you're smitten!' she hooted. The biter bit? She wanted to laugh and couldn't, feeling instead only an uncomplicated rush of affection. It had been bound to happen some time, even to her dear self-obsessed cousin. He'd fallen in love. But wasn't that meant to be wonderful?

'She's gorgeous, Sam,' he groaned, giving the impression that falling in love was anything but. 'I can't stop thinking about her, what ever I'm doing, even when I'm playing!'

Sam, at least, knew how much football meant to Paris. She had to smile at this.

'That's how we all feel at the start of a relationship,' she pointed out gently, amused that she had to. She wasn't talking about the sort of casual affair Paris more usually indulged in, either.

The circling of his thumb increased in

tempo. He looked up, his eyes fastening on hers.

'Paris! She isn't married?' Alarm spread across her face.

'Of course she's not married!' he retorted. 'At least . . . not as far as I know. No . . . it's worse than that!' He gulped his drink, composing himself. 'I don't know who she is. I mean her name or anything. I've no idea how to get in touch with her . . . '

Seeing Sam's blank look of incomprehension, falteringly, brokenly he began to explain. He'd met her on the last day of his holiday, an English girl working in the hotel as some kind of a maid. It had been her last day too, before flying home. Before he'd had the chance to discover a thing about her, she'd disappeared. He'd tried everything; talked to everyone he could think of, but it was no good. She might never have existed, a figment of his imagination!

Unforgivably, after their all too brief conversation, he'd fallen asleep. If only he hadn't had the mother of all hangovers and he'd have got up, there and then, to see where she'd gone.

'I didn't realize I was never going to see her again!' he wailed, as if he was hoping that somehow, miraculously, Sam could conjure her up for him. 'It isn't infatuation, if that's what you're thinking,' he cried, catching her bemused expression and looking aggrieved. 'I know it sounds crazy — '

'You're right. It does.' She knew him too well. He settled on so little. This was bound to be another of his temporary fancies. 'Why are you so gone on her?' she asked curious to know.

Paris shrugged. 'We talked and . . . that was all really. We just talked and I really liked her . . . '

'Surely the hotel could furnish you with a contact number?' she suggested, applying logic to the problem.

'They won't cough up. I've already tried!' he confessed, grinning sheepishly. 'There were only two flights out the day she left and I was on the last. She said she was returning to England but . . . Let's face it, Sam. She could be anywhere.' A girl who would go where she pleased, when she pleased. He'd no idea how he was going to find her again and it was driving him mad. His colour deepened.

'What can I do?'

'I don't see there's much you can do,' Sam answered, ever practical and sorry she couldn't be more encouraging. It did sound hopeless. 'Try and not worry. Something will turn up.'

'Hey, there are loads of girls out there.' His

expression belied his flippancy. He pushed the empty glass across the bar. 'Can we talk about something else? Tell me about Uncle Gerry . . . '

It would at least take his mind off things.

'I can't tell you what my father's up to at present.' She sighed. 'I've heard nothing other than a measly phone call.' They had had a single, garbled conversation on a crackly line, following on from her fruitless visit to Spain early in the autumn. He'd been so cagey, refusing to tell her where he was currently living. She'd no idea what possible reason could have driven him into abandoning his flat overlooking Seville and, worse, leaving his property business to run itself. The flat was beautiful. His work was his life. None of it made sense. She had to accept that, for some reason, he didn't want to be found. No one at his office had seemed in the slightest minded to help her out, leaving her with the impression that they'd been warned off, probably by Gerry himself, though she'd no idea why this should be.

'He told me not to worry,' she went on. She had wondered how he could expect her to do anything else. If he was in trouble she wanted to be there for him. He must know it!

'What a pair!' Paris ran a hand through his hair, grinning wearily. 'He'll be all right, Sam.

Me too, I expect. Somehow . . . '

'Sam . . . ?'

Their so unexpected confidential moment was broken. She swung round, her face dissolving into a smile of undisguised pleasure, surmounting everything, even her present worries. 'Steph!' she breathed, jumping down and sliding her arm through his. He patted it encouragingly, his ready smile reflecting hers.

'Sorry, Sam, I keep you waiting. I make it up!'

'You're going to, don't worry!' she warned, jokingly. 'We're late, we'd best get a move on. Sure you don't want to come, Paris?'

Paris shook his head, pulling a face.

'Nah. Have fun, you two . . . '

At that moment George Carter emerged through the swing doors and, looking unnaturally dour, appeared to wish them anything but fun.

Uncomfortably intuiting the young man's feelings for her, Sam stifled a momentary pang of guilt. She did like him. Let's face it, there was nothing to dislike about George. She hadn't reckoned on Stephanio, that was all. They stopped, making small chat, then passed on, her grip tightening on Stephanio's arm, George already selfishly forgotten and her spirits rising at thoughts of the evening to come.

Bobbie Vernon stopped to pull up her collar before stepping smartly outside into the December evening. Cold slapped against her face, sharpening senses made dull by overwork. It had been a tough week, following on from a tough last few months but it was a battle she hoped she was winning.

A warm glow flowed through her, making her oblivious to the wintry weather, with the frost already riming the stands of this famous old ground. The glowing feeling had been reinforced by a thing wonderful to Bobbie, more so because it had been so totally unexpected. She had gained respect in the eyes of her work colleagues, to a man, the one group of people among whom she'd never thought to see it, urging her on as nothing else could have done.

She still had a lot to prove, and she meant to prove it, hence the working late. She didn't have to remind herself she'd yet to get home, wash, change and somehow get herself to Susie Lamoure's place by sometime half an hour ago.

Under the pool of light thrown from the streetlight across from the ground, the figure of a man emerged from the bus shelter under which he'd been sheltering, pulling down his hat before crossing the road towards her.

'Alan?' Her face must have registered her surprise. Alan Campion stopped in his tracks, watching her warily, unsure of her response, or indeed, what his own should be. He'd been nowhere near the ground since he'd so abruptly resigned from the club. She had no idea, she realized now, how he must feel about her taking over his old job. Annoyed, she imagined. She stood, regarding him warily, relaxing when she saw there was really no need for concern. He smiled, his hand brushing her arm.

'Bobbie . . . I was hoping I'd see you. Have you time for a coffee?'

She hadn't, but how could she refuse?

Ted Bovey's was a dingy backstreet café supporters used on match day, thereby swelling the coffers to cover the lack of takings during the rest of the week. Inside the warm and strangely welcoming confines of the burly ex-footballer's tiny front room, Bobbie unfastened her coat and sat down to stare into the murky depths of a beverage of dubious quality, waiting patiently for the man across the table to tell her what this was about. Her conscience was already reproaching her. She'd been meaning to ring him, something else she hadn't had time to get round to yet. He must feel he'd been abandoned.

She stirred her coffee, embarrassed about it, conceding now that what Eleanor had complained about only the previous evening was perfectly true. She'd become so consumed in all things Rislington of late that everything else was passing her by. This shy and gentle man's predicament for one.

'How are you?' she began. 'I mean . . . ' she smiled helplessly, 'what I'm trying to say is . . . how are you coping?'

'Just!' he acknowledged ruefully. 'Ronnie cut me dead in the street this morning but it's good to know who your friends are! I've certainly found out that much.'

She pulled a sympathetic face, exasperated, if not surprised that the Rogues manager should assume their old friend's guilt before the affair had even gone to trial. 'If it helps, I'm having trouble with him too,' she said encouragingly, trying to take his mind off his troubles. 'You've heard we've drawn Villains in the third round?'

She ought, like Ronnie, to have been thrilled, but instead had been faintly repelled by the unpleasing sight of her manager dancing round the office radio the moment the draw was heard. Supporters too, desperate for a crack at a Premiership scalp, had never left off ringing to express their jubilation at the news.

For the first time in her life Bobbie was seeing things from a different angle. Their squad was too lightweight, certainly not strong enough to maintain their current, unexpectedly high league position with a cup run. Alan would know exactly where she was coming from.

'Ronnie pleased, was he?' her old colleague conjectured.

'Too pleased!' she groaned, recollecting with a sharp stab of disapproval his refusal to listen to her heartfelt exhortations urging caution. 'Fiddlesticks, woman!' he'd retorted, his very expression suggesting she knew nothing about it. She was a woman; the fact spoke volumes where Ronnie was concerned.

Only a growing awareness that her relationship with her erstwhile manager was rocky enough as it was had stopped her temper from spilling over.

'What's more important, Alan, league or cup?' she demanded hotly, all her ill feelings stirred anew at thoughts of Ronnie's intransigence. 'The Premiership's where the money is; we can't possibly do both — '

'The league of course!' Alan responded supportively, understanding exactly. 'And I can well imagine Ronnie's reaction when you put him right . . . ' For the first time during the course of the conversation, Alan Campion smiled. He'd had his battles with Ronnie too. Who hadn't?

'I suggested fielding a weakened team!' Bobbie's eyes rolled at recollection of her temerity. It was euphemistically called squad rotation. Every club did it nowadays and Ronnie should have known it more than anyone. Instead he was placing his own personal dreams of glory before what was best for the club.

Trouble was looming and would have to be tackled sooner rather than later.

'Hearing things like that makes me glad I'm out of it, Bobbie,' Alan muttered, taking a gulp of coffee.

There was a pointed silence. Was there something else? Something must have brought him back to his old stamping-ground.

'Alan, if there's anything I can do?' she prompted.

'Actually, Bobbie . . . there is. I want you to help clear my name!'

This last was spoken forcefully, animating Alan Campion's thin features with a surprising vigour. The old Alan. Bobbie leaned forward, elbows on the table, hands clasped together.

'Alan, I'd do anything . . . ' she said slowly, her mind working in overdrive.

Despite her desire to believe, a tiny sliver of doubt would insist on surfacing. The police had charged him. They must have some evidence!

Her face was an open book. 'You too, Bobbie?' he muttered, staring at her miserably. 'Of course, you're bound to think — '

'I don't think anything!' she interjected hotly.

'I was in a mess financially at the time the money went missing — '

'You don't have to explain . . .' she mumbled wretchedly, feeling terrible, wishing they weren't having this conversation. Alan was worried sick and had every right to be.

'It's OK, I want to tell you.' He sat back, running a tired hand through his hair. 'I'm not the first to take on too much and find the ends don't meet. Debt's a fool's game and a fool fell into a trap. My rotten bad luck, the stuff the police have managed to unearth, given the interpretation they were bound to put upon it.'

Impulsively Bobbie reached across the table and covered his hand with hers, her gut instinct assuring her of his honesty; she was relieved when his face relaxed.

'If you could just go through some of the old office records?' he pleaded. 'Something, anything you can find you think might help!'

She could certainly. Then she sat back, frowning, overwhelmed by an unexpected and unpalatable thought . . . She had no right to be here! She shouldn't be talking to anyone about club finances and never with Alan, Alan less than anyone. Everything happening to him at this moment was a matter for a court of law.

'There's bound to be something on a file somewhere . . . ' He stopped, faltered, aware something was wrong. 'I was saying — '

'I know what you were saying, Alan.' Slowly, wretchedly, sick with guilt, Bobbie pushed back her chair and stood up, only too aware that, father on the board or not, if the club's lawyers were to get the slightest wind of her being here she'd be dismissed instantly. Why hadn't she thought?

'You'll help me, surely?' He frowned, still not understanding.

'I'm sorry. I can't. You must know why . . . '

With no thought in her head now other than to get away she stumbled forward, knocking against the chair in her haste, hardly aware of Alan's pained face, the clatter of teacups, of Ted banging about in the back and the steady hum of traffic outside the ground, penetrating even the walls of this grubby little café.

Her face was hot with confusion. Alan was

109

her friend, Landon's too. Despite what her every instinct told her, her steps faltered. Hand on the door, she turned, looking back wretchedly to where Alan sat, thin shoulders slumped, head buried in his hands, an aura of despair surrounding him, it broke her heart to see him. Her old friend. Landon's friend and part of her childhood.

Was she really becoming the kind of person who'd turn their back on an old friend in trouble because sticking up for him was awkward, impossible even? Was there even a decision?

Hang the lawyers and the football club! She went back, past caring anyway, her hand falling lightly on his shoulder. He looked up instantly, a tremulous hope illuminating his face.

'Don't worry. I'll do what I can,' she murmured quietly, relief flooding her voice. 'Just for goodness' sake, don't tell anyone, that's all.'

★   ★   ★

'How do I look?'

Eleanor emerged from upstairs in the dress she'd spent an age in choosing, executing a neat twirl in front of Landon, where he sat at the writing bureau, finishing the last of the work he'd brought home from the board-room. The hem was below knee-length, and the dress had a high bodice and flowing skirt in the kind of pale blue that matched her eyes. At one time, Landon's eyes would have been on stalks, to see her in a dress like this. Was she being oversensitive, anticipating a slight where none was intended? He glanced up quickly, running a hand through his thick grey hair.

'You look lovely,' he remarked, returning immediately to the list of accounts that wouldn't quite add up, no matter how long he fretted over them.

'You might sound like you mean it.' She frowned.

He threw down his pen and stood up. It could wait, he'd had enough. He was tired, this blessed charity do of the Lamoures was the last thing he felt like.

'I might have guessed you wouldn't want to go,' Eleanor observed, seeing his ill-temper. Discontent crept into her voice.

'To be honest, I don't,' Landon complained, speaking his mind, then, watching her face fall, wishing he hadn't. 'Oh hang it, Eleanor,' he blustered testily, 'must you be so embroiled with the Lamoures? I can't stand them, if you must know!'

She came to stand by the Christmas tree she'd spent the afternoon dressing, her voice full of the hurt she was battling to restrain.

'You have no right to say such things. You hardly know them,' she murmured, not understanding why he'd become so unjust of late. He never used to be.

'You've been spending an awful lot of time there, that was all I meant,' he answered, a barely suppressed indignation rising to the fore.

'Why shouldn't I?' Even Landon heard the edge to her voice.

Too late, he tried to backtrack. 'I'm not saying it's bad for you to have a hobby,' he blustered. 'I mean, all the charity work you and Susie get up to — '

'Get up to?' she queried hotly, sensing injustice, determined to winkle it out.

Landon took a deep breath, nettled that the Lamoures had been the start of all this, that if they'd never asked Eleanor along on their blessed cruise, none of this, whatever it was that was wrong with his marriage, would ever have boiled over.

He and Eleanor seemed to do nothing but fall out nowadays. She couldn't want it this way. He surveyed her hopelessly, wishing he could snap his fingers and put things right. He could at least, he decided swiftly, be honest about how he felt.

'I've been meaning to say it for a while. It's taking up too much of your time.' He stood

112

back, frowning, waiting for the eruption he knew was bound to follow. Eleanor had always been volatile and once, strangely, he had loved her for it. Now he'd rather anything than that she should go off on one of her tantrums.

He was getting old; he wanted a quiet life! Was it too much to ask?

'Football takes up nothing of your time, I presume?'

Rather than exploding her tone was icy, wrong-footing him.

'I knew you'd have to drag football into it — '

'We're late. Are you ready?'

She turned away forlornly, reaching for her evening bag, thrown carelessly on the chair, so he wanted instantly to reach out too, if only to pull her into his arms and hold her close. Love all their troubles away. He didn't. It was too late. They'd reached an impasse, something that they were doing too much of lately.

He drove in a silence in keeping with the large fat snowflakes which, having threatened all day, were falling at last, hissing against the windscreen, and covering the world in white. The night sky was clouded, the moon non-existent. Eleanor sat stiffly in the passenger seat, distant and preoccupied,

113

responding to his blunt and painfully obvious attempts at retrieving the situation with mostly monosyllables. Now and then he shot her a worried glance.

'Are you all right?' he asked, at last.

'Of course,' she snapped coldly, obviously not.

Stubbornly she refused to tell him what the problem really was. Why had they lost the ability to talk? They always used to talk! He sighed heavily, aware that he'd managed, yet again, to disappoint her and that he'd done it when she'd so been looking forward to this evening. Couldn't he just, for once, have kept his reservations to himself? Could he help it, if she was behaving like a small and petulant child?

The Lamoures' mansion loomed, a beacon of light. Relieved, he swung the car through the gates and parked up along the already thronged driveway. He took Eleanor's arm and hustled her inside, to be greeted by the sight of a huge Christmas tree shimmering in the hallway. A butler divested them of outer clothing and directed their way through the hall and towards a room from which emanated the happy hum of voices, of people having fun. Momentarily, Landon's low spirits lifted.

'There you are, Eleanor!' Immediately Susie Lamoure made a beeline for Eleanor, hustling her away, leaving him alone and awkward again, feeling deserted, any pretence at enjoyment dissolving instantly. He hated large social gatherings and this sort more than most.

'Vernon!'

He swung round, relieved to find Eddie Lamoure's burly figure at his elbow. So he didn't like him. It was someone to talk to. His face fell into a weak attempt at a smile.

'Good you've come, man! I've been meaning to have a word . . . ' Smoothly, Eddie took his arm, steering him back the way he'd just come and up the curling stairway facing the hall to a seemingly endless corridor and a room that was obviously his private study. He shut the door, instantly and wonderfully to Landon's mind, fastening the lid to, on the blaring music and the sounds of burgeoning revelry. Peace. He relaxed instantly, taking his time to absorb his surroundings so he'd have something to tell Eleanor later; he was sure she'd never been so far into the house as to penetrate the space of Lamoure's private sanctuary. It was a large and comfortable room, panelled in oak and lined with books he was sure Eddie Lamoure never took the trouble to read; he wasn't the type. There was a desk, and a sofa, chairs were dotted about and a drinks cabinet was

115

nearly as big as his own study at home. The works of art hanging on the one spare wall were, he guessed, priceless, but, surprisingly, they were interspersed with pictures of Eddie Lamoure at the various stages of his life, to what he was now, entrepreneur and hard-nosed businessman.

No one tangled with Eddie Lamoure by choice. Landon, experienced as he was, had no illusions about the middle-aged man who lowered himself into the chair on the far side of the desk. He leaned back to light up a large fat cigar, puffing clouds of blue-grey smoke in his direction.

It had been a long day. Uneasily, he sat down on a vast sofa into which he all but disappeared, pondering what this was about. He and Lamoure hardly inhabited the same sphere. He was a football man, romance was in his soul, his companion was a moneymaking machine, dealing in amounts of money that Landon considered obscene. They'd not a thing in common.

Lamoure scrubbed a large hand across his face. 'I've a business proposition,' he barked abruptly, plunging straight to the point. 'What do you want for your shares?'

'My shares?' Had he missed the point somewhere? Landon stared at the wretched man in blank incomprehension.

'Your shares, man!' The businessman leaned forward to rest his elbows on the desk, fixing Landon with a calculating stare. 'I'm head of a consortium interested in buying up the football club. Rislington Rovers FC. What do you say? We're offering a good price; you'll not lose out, mind!'

'What do I say?' Sell his lifeblood? Landon sprang to his feet, shock causing the colour to flee from his face, any illusion of good cheer shattering instantly. 'I say you're out of your tiny mind, man!'

★ ★ ★

Bobbie parked amongst the general assemblage of Jags and Mercedes and jumped out of the car, arriving at the Lamoures' impressive front door at the same time as Babs and Taylor. They might as well have come in the same car, but the fact that it had never entered their respective heads spoke volumes for the way things were between them.

'Looks like we've landed in fairyland!' Babs chuckled, nodding towards the tree, good humour bubbling up inside her. It was a beautiful tree and she'd always loved Christmas. Eleanor always made such a lot of this time of year.

She clung to Taylor's arm, even now

surprised that he'd agreed to accompany her. Charity events weren't normally Taylor's thing. She'd won him round by pointing out that it was good for trade for the two of them to be seen together and at such a prestigious occasion. Taylor knew as well as she did that Cedars' success depended on nights such as this.

At the same time she was aware of Bobbie's shooting her a look of reproach. She couldn't still be sore over Todd's decision to go professional? It seemed she was.

'How's Todd?' Babs enquired innocently, reluctantly letting go of Taylor's arm. The two women divested themselves of their coats before the little party made its way into the function room, Babs in a swirling ankle-length of powder-blue that suited her complexion exactly, Bobbie in a neat white blouse and a black pencil-skirt that her sister considered too severe.

'How do you think?' Bobbie retorted, more sharply than she'd intended. She hadn't come here to argue, but her dear son was existing currently in a crumbling bedsit, struggling to make ends meet. True, he was making a name for himself, winning one or two of the smaller, more local tournaments, but it was still a far cry from his ultimate goal, which was successfully to apply to join the PGA. He ought to have realized, long ago, exactly where this crazy venture was heading and Bobbie would be failing in her duty as his mother if she didn't point it out. Babs had no right to egg him on.

Bobbie was consumed with a guilty feeling that she had no right to cast cold water on her son's dreams either; that it would be better if she supported him whole heartedly, whatever he wanted to do or be.

'I do wish you hadn't encouraged him in this foolhardiness, Babs,' she muttered, unable to help herself for blaming Babs.

'I? Encourage him?' Babs face flamed red.

'You know this is a pipe dream! Not what I wanted for him.'

'Isn't it about what Todd wants?' Babs responded, shocked that she had to point it out.

'How about I take your big sister for a dance?' Taylor cried, intervening before a full-scale family row erupted. He hustled a protesting Bobbie quickly away and on to the dance floor. It was the last thing she felt like when she'd already decided on one quick drink and home!

'Let yourself go. Relax!' he urged, slipping his arm around her waist. Ignoring Babs's obvious disapproval, he guided her with consummate ease around the floor. He was a good dancer with an athlete's natural sense of rhythm. Her good humour restored; Bobbie gave in with good grace. Despite his reputation, she liked Taylor and always had. Her nimble feet followed his as she enjoyed for a moment the feeling of big-brother reliability that he'd always, surprisingly, aroused in her. There was more to Taylor than met the eye, she mused, aware at the same time that after the sort of week she'd had she was too tired for this and would rather be at home, tucked up in bed. The music finished. She reached up and kissed her escort lightly and placatingly on the cheek.

'Dance with Babs!' she ordered, chuckling at his wry expression. A niggling doubt surfaced, maybe her sister's marriage wasn't as stable as Babs would have wished it. And neither was that of her parents, come to that, she reflected, making her way to the bar and considering the unpalatable fact: how few relationships in her family were currently unmarred by discord.

'Here, let me!' As if by magic, Davie Mackenzie appeared at her side, looking surprisingly pleased to see her and giving every impression that he'd been awaiting his moment. She couldn't deny, despite her tiredness, the thrill shooting through her at the sight of his lean, hard figure, distinguished in tuxedo. She'd known he was going to be here. It seemed she couldn't even acknowledge to herself the truth: she'd been on the lookout for him ever since she'd walked into the room.

He ordered a white-wine spritzer, her usual drink.

'There was no need,' she frowned, disarmed as his hand lightly and, it seemed, deliberately brushed hers as he passed her glass.

'There was every need,' he countered. 'Bobbie, we can't carry on this way . . . '

He referred to the way they'd been avoiding each other of late.

She stood, holding her glass awkwardly in both hands, wondering how to respond. Being around Davie nowadays, she was discovering, made it hard to think. Ruefully she acknowledged that she was still attracted to him and, no matter how he tried to deny it; she sensed that he was still attracted to her.

She sipped her drink, accepting that it was still no good. Even if either of them wanted to rekindle their old affair, there was always the small matter of her job. The press would have a field day if she took up with one of her own players.

It shouldn't matter, but of course it did. She'd enough on her plate.

'I don't mean to avoid you, Davie,' she prevaricated.

'You just look like you do,' he countered, watching her broodingly, unable to hide the spark of desire that sprang into his eyes. With a shock, she realized that he wanted her, just as much as she wanted him.

'It's just . . . awkward.'

'Of course it is but we can be grown up about it, surely?'

'Come and dance, Davie . . . '

A young girl whom Bobbie recognized as one of Susie Lamoures' many nieces, had pushed her way through the crowd milling round the bar. Pretty, long-haired, she grabbed Davie's arm and pulled him on to the dance floor. Too easily, he let himself be led away, turning to throw Bobbie a rueful glance. Or was it one of relief? Suddenly Bobbie didn't know. He knew the score between them. His dancing partner must have been a timely intervention when it appeared that all he wanted was to warn Bobbie off. A good working relationship, that was all he intended. She was a fool if she thought his unexpected attention meant anything else.

Bobbie stood, frozen into immobility, unwilling to watch, but unable to help herself, hating to see his arm placed round the girl's slim waist and the way he was holding her so unnecessarily close.

If he'd wanted to make a point, he'd made it.

A hot tide of emotion surged through her, which she recognized immediately for the jealousy it was. Why shouldn't Davie Mackenzie dance with other girls? Unattached girls unburdened by emotional baggage and a job that never gave them time to think.

She turned away and put down her glass, her eyes full of bitter and unexplainable tears.

★ ★ ★

Landon fled from Lamoure's study and hurried across the hallway to the function room, where he found Eleanor at last, chatting to some of her fellow charity workers. Grimly, he pushed his way towards her and took hold of her arm.

'We're going — '

'We are not!' Irritated, she broke free and stepped back to stare up at him, perplexity gradually giving way to alarm.

'Landon? Are you all right? You've gone very pale — '

'I'm not all right!' he snapped. He pulled her away, out of earshot and glowered down at her as if it were all her fault. Hang it, it *was* her fault! A vague disquiet surfaced. Eleanor was in such cahoots with the Lamoures nowadays, she must have known about Eddie's offer all along. 'Offered to buy my shares . . . Eddie Lamoure . . . pompous ass!' He was almost apoplectic. 'Knock-down price too, I expect! Does the man take me for a fool? And don't tell me you knew nothing about it . . . ' People were beginning to stare. He took a deep breath, urging his heart to stop hammering.

'I've no idea what you're talking about.' Eleanor was bewildered. Here he was, charging out here like a rampaging bull, just when she'd thought things were going so well. 'I wondered where you'd got to.' She frowned. 'I might have known it was business!'

'Eddie Lamoure's just offered to buy me out of the football club,' he repeated more calmly, at last beginning to make sense. Furiously, his eyes fastened on hers.

Eleanor's face cleared as comprehension dawned, bringing with it a wild joy that she made no effort to hide. There was no reason to when Landon knew precisely how she felt about his involvement in all things football, and Rislington Rovers football club in particular.

'But darling, what a wonderful opportunity!' she enthused, her face immediately shining and bright as a young girl's. 'Oh, but you will, won't you? Think of all the extra time we'd have to spend together . . . '

Landon's whole body stiffened. She'd

betrayed him, colluded to get him here and now she was making things even worse. 'Of course I won't accept,' he answered quietly. 'You mean, sell out to a moneymaking machine like Eddie Lamoure? Surely you know me better?'

Oh, she knew him! Hope died instantly in Eleanor's breast. She was a middle-aged woman again and, even worse, one not particularly desired. She shook her head bitterly.

'Why, Landon, whatever should give me the impression that you might just once, *once* in your whole blessed life, put me before your precious football club?'

Aware only of Landon's shocked, white face, and needing desperately to put distance between it and herself, she blundered away, only to pull up short against a tall and reassuringly familiar figure. Relief shot through her. Accompanying a cry of surprise, Giles Barnard's hands fell to her shoulders, pulling her close.

'Eleanor! Are you all right? Oh, but it is good to see you again!'

Aware of Landon in hot pursuit, she leaned into him.

She hadn't seen Giles since the cruise. Despite their differences, the awkwardness caused by his misguided passion for all things

Eleanor, she had eventually managed to persuade him that her marriage was the most important thing in her life. Or, at least, it had once been, she raged inside herself now, unable to make sense of the jumble that her feelings were in.

At this moment, Giles was a port in a storm, and any port was needed now.

'Giles! Am I pleased to see you!' Her tone was heartfelt.

'Problems?' His gaze searched hers, his face expressive only of his delight at seeing her again.

Aware of Landon on the periphery of her vision, she nodded dumbly, horribly aware too of a tear spilling over, tracing the line of her cheekbone. She dashed it away angrily. 'Take me somewhere quiet, Giles, please,' she implored, relieved when, without further ado, he led her to a secluded alcove where they both sat down.

'Tell me?' he prompted, seizing her hand and stroking it gently.

'I'm being ridiculous,' she muttered, certain that she wasn't. She tugged free and fumbled in her bag for a hanky to blow her nose. Hot feelings rose, demanding outlet. 'Eddie's made a bid for Landon's shares in the football club!' she blurted out miserably, though still with wits enough to register her companion's calm acceptance of the news. Giles knew about this already?

'Ah . . . Eddie's managed to corner him, then?' he responded, confirming the suspicion.

'You knew?' she demanded, perplexed and wondering how it had become such common knowledge.

'You could say!' Giles laughed easily, angling his long frame towards her. 'Of course I know! Didn't you realize? I'm part of the consortium and if you could only persuade your dear husband to sell up, you'd actually be doing me one huge favour. He isn't too hot on the idea, I take it?' He seemed to find the idea amusing.

'Ice-cold, I'd say,' she muttered, treacherously. Suddenly, she didn't care. 'Landon does as Landon wants and never mind what I might think!' she cried angrily. 'Oh, but Giles, it would leave us so much time to spend together. It would be simply wonderful if only he could see it! But it seems I don't matter to him, not even as much as I thought . . . '

It was unforgivable to be saying these things to Giles, but Giles was here and listening sympathetically, unlike Landon who wasn't, and who didn't listen anyway. The crowd dimmed, receded; at long last her anger, unquenchable, boiled over. Football had had such a terrible, unforgivable effect on her family over the years. Bobbie had never a moment to spare, Babs and Taylor were at constant loggerheads. Paris was running wild, with too much money, and not enough sense to see where it was leading.

She hated it. She hated football!

Her eyes brimmed with tears she no longer took the trouble to hide. As far as she could see, prising this family away from its over-involvement with Rislington Rovers football club would be the best thing, the most wonderful thing that could possibly come to pass.

5

From the far corner of Rislington Rovers' famous old football pitch came the bellowed orders of Bryn Mackay, head coach, putting the first team through its paces. It was the fourth round of the Cup on Saturday and, contrary to expectations, the Rogues were still in it, with a chance of progressing against fellow championship side, Borden United.

On her way back to work after a lunchtime meeting with Eleanor in The Cedars' stylish new spa centre, Bobbie plunged her hands deep into the pockets of her sheepskin coat. The extra matches caused by the cup run and Ronnie's insistence on playing the first team throughout had put an unnecessary burden on what was basically a small squad. Too many games equalled too many first team members injured, Davie Mackenzie amongst them. It wasn't a coincidence they'd lost the mid-week league match, dropping places in the league and out of the top six positions ensuring their place in the play-off for promotion at the end of the season. Even Robbie Hubberfield couldn't argue that his policy of fielding the first team in the cup games was causing discontent amongst the reserves, denied their customary chance of a game in which to stake their claims for a regular spot.

Anarchy threatened.

'All right, Bobbie?'

Ronnie Hubberfield broke away from supervising the five players designated to take penalties in the event of a draw, throwing a condescending smile her way.

Someone ought to point out that bobble-hats and shorts didn't suit middle-aged men, revealing knees scarlet with cold. The chance to have a word was too good to miss. Boots sinking into the hallowed turf, she marched briskly across the pitch.

'Are you giving the reserves a chance, Saturday, Ronnie?' she demanded, knowing the answer already and already out of patience.

'I shouldn't think so!' he responded sharply. He stood, jogging on the spot, thumping his hands under his arms to keep warm. Snow threatened. Unfortunately, not threatening enough to get the match cancelled and rearranged to some more convenient date when the treatment room wouldn't be quite so crowded.

'And what about the league?' she demanded indignantly.

'I know which the supporters want most . . . ' he goaded, enjoying her discomfiture.

'The fans want Premiership football — '

'As if you'd know.'

She knew nothing obviously! She was a woman and everyone knew what Ronnie Hubberfield thought about women and football. Chauvinistic wasn't in it. Bobbie's temper, never far from the surface when she was near Ronnie, threatened to spill over.

'We'll see what Jimmy has to say, shall we?' she answered coolly.

'You needn't go blatherin' to the chairman!'

Ronnie's colour was high but whether that was down to the exercise or to the doubles he'd downed in quick succession at lunch she couldn't tell. She hoped his drinking wasn't getting out of control. Unless there was something else?

Heads turned. Glad of the diversion, players stood hands on hips, breathing hard and watching them curiously.

'You might find you've taken on more than you expected,' Ronnie added maliciously.

'Meaning?'

'Meaning you were seen talking to Alan.'

Even allowing for her heels, he was a good head taller than she was. His manner was threatening, challenging her to cross him if she dared. She did dare. She had to.

'I shall talk to exactly whom I please!' she retorted, resisting the urge to step back, perfectly aware, as was Ronnie, that her unsanctioned communion with Alan Campion could land her in terrible trouble. Her secret was out, in the worst hands possible and she couldn't do a thing about it. What she could do, however, was stop this irascible old Yorkshireman from treating the club as if it were his own personal plaything.

'You might be prepared to trample over old friends, Ronnie,' she went on quietly, 'but you could at least cast an eye over the treatment room before you scupper any chance of success we have in the league. Tell our chairman that, too, whilst you're about it!'

Not waiting to see the effect of her tirade, she turned, pinkfaced, and stalked away, back through the players' tunnel and up towards the offices. She was trembling, her confidence at zero point. Reaching the sanctuary of her room, her bolthole as she'd come to think of it, she was miserably conscious this was the second unlooked for set-to she'd suffered already that day. Did the fact that the first had involved her mother make it better or worse?

★ ★ ★

The aromatherapy massage, a long-standing arrangement that Eleanor had persuaded Bobbie into when once, fondly, she'd imagined she had a life outside Rislington Rovers, had today been meant to stretch to a pedicure and a light lunch with Babs. She'd rushed the massage, cried off the rest and only the fact she'd seen so little of her mother lately, persuaded her to keep the massage appointment.

'You're never dashing off already . . . ?'

Frowning, clutching the large pink bath-towel provided for the guests, Eleanor eased herself up from the masseuse's couch.

'Sorry, Mum . . . ' Bobbie, done and dusted and keen to be off, was already backing towards the door.

'Lavender is meant to be relaxing, darling.'

'So that was what it was?' She grinned.

'See you next week, Eleanor,' Sue, the head masseuse, snapped the lid on her case of unguents before hurrying away to her next appointment.

Eleanor sat back, feet dangling, looking suddenly so sorry for herself that all thoughts of the mid-season statement of accounts, which Bobbie had promised Jimmy yesterday, shot from her mind.

'You and Dad did sort out that silly business over the shares, didn't you?' she murmured. 'You understand he can't possibly sell out to Eddie, no matter what's been offered?'

Eleanor slid off the couch, feet fumbling for her slippers. Her expression made it clear that she hadn't accepted it, was still fuming in fact and holding it in, in a way entirely at odds with her usual forthright manner.

'We did what your father wanted — as usual,' she said savagely. 'Goodness me, why should any man choose to pay a little attention to his wife!'

Her tone was so bitter, so not Eleanor, it took Bobbie's breath away.

'There's far more to it than — '

'He doesn't care about the extra time it would give us together!' she interrupted peevishly. Nothing had changed. She wanted to sell. Landon didn't. Their mutual resentment was plain to see. Stubbornly, unforgivably he refused to see that Eleanor wanted this for them both. 'You might back me up for once, Bobbie,' she finished, forlornly.

Something in her tone made Bobbie's heart ache. She dreaded to think what this business was doing to her family. She spoke gently, willing this sometimes obstinate woman to understand. 'It would be terrible if we lost our family holdings. Please, Mum . . . You've got to at least try and see Dad's viewpoint.'

'Giles says it would be the best thing that could possibly happen!' came the swift response. 'An injection of cash, new faces, fresh ideas — '

Bobbie's temper, stirred by too much to do and not enough time to do it in, for once and unusually for her, spilled over. 'What's Giles Barnard to do with this?' She frowned. 'I know he's in Eddie's consortium, but you shouldn't be listening to him, Mum! It's . . . it's disloyal!'

'Hah! And I'm supposed to stand back whilst your father works himself into an early grave?' Her mother's large, still vivid blue eyes, widened in dismay. 'I know it's hard having to face the fact that he's not as well as he used to be — '

'His angina's no worse?' Bobbie couldn't bear the thoughts of anything happening to Landon. Landon was the one constant in her life; it was unfair of her mother to play on her fears.

Eleanor shook her head. 'Not worse exactly, darling, but all this business isn't helping. He ought to be slowing down, taking things easy. I would have thought you'd be trying to make him see sense.'

'Sell our shares you mean?' Bobbie's voice dropped an octave.

Eleanor's sense of injustice finally and unforgivably boiled over.

'Of course I mean sell our shares and good riddance!'

The recollection of her mother's last words still ringing in her ears, Bobbie crossed the office and flicked the switch on the kettle. That, it turned out, had been that. Eleanor had disappeared off to her pedicure; Bobbie had called a hasty goodbye to Babs in reception and hurried back to work.

She poured boiling water on coffee granules, reached for milk, sugar, her mind in turmoil. Was her mother right? Was she, Bobbie, choosing to ignore the effect this whole business was having on her father's already fragile health?

There was no doubting he had looked strained of late.

★ ★ ★

'She only ever sees your father's point of view . . . '

Despite her lingering resentment over Bobbie, Eleanor Vernon finished the last of her crispy chicken with pancetta, with a soft sigh of pleasure. A morning spent in the

136

health spa had whetted her appetite. It had done her good to get out and take her mind off things.

There was no response. Babs was staring forlornly across the room and through into the foyer where Taylor lounged against the reception desk, sharing a joke with the new receptionist. Eleanor swivelled round, unsurprised to see the pair laughing, heads bent too close together and obviously sharing an intimate moment. Typical Taylor!

'Everything all right with you two, love?' she asked, turning back, her expression troubled. Momentarily she forgot her own woes.

Babs jumped, visibly startled, putting down her knife and fork and giving up any pretence of eating. 'I think he forgets I'm here sometimes, Mum,' she murmured, wistfully.

'You two ought to get out more,' Eleanor smiled. 'Why don't you take the evening off? Get away from this place!'

'Oddly enough, I've already suggested it. He's out with an old teammate tonight.' Babs was still unsure whether she believed it or not and took no trouble now to conceal her bitterness. There was no point, Eleanor was aware of it anyway. Her wide blue eyes, Eleanor's eyes, filled with pain.

And then, just as suddenly, she relaxed.

'Oh, take no notice of me, Mum. I'm being over-sensitive.' She smiled weakly. 'I only wanted to talk business. When else do Taylor and I get a chance?'

'He ought to take more care of things.' And you too, Eleanor thought hotly, not saying it, seeing Babs hurt enough already. Instead she poured the coffee. 'Everything *is* all right, darling?'

Ruefully, Babs gestured to the empty tables around them.

'You mean more than the usual post-Christmas slump? The fact that the health spa hasn't exactly taken off and I can't get the books to balance?'

'Oh dear, Babs . . . '

'Don't worry. I'm joking!' Was she? Again, Babs no longer knew. She sipped her coffee, frowning thoughtfully and accepting that she wasn't sure about anything any more. With a supreme effort she forced her mind back to her big sister's unswerving and entirely typical support for their father. 'You can't expect Dad to give up his shares, Mum. Nor expect Bobbie not to back him,' she added, as an afterthought, trying to be fair, even now, when Bobbie hardly deserved it.

She sat back, a small pout of discontent niggling to the surface.

'Why was Bobbie the only one who

thought to tell me about this share business?' she demanded. 'It should have been Dad, only I don't suppose he gave me a second thought.' Her voice rose, colour flooding her face at recollection of Landon's insensitivity. Typical Landon! Typical Bobbie too, taking charge and not giving a thought to Babs. 'He'll have talked to Bobbie, of course!' she muttered angrily. 'He's always favoured Bobbie. This is just another prime example . . . '

Eleanor Vernon wrapped her hands round her coffee cup and sat back; regarding her younger daughter in dismay and mortified now that she hadn't picked up on it. How long had she been bottling this up?

'You know how busy we were at Christmas,' she urged, in a belated attempt to repair the damage Landon had obviously, so thoughtlessly done. 'You were rushed off your feet at Cedars. Your father hardly saw you, love, to be fair.'

The worst thing was, Babs did have a point. Christmas had been a disaster. Landon and Bobbie had spent it in a close discussion which ceased immediately anyone else came near. Even Eleanor had begun to feel pushed out.

'Love, he doesn't mean to be unkind,' she pressed on. 'He has a lot on his mind. We all do.'

'It still doesn't make it right — '

'It doesn't and I'm sorry, and I will have a word with him but . . . ' Eleanor put down her cup, tilted her head to one side and fixed her daughter with the sort of gaze that sent Babs spinning instantly back to her childhood. She had an opinion she was determined to air, whether Babs cared to hear it or not. She leaned forwards, her voice filled with excitement. 'Have you thought how much we'd get, if only we did sell those blasted shares?'

Oddly, given that they were in a business dealing so much with it, the question of money had never entered Babs's head. In the pause that followed, for the first time she did consider it.

'But what are you saying?' She frowned, puzzled. There was no doubting that she could do with some extra cash. She'd only to think of all that needed doing round this place.

Astute enough to realize that she'd made her point, her mother gave a laugh that carried all before her, even Babs. 'A chance to fulfil your every dream, darling, that's what I'm saying!' she cried. 'You and Bobbie would come into your inheritance, darling. Just think. And at a time when you're still young enough to make the best of it. You're worried about the health spa . . . Have you thought my dear, darling daughter, of all you'd be able to do here, with such a massive injection of cash?'

* * *

'Grief! We must have won the Cup already!'

Sam Vernon stood in the foyer, transfixed by sight of the scrum of reporters outside on the steps. Television lights flared, flashes exploded. She swung round; all was made instantly clear as Paris, grinning inanely, emerged from the players' bar. Sam had heard about his call-up to the full England squad before the team's all-important European Cup qualifying match. Believing nothing beat experience, Billy Ascot, the England manager often selected one of his more promising players from the U21 set-up, prompted on this occasion by the wonder goal Paris had scored to take the Rogues through to the fifth round of the Cup. Borden had folded like a pack of cards. A winning goal didn't normally create this kind of furore but then what did Paris ever do that could even vaguely be construed as normal?

'There you are, Mr Pryce-Martin!' A beaming Fred Vinter snapped to attention, pulling open the glass-fronted doors. 'Ready for the fray?'

Had they a choice? Paris's reply, if any, was drowned, his arms folding protectively round Sam's waist as they plunged into the mêlée, deafened by the shouts and yells as every journalist, intent on a scoop for the morning's papers, vied to outbid the others. 'How are you feeling about your England call-up, Paris? Has the England manager told you his plans? What does he reckon to your lifestyle, Paris?'

There was nothing else for it. Glimpsing a gap in the scrum, Paris pushed Sam roughly through it, seized her hand and ran as hard as he could. Pulled recklessly along, Sam felt only an irrepressible urge to laugh. But this was crazy, madness. Where was he taking her?

They ran helter-skelter, press pack in hot pursuit, hugging the edges of the ground before bursting, laughing and breathless, into the car park and Paris's BMW. Camera lights snapped, instantly blinding. The car roared through the gates.

In disbelief, Sam craned her neck to view the assortment of pressmen, running like a pack of wild animals, down the road behind them, eventually careering to a frustrated halt. She had no idea how Paris coped with this.

Not for the first time, she felt some sympathy towards him. Nothing could have prepared him for this.

'Paris, please stop! Drop me off . . . I'll walk back.'

'Oh, c'mon Cos,' he wheedled, shooting her a desperate glance. 'I need you! Don't let me down now . . . '

He'd always been able to wrap her round his little finger. Resigned, she reached for her seat belt. All she had on her diary that evening was a date with a book and a hot bath, nothing pressing. Stephanio was back home in Italy on compassionate leave. His mother was ill, fortunately nothing too serious.

'Where are we going?' she enquired, giving in, while reflecting that Paris got his own way too often and it wasn't good for him.

He grinned happily, cruising down the slipway and on to the A6 before answering.

'Brookfield, that's where. Aunty Bobs has fixed for me to present awards at a youth club. It's good for me, apparently, though she might have spared me the lecture. Look at the coverage the club's had over my England call-up. But there you go . . . the press knows where the real interest lies.'

'The football in the community project?' Sam demanded, ignoring the boast and returning the conversation to the scheme that, she knew, was close to her mother's heart. Bobbie was adamant that the club should at least try and put something back into the community, supporting it, especially in an area like Brookfield, where it was so desperately needed. A vast sprawl of urban dereliction, defunct factories and delapidated high-rise flats surrounding run-down shops. Nothing for the kids to do but get into trouble. 'Mum's right,' she scolded. 'It's about time you realized how normal people live . . . '

She was wasting her breath. She turned towards him, her gaze admonitory, pleased of an opportunity to tell him exactly what she thought. Every time she'd picked up a paper lately there'd been a snap of Paris, surrounded by a posse of girls and emerging, bleary-eyed, from some nightclub. Ronnie Hubberfield was apoplectic. His protégé was back to his bad old ways — and with a vengeance. So much for his mystery girl!

'It's not my fault girls like to kiss and tell!' he muttered, looking for a moment like a petulant child. He changed gear, jammed his foot down on the accelerator. The car speeded up.

'Perhaps not,' she conceded. But that wasn't the point . . . or was it? 'Don't you

ever think someone will end up getting hurt?'
She frowned.

'I don't mean anything,' he muttered,
sheepishly. 'They use me because they think
my life's exciting. They want a piece of it.
They don't really know what it's like. No one
does . . . ' His eyes skewed sideways, pleading
understanding. 'I suppose I'm flattered. I like
beautiful girls chasing after me. Who
wouldn't?'

As a point of view, it had a certain sense,
albeit a one-sided one. Sam was in a mood to
humour him. The atmosphere in the car was
warm; they were cocooned against the
growing darkness, inviting confidences. She
leaned back, stretching her legs and suddenly
relaxing.

'It doesn't make it right,' she proffered,
surprised when he nodded in agreement.

'If only I could find that girl, Sam! I'm not
making excuses but . . . what else can I do,
but try and take my mind off things? I've no
chance of finding her again.'

'I see.' She sighed. Or at least she thought
she saw. But why did she find it so hard to
feel sorry for him? He had no right to use
other people to make himself feel good. When
she thought of Todd striving to make the
most of every ounce of talent he possessed, it
was no wonder she got so cross with Paris.

'You must be missing Steph?' Sensing disapproval, abruptly he changed subject, turning her attention to the one thing she'd been doing her best to avoid.

'I've not really had chance to miss him yet,' she fibbed. Of course she missed him, desperately. She couldn't stop thinking about him and was illogically angry with him because of it. She leaned forward, fiddling with the car radio until the sound of James Blunt came, hauntingly, over the airwaves. Dark patches of open countryside quickly transformed to streets and housing, grim warehouses were lit by pools of orange light. Paris found her hand and squeezed it. She took a deep breath, composing herself.

Could she trust him? She had a sudden blinding desire to tell someone, even Paris.

'I love him,' she said simply. 'I haven't told him yet. I don't even know if I will.'

'Why ever not?' he demanded, sounding amused.

Trust Paris not to understand. And yet she could hardly blame him when she struggled to understand her reticence herself. She shot him a desperate glance. 'It would complicate things,' she prevaricated. She was hardly likely to move things on when she still wasn't yet sure, exactly what she wanted. And neither was Stephanio. Stephanio was too

146

wrapped up in his career and hopes of breaking into the first team. Football always complicated things. 'Life shouldn't be like this . . . ' she muttered, more to herself than to Paris.

'Life *is* exactly like this, Sam!'

How come Paris had grown so wise? It was turning into a night of surprises. 'I'm worried about Dad, too,' she confessed, all her woes rising as one. Despite all their efforts, they'd heard nothing. He still hadn't turned up at his office and the caretaker at his flat whom she'd managed to track down yesterday, informed her, in broken English, that Gerry had only told him he was going away and to keep an eye on the place.

Bobbie would have none of it, but Todd was talking about the police, involving Interpol, anything other than this frustrated hanging around.

'Where can he be?' she moaned.

'Perhaps he just needed time out?'

'Then why not say so? He must know we'd be worried!'

Paris's grip on her hand tightened. 'No point me telling you not to worry but . . . He'll turn up. Don't ask me how I know, I just do . . . ' He broke off. They'd reached their destination.

Halfway down the street of derelict housing along which they'd just turned was a gap between a boarded-up shop and the end of a row of houses. Paris nosed the car through it, coming to a halt outside a large warehouse set back on waste ground. Lights from the windows illuminated a grubby forecourt. They got out. Immediately a middle-aged man, wearing a tracksuit and with a shock of thick white hair, came hurrying towards them. He could have been anyone. His voice, at least, was reassuring.

'Paris Pryce-Martin? Tom Burnett! I run the youth centre. This is inordinately good of you. Please . . . come inside . . . ' He threw Sam a glance which made her feel instantly superfluous and held out a large hand before ushering them inside and through a dimly lit hallway. This led to a large and functional room, the starkness of which was relieved by a number of brightly painted posters adorning the walls. The effect was unexpectedly lively. A number of young people were variously grouped round computer screens, playing table tennis or merely sitting chatting and drinking coffee. Music blared. Near the door stood a group of teenage girls, obviously waiting for Paris. They headed in a rush towards him. Used to it, resigned, Sam trailed after him,

148

wondering, for the umpteenth time, exactly what she was doing here.

'The girls' under-eighteen football team!' Tom Burnett raised his voice above the mêlée. 'Sorry lad! They'll calm down, shortly. Girls, put him down, do . . . Come and have a drink if you can manage to extricate yourself. Then we'll make a start . . . '

Somehow he managed to manoeuvre them towards a large urn on a wheeled trolley where a young woman stood, dispensing drinks. She was a striking-looking girl, with a shock of copper hair. Startled by the commotion, she spun round. Even Sam had to concede it was some entrance.

Paris gasped, his knees buckling, whilst at the same time he tried and failed miserably to extricate himself from the clutches of the girls hanging on to his arms, pulling at his jacket, rifling through his pockets, hell-bent on some kind of trophy.

An expression of scorn, mixed in with a hefty slice of disbelief settled across the girl's mobile, wildly attractive face. The face he'd seen so often in his dreams. So much so that some mornings he even begrudged waking up.

The last time he'd seen her she'd been wielding a vacuum cleaner. She thrust a cup of tea towards him with a remarkably steady hand as, unbelievably, wondering, Paris found himself staring into the eyes of his mystery girl.

★　★　★

Bobbie leaned wearily over the steering-wheel, trying to summon enough strength into her tired limbs to leave the car. A freezing January evening lay waiting, whipping stingingly sharp flakes of snow against the windscreen and the bright mullioned windows of Jimmy Proudfoot's sumptuous home, outside which she'd just pulled up. Beyond, the hills and valleys of some stunningly beautiful Peak District countryside faded into darkness. She didn't even know whether she'd done right to come. Jimmy wasn't expecting her. Her excuse, the reports he'd requested earlier, lay on the back seat. She reached back to gather them up and got out of the car, bracing herself against the wind that was blustering snow so spitefully against her face, before heading up the drive towards the porticoed door.

What she was about to say to Rislington Rover's club chairman about their team manager was for his ears only, and was so inflammatory that it would rock the club to its foundations should it ever get out. It had to be said. She was the one to say it. No one had ever said this job would be easy!

Her hand reached for the bell. The door was flung open, startling her and spilling bright light from the hallway into the porch where she stood.

'Bobbie? Good to see you!' To her amazement, Eddie Lamoure, large as ever and beaming broadly, swept past her and outside, heading determinedly towards a silver Rolls parked on the far side of the drive. Eddie's car. She remembered it now.

'Bobbie?' Jimmy's face loomed anxiously behind the doorway, staring at his chief executive with dismay. She'd interrupted something, but what, exactly? That the two were acquainted she knew. She'd had no idea they ever met on any kind of a social footing.

'Jimmy! I'd finished the reports. I thought I might as well bring them round. I hope you don't mind me calling without ringing first?' Aware that she was babbling, she stepped past her chairman and into the hall, blinking against the lights and too rattled by sight of Eddie to be much aware of her surroundings. Oak-panelled walls and gilded fittings. The comfortable sense of money at ease with itself.

Jimmy led her through into the sitting room, standing awkwardly and obviously

151

unhappy that he'd been caught out. She'd no idea what Eddie could have been doing here. All thoughts of the discussion she'd intended to hold fled from her mind. A shocking thought surfaced, overwhelming all else.

'Was Eddie here about this crazy idea of buying into the club?' she cried. Her voice trembled with emotion; even now she was unable to believe she was saying this.

Jimmy started.

'Why . . . Bobbie . . . of course not!' he blustered unconvincingly. 'We'd charity work to discuss, nowt else!'

'I'm not a fool, Jimmy.'

'I never said you were.' He rocked back on his heels, thrusting his hands in his pockets, guilt, indecision, the lure of the kind of money Eddie would be offering for his shares, writ large on his face.

Bobbie stood, lost for words, more convinced than ever that buying into the club was exactly what Eddie had been here about. It was an appalling thought. Jimmy loved this club as much as Landon did. At least she'd always thought he did. Suddenly she wasn't so sure.

'Where will it leave my father!' she cried, angrily. 'Does he even know? Oh how could you, Jimmy!'

'Don't take on, lass. Things might not be

what they seem!' The chairman's grizzled head jutted forwards. 'I've the right to see who I like . . . '

He protested too much and she didn't believe a word of it.

'The press will have a field day if this ever gets out!' she muttered, red-faced and miserable, wishing she hadn't come. Indignantly she thrust the reports towards him. 'Here, you'd better take these.'

They stood in bullish confrontation. She needed to get away and find herself some fresh air. Throwing him the kind of look that would have made a boardroom of Jimmy Proudfoots quail, she spun round and headed for the door and flung outside. She half-expected Jimmy to come chasing after her. That he didn't spoke volumes.

Cold air slapped against her face, snow stung her eyes and lashes and tasted bitter in her mouth. It had happened. She had to deal with it.

She jumped in the car and drove off, too fast, stopping in a lay-by to ring Landon. She needed his advice, his calm, good common sense. Quickly she explained what had happened, what she'd seen, how shocked she felt.

There was a pause whilst he digested the news.

'Eddie was bound to have approached Jimmy sometime,' he answered, the line crackling with his indignation. He and Jimmy had been friends since school. Landon more than anyone would feel betrayed. 'I naturally assumed he'd refuse, that things would die down. It takes some beating, this, Bobbie!'

'How could he, Dad?' she cried angrily. 'And what's in it for Eddie? I don't understand — '

'It's business,' Landon answered sharply. 'I reckoned Jimmy would resist any inducements, but who knows. He's old. Things may have got too much for him and he wants out . . . ' There was a pause. She could see him in her mind's eye, her dear father, face troubled, shaking his head at all this. 'Eddie's taking a gamble on the new television deal . . . ' His voice when it came was filled with urgency, adding weight to his words. 'The amount of money the sport channels are prepared to chuck at things is obscene. If the Rogues do achieve the impossible and go up, a good chunk of it'll be headed our way, too. Eddie and his cronies are banking on it. They couldn't give a toss about the club!'

'I see . . . ' Suddenly she did. Everything was all too horrifyingly clear.

'Try and not worry.' Landon's voice, all calm reassurance, broke into her thoughts.

'I'll talk to Jimmy in the morning. See if I can't talk some sense into him. There's nothing else we can do.'

He was right. Landon usually was where football was concerned. Bobbie switched off her mobile and dropped it back into her bag. Going home to the early night she'd planned seemed the last thing she needed right now. Without hesitation she turned the car round and headed back towards Rislington and the football ground. Half an hour later found her sitting absorbed at a desk in a records office comfortingly deserted, thoughts of Eddie Lamoure finally and successfully banished whilst she sifted through back-dated files looking for something that might possibly help her old friend, Alan. Now was the perfect opportunity and she had promised she'd do all she could.

At once she sat back, brushing a hand through her unruly mass of hair. It had been some night. She did so want to help but what exactly was she looking for here? She stood up, made coffee, and stood by the window to drink it, her fingers curled around the mug. She stared balefully out into the darkness as a fresh squall of snow came blustering over the pitch, and splattered against the glass. She'd have to do something before Ronnie spilt the beans to Jimmy.

Fighting an almost overwhelming tiredness, she returned to the cabinet and pulled open another drawer.

'Not gone home yet, Bobbie?'

The familiar voice made her jump, causing her heart to patter painfully against her ribcage. She spun round, almost guiltily, to see Davie Mackenzie silhouetted in the doorway.

'Davie! You startled me . . . '

'Must be a guilty conscience?' He laughed, taking the sting from his words but nearer the mark than he realized. She shouldn't be here. She shouldn't be doing what she was doing! He limped into the room, reminding her that he wasn't yet fully recovered from the injury he'd sustained before the win against Borden.

'I've been doing some work in the gym . . . I saw the light. Don't ask me why I thought of you. What are you up to?' he asked curiously, his gaze taking in the files littering her desk, her general air of despair which she was far too tired to hide. She shut the drawer, turned to lean back against the cabinet and wondered whether she ought to confess. It wasn't any of Davie's business. But, whatever problems there were between them, Davie was an honest, generous man and she did need to talk.

'I'm trying to find something to help Alan,' she answered steadily. 'Someone's got to do something. I can't believe he swindled the club.'

Davie limped painfully towards the desk. He picked up one of the files and leafed through it, taking his time before he answered.

'I must admit I'm with you,' he said. 'The Alan Campion I remember must have changed an awful lot, if even half of what the police are suggesting is true.' He glanced up, his gaze fixing thoughtfully on hers. 'Do you even know what you're looking for?'

'Not exactly,' she admitted, shamefaced.

'Typical Bobbie, jumping in where angels fear to tread.' He replaced the file, then moved towards her with surprising agility considering his injury. He came to a halt directly in front of her, his hands resting on each side of the cabinet. She was trapped, taken by surprise, unable to escape even if she'd wanted to. Did she want to?

Long seconds lingered, seconds in which she was only too aware of how close he was and of her own unexpected, irresistible longing. It was impossible. They both knew the state of play. Club executive, star player? How could that possibly work?

'Isn't it time we stopped playing games, Bobbie?'

'I've no idea what you mean.'

'You have and we are!' His words acknowledged both the truth and his right to say it. Wasn't she tired of running away? Didn't this thing between them, old, unfinished business, have to be acknowledged and faced?

'It would never work,' she moaned, made miserable at the thought that there were questions concerning their relationship that she simply couldn't face. There was too much else in her life. Her job for one thing, the takeover bid, this worrying uncertainty over Alan, even the troubles of her parents' marriage! Why had he to start this up again and now?

'We're grown-up people, for goodness' sake! We have grown-up needs . . . ' His voice was unsteady and edged with passion, impatient because he couldn't find the right words. He'd never been good at words! Football was his game.

His breath was warm on her face. She wanted him to stop and leave her alone! Whom was she trying to fool? She closed her eyes, on the point of giving in.

'But you said it was too late!' she moaned, her eyes fluttering open again. She struggled

158

to come up for air, aware only of unexplainable currents pulling her back down.

'I know what I said!' he answered roughly. It didn't account for how he felt now. Away from her all those years, it had been easy to push his feelings away and pretend they didn't exist. His hands relaxed, leaving her free to escape if she wanted to. She didn't. In a desperate and unforgivable moment of weakness she swayed against him, aware only of his breath quickening, unsurprised when his arms folded around her, pulling her close. For one long and glorious moment, she laid her weary head against his chest.

'Bobbie? It is Bobbie isn't it?'

The voice, a blast from her past if anything was, crashed into her consciousness.

She pushed Davie away and stepped back, banging clumsily against the cabinet. Shocked surprise registered on her face as she saw Gerry Mansfield, her ex-husband and the father of her children, watching them from the doorway, an expression of worryingly benign good-humour on his handsome face.

6

Todd Vernon pushed open the door to the club's supporters' shop, neatly tucked into one corner of the Albert Vernon memorial stand, and made a beeline for Sam, who was standing at the counter, sorting through samples of new merchandise. A sprinkling of supporters browsed through the displays, half an eye on the door in case one of the players should appear

'Ready, Sis?' he called.

She looked up, surprised.

'I thought I was picking you up?'

'Couldn't wait; too on edge!' He grinned, making a conscious effort to calm down. 'Tell me what Dad said again . . . ?'

'He said very little. You know Dad, Todd, evasive as ever.' Her eyes rolled, filled with the incredulity she still felt following Bobbie's return home with the startling news that their father had turned up, was booked in at Cedars and longing to see them both. Sam had got straight on the phone, would have dashed straight over to see him too, if only, frustratingly, he hadn't pointed out that it was late, he was dead beat after the flight, they'd have all the time in the world to talk in the morning. 'Give me a chance to pull myself together, Sam,' he'd grumbled, seeming to have no clear idea of the worry his disappearance had occasioned his children. If he had, he'd ignored it. Much as she loved him, Sam had no illusions. They were meeting at Cedars.

Sleep had been impossible. She'd risen early and driven to the ground, determined to put the time before she needed to go to Cedars to good use. 'Todd, it was so wonderful to hear him!' she enthused. 'I just wish he'd told me what he's been up to all this time.' It was bugging them all, even Bobbie, who'd seemed more than a little distracted last night.

'He'll tell us, don't you worry,' Todd growled, at that moment looking remarkably like their mother. Their eyes caught, holding mutual amusement, relief and a burning curiosity. It would be some meeting, some explanation!

'How about I take him one of these?' She held up the T-shirt in her hands, the front of which was stencilled with an aerial view of Rislington's ground, ringed round with the slogan 'Jimmy Hubberfield's' Barmy Army'. 'Mum's considering putting a run through.' This would be a financial risk and Sam was still unsure about it.

'Barmy about describes it. What a mouthful!' Todd frowned. 'Are you all right, Sam?'

Her little brother could be surprisingly sensitive at times. She had been feeling on edge and not just about their father. She folded up the T-shirt, replacing it in its Cellophane cover.

'Steph's back,' she answered quietly.

'But that's good, isn't it?' Todd demanded, surprised at her lack of enthusiasm.

'He just . . . didn't seem hugely pleased to see me.'

An understatement. The young woman's eyes clouded with unhappiness. If she hadn't bumped into George at the ground, she wouldn't even have known Stephanio was back. She'd rushed straight round to the digs he shared with George, desperate to see him, worrying why she hadn't heard. And to think she'd imagined the grand reunion!

How let down she'd been.

'Sam, I was going to phone,' he muttered, his gaze curiously evasive. He held the door open and followed her through into the dingy little sitting room. Discarded clothes, papers, dirty mugs were lying about. A typical bachelor flat.

'How's your mother?' she demanded, afraid that this might be the problem.

'My mother — she's fine. A bad chest infection. No more.'

'Steph, that's wonderful news,' she cried. 'I'm so pleased! I'm pleased you're back, too. I've . . . I've missed you.' Shouldn't he be saying as much to her? Nothing was forthcoming. Something was wrong. A chest infection seemed such a small thing to have gone chasing all the way back to Italy for.

'Have you missed me?' His hand rose, brushing the line of her cheek before dropping harmlessly away. She'd caught him unpacking. Clothes and books all over the place, his shaving gear dumped out on the table. He turned to finish his task, too quickly absorbed, as if she wasn't there. He hadn't even kissed her, she realized miserably. Was he tiring of their relationship already and didn't know how to say it? And just when she'd nerved herself to tell him how she felt!

She felt too much, it appeared.

'He'll be whacked' Todd sympathized. 'You know what travelling's like . . . '

She did and she expected he was right. 'Let's go.' She frowned and reached for her coat, slung over the back of the chair. She wasn't intending to go chasing after him to find out how things stood. It was up to Steph to make the next move.

The receptionist at the desk at The Cedars directed them to the conservatory, a glass extension to the main building, that Babs had commissioned two years previously. It was proving popular amongst the guests, who enjoyed relaxing in its spacious confines.

'There you are!' Beaming broadly, Gerry Mansfield put down the pot from which he'd been helping himself to more coffee and leapt to his feet. Sam threw herself into his arms.

'Dad! Where've you been? How are you? Oh, I have missed you! Have you any idea how worried we've been?'

'Whoa . . . Which first?' Somehow he extricated himself enough to give Todd a hug too. He'd lost weight. Otherwise he looked tanned and fit. As usual, he took charge, ordering more coffee, settling the party down at the table overlooking the greens. That was her dad, arranging everything to his satisfaction. Sam felt the first faint stirrings of exasperation.

'Where've you been?' she moaned softly. What did he mean by turning up so breezily as if there was nothing wrong? He didn't seem to care what he'd put them through.

Gerry poured coffee. 'I didn't mean to worry you,' he said. 'Things have been

164

. . . difficult.' His restless gaze settled on the course and a party of residents playing the last hole.

'For goodness' sake, Dad!'

He sat, fiddling with the coffee pot and looking faintly embarrassed. 'If you must know . . . I've been at a retreat,' he announced, running all the words together. He turned his gaze towards them, full of apology. Then he frowned and picked up his cup with a hand that wasn't quite steady.

'A what?' Todd's expression mirrored Sam's. Shock, disbelief, the last thing they'd expected.

'Seville. A monastery in the hills,' he enlarged. 'I . . . had some things to think over.' Gerry Mansfield sat back, drinking his coffee, trying to gauge his children's reaction and wondering how much he could get away with without telling them. Things were proving more difficult than he'd expected. Gone was the suave, confident man they knew, replaced momentarily by a middle-aged man, rather frayed round the edges, one they didn't know nearly so well. The real Gerry Mansfield. It was a worrying thought and Sam felt the first faint stirrings of an unexpected emotion. Pity was the last thing she'd expected to feel.

'The business was struggling,' he went on,

uneasily. 'I made a bad investment, a new development which went bust. The Spanish government didn't like it and were threatening to move in and take control. No matter how hard I worked I couldn't pull things round. It just . . . got on top of me.'

'How exactly?' Todd prompted. Sam shot him a look of exasperation.

'Do I really have to spell it out?' He hated talking about something which made him sound so weak. 'I was at breaking-point, if you must know. Going away was the best thing I ever did . . . '

How alone he must have felt! 'Why didn't you tell us?' Sam demanded, hating to think what he'd been through and, worse, what it said about their relationship, which she'd always so fondly, and despite her parents break-up, imagined a good one. Bobbie had always encouraged her to feel a part of her father's life. 'I'd have wanted to help!' she blurted out indignantly.

He shifted uncomfortably. 'I couldn't let word get out. Not even to you. The business was in such a bad way, Sam. People aren't always sympathetic, particularly when money's involved.'

'More fools they!' Todd interjected. 'It's better out in the open. Nothing's worth your health, Dad . . . '

'But how did you cope?' A bizarre image entered Sam's head. What had the monks made of her father? What had he made of them? Even given the seriousness of all he'd told her, the corners of her lips tugged upwards. It was the best thing she could have done. The tension relaxed.

'Don't mock, young lady,' he warned, catching the look, laughing too now. He leaned back, stretching his arms, exulting in his body's new-found fitness. 'The order encouraged . . . a oneness with nature. I tended the vegetable patch, weeded, tidied up, that kind of thing!' His arms dropped, his expression became serious again. 'It gave me time to think. All kinds of stuff I'd shoved to the back of my mind surfaced. Things I should have paid attention to. Like how unfair I've been to you two . . . '

'Unfair? But how? Dad, of course you haven't!' Sam declared, too hotly. She looked away quickly, not wanting him to see the truth. Typical Sam. Always willing to see the best in everyone. Gerry Mansfield experienced a momentary pang of conscience, knowing he was responsible for that too.

'I've allowed business to take over my life,' he asserted doggedly. 'You've both suffered for it. But don't worry, things are going to change!' His voice had risen and heads turned. He went on, more quietly, 'I mean, I'll make it up to you, if I can.' He took their obvious astonishment as agreement, laughing pleasantly. 'How's your mother?' he demanded, changing tack in the abrupt way they both remembered, giving some comfort, at least, that a little of the old Gerry remained.

Both she and Todd were wary of talking about either parent to the other. 'Mum's OK,' Sam answered, guardedly.

'I didn't know she was with Davie Mackenzie! I thought he was still playing for the Gunners?'

'There's nothing between Mum and Davie! He's only back, signed up with the Rogues,' Sam explained impatiently, surprised to be asked, but confident Bobbie would have told her if there'd been the slightest thing going on in her love life. Quietly and with a rising excitement, she noted her father's interest. Had he decided, at long and wonderful last, that he wanted them to give it another go?

There was so much she wanted to ask! Now, unfortunately, with Todd all ears, wasn't the time and, in any case, it was time to go. Todd had a date at the driving range; she had to get back to work. College restarted the following week.

Reluctantly they said their goodbyes,

promising to meet later for dinner.

'Do you think there's a chance Mum and Dad'll ever get back together?' Sam wondered as soon as they were outside and out of earshot. Gerry Mansfield stood at the entrance and gave them a lazy wave before disappearing back into the foyer.

Todd laughed out loud.

'There's more chance I'll win the Open!'

His calm, good humour put a damper on her daydreams, but even then she couldn't let go of the idea. She'd always lived in hope, always dreamed the impossible. She drove Todd to the range and carried on into work, her mind whirring. Her parents together, where they ought to be! Something must have brought her father rushing back to England other than this half-baked notion of making things up to his children.

★   ★   ★

Davie Mackenzie crossed the floor of Bobbie's office and folded her into his arms.

'I couldn't wait to see you,' he breathed into the scented thickness of her hair. Leaning into him, for the first time that morning Bobbie relaxed. Even Gerry turning up, so shockingly and at such an interesting point in the previous evening's proceedings,

169

had failed to dampen the joy she'd felt at old feelings rekindled. So much so that she'd woken that morning wondering whether she'd dreamed it all. Much as Davie insisted he'd returned for footballing reasons, even he couldn't deny the attraction between them. Things were happening too fast.

Gerry's arrival had been well-timed. Who knew where last night might have ended, what she'd be regretting? She stepped back, away from the temptation of Davie's arms. 'Davie, we have to be careful.' She frowned.

'Must we?'

She nodded, deadly serious.

'I'd hate the press to get hold of it. Think of the headlines!'

'Get hold of what, Bobbie?' Babs stood in the doorway, watching them, a look of intense speculation on her pretty face. It seemed they were fated.

'Something and nothing . . . ' Bobbie responded, hoping she didn't look as guilty as she felt. Davie was already edging towards the door.

'I'll get back. Ronnie's organized an extra training session. There's no rest!' He threw Bobbie a rueful glance, his eyes holding a promise that only caused her heart to thud the more. He squeezed past a sadly smirking Babs and fled.

'Something I said?' She laughed and closed the door with exaggerated care. 'I'd no idea you and Davie were an item again?'

'We're not! That is . . . ' Bobbie stopped, flushed up, not sure how much, if anything, Babs had actually seen. Did it matter? Could she trust her little sister to keep it to herself? Things hadn't exactly been easy between them lately.

She retreated behind her desk, taking a deep and steadying breath, longing suddenly to talk to someone, even Babs. She and Davie were too new, too wonderful to keep to herself.

'Babs . . . not a word of this must get out but . . . Davie and I — '

'Yes? You and Davie?' Babs face sparkled with good humour.

'Oh, I still like him, Babs!' she cried, experiencing a great rush of relief to let it out. It went some way to describing it and how good it felt to say!

'You don't say!' Babs laughed. 'He still likes you, too, by the looks of it!'

She *had* seen. Some of the euphoria occasioned by Davie's embrace was already beginning to wear off. 'Is it such a good idea, getting back together, Babs, do you think?' Bobbie frowned.

'What have you got to lose?' Babs

murmured. 'If you still have feelings for each other and it works, what harm can it do?'

Calm, good common sense. Exactly what she needed. She'd go with it, see what happened. Bobbie's face cleared at last. 'Oh Babs!' she cried, her voice full of a surprising affection. 'It is good to talk!' Their gazes caught and held, both women abruptly and delightfully plunged back to their teenage years and the hours they'd spent discussing hair, make-up, their latest boyfriends. What a shame they couldn't get back to how things used to be.

'I wish you well of it.' Babs smiled, coming right into the room. She stood to look about her, her admiration plain. For Babs match days were more usually confined to the directors' box and the half-time cup of tea in the boardroom; she hadn't been up here since Bobbie had moved into the chief executive's office. Things had changed more than she would have believed possible.

'You've done well, Bobs!' The unlooked-for approval, and coming from Babs, her sworn enemy of late, startled them both.

Bobbie got up and flicked the switch on the kettle.

'You look like you need one,' she commented drily, for the first time acknowledging the dark circles under her sister's eyes.

'That obvious, huh? I've popped in to return these . . . ' Babs dumped the files she'd brought on to Bobbie's desk and stood, unloosening her coat.

'You've had chance to look through them already?' It had been Davie's brainwave. If Bobbie couldn't find anything to help Alan Campion's case, perhaps Babs with all her experience of running The Cedars single-handed would be able to help? Dead beat as she'd been last night, her head spinning with Gerry's emergence, she'd still found time to act on the suggestion, calling round at The Cedars before she turned in. Surprisingly, Babs had appeared only too keen to help.

'I've only had time for a cursory look but there's something there, Bobs . . . ' Her voice quickened with excitement. 'A company called Aldergate Holdings keeps cropping up . . . '

'Something to do with the corporate entertainment side,' Bobbie agreed, remembering it only as one of the many companies the club had used. What was it about this one that stuck out?

'The payments stopped all at once?'

'I expect we moved on, found someone else.'

'Someone more competitive?' Babs's eyes narrowed, her fingers drummed on the desk.

'There are some irregular payments, either too close together or too far apart. It isn't as if anyone else crops up once they disappear altogether. Call it intuition if you like, Bobbie but . . . leave this with me, will you? I'll make a few enquiries and see what I can find.' Her gaze settled firmly on her sister, indicative of the other, more pressing reason why she'd called. 'What do you really reckon to this share business, Bobbie?' she asked, abruptly. They'd both been too tired to talk it over much last night, but it was still playing on her mind. Bobbie's too, she suspected. It was time they talked it through. Bobbie poured boiling water on to coffee granules, thinking carefully before she spoke.

'Are we talking personally or professionally here?'

'Both . . . I think . . . ' Babs frowned.

'Then personally, I think it's a terrible idea!' Bobbie pulled a face. 'Think how many years the family's been involved with this club. Selling out would just about finish Dad off. I understand how Mum feels about his health, but she's not thinking this through . . . '

'She's worried. We all are. What a mess, Bobbie!'

For once they were in agreement. A mess described it. Worse, it was one no one appeared to know how to sort out. 'Eddie Lamoure's a shark, out for himself . . . ' Bobbie mused. 'You could argue the club might go along for the ride; the extra cash would certainly help us into the Premiership. Once there, he'd ditch us and then where would we be?'

'In a stronger position?' Babs suggested forcefully.

'Possibly! The club would be a viable concern.' Despite the seriousness of the subject under discussion, Babs's eyes began to twinkle. 'In the Premiership, no captain at the helm, fodder for a passing sheikh or anyone else interested in making pots of money. We both know there's so much more to football than that! We have a responsibility to the community . . . ' she concluded thoughtfully.

Babs took her mug and sat down behind the desk.

'Mum reckons we'd be fools to turn down the sort of money Eddie's talking,' she said carefully, one elegant finger circling the rim of her mug. 'She has a point, Bobbie. Cedars could certainly do with a cash injection. The overheads are astronomical — '

'You aren't struggling?' Bobbie demanded.

'Not struggling exactly!' Babs smiled. 'We make ends meet. We could do better.'

'I just wish Eddie had never offered to buy Jimmy out!'

'You mean he's offered to buy Jimmy out too?' This was news to Babs. She frowned, not trusting herself to speak until she had her emotions more firmly under control. 'Why am I always the last to hear?' she asked more quietly, nursing her mug between her hands. The air was thick with things unsaid, undercurrents probably best left where they were. 'Forget I said it,' she muttered awkwardly.

'Isn't that a bit late?' Bobbie pointed out, privately acknowledging that she had a point. There was no denying she'd grown close to her father of late. Babs must have picked up on it and begun to feel left out. 'He doesn't mean anything,' she proffered, feeling oddly guilty. 'It was my fault, in any case. I caught Eddie coming out of Jimmy's yesterday. I told Dad and . . . You know Dad, Babs! Half a thought and it's suddenly a certainty. I'm just the one here, the one crazy about football — '

'But I love football too,' Babs cried, not caring how childish it sounded. Her big sister was always getting more attention and it wasn't fair! It had always rankled, always left her feeling oddly inadequate.

'You're right. It isn't fair.' What more could she say? Babs had a point. Landon being

Landon wouldn't even be aware that Babs felt left out in the cold. From the depths of the jumble inside her handbag, her mobile rang. Perfectly timed, Landon's voice came loud and clear.

'I've spent the last hour at Jimmy's. Can we meet? We need to talk — '

'Dad, Babs is here with me — '

'What?'

'We've been discussing the takeover.'

'You'd better bring her, then. I'll see you back home.'

The connection broke. Whatever information he'd gleaned from Jimmy Proudfoot, it was important. 'He wants us to meet at Mum's,' she murmured, her head spinning.

'You mean he wants you.' Babs frowned.

'He wants us both!' Bobbie answered sharply, already reaching for her coat.

* * *

'Oh Lord, what have I done now?' Too late, her young face a picture of perplexity, Anna dropped the phone. She must have had a brainstorm, a moment of madness! Calm, sensible Anna Kirkby, who at any given moment knew exactly what she was doing, where she was headed, had done something inexplicably impulsive. One day it would get

177

her into trouble. Perhaps it already had.

Around her the Social Services Department of Brookfield Borough Council lapsed into the lull of a well deserved, mid-morning coffee break.

'Trouble?' Katie, her friend and colleague, enquired.

'The footballer I met again at the youth club, last night. That was him! He's asked me out for lunch. He must have got my details from one of the lads. I certainly didn't give him any . . . ' She frowned, momentarily overwhelmed with the mess she'd just landed herself in. 'Why did I say yes?'

'Because he's famous and you liked him?' Katie suggested brightly.

Anna laughed out loud. 'He's the most conceited, impossible, arrogant . . . '

Used to her friend's passionate displays of emotion, Katie grinned.

'That good, huh? Tell me about it when you get back.'

Anna was still puzzling over why she'd agreed instead of telling him to take a running jump, when the long bell in the high clocktower above the slate-grey roof of the large Victorian building converted for Brookfield Borough Council use, struck the mid-day hour. She was late. She grabbed her coat and scarf and was still struggling into

178

them as she emerged from the main entrance and ran down the steps. Her heart lurched. Ignoring the smiles of recognition from the council workers streaming past, Paris stood waiting on the pavement. Seeing her, his face lit up.

'I wasn't sure you'd come,' he ventured, sounding surprisingly unconfident.

'I'm only going to the park,' she retorted, more sharply than she'd intended.

At this time of year? In this cold? 'The park will be lovely,' he insisted, falling into step, matching his stride to hers.

The park to which she referred was a municipal one, reached through a set of gates in a large yew hedge that ran the length of the pavement and screening the park from the road. Not much of a park, Paris considered, eagerly following her through. A few dead leaves and tired winter pansies were scattered on the borders beneath the trees. A path led down to a lake of greenish water on which floated an elderly swan and two or three cygnets shaking their tails against the cold.

'I hate being stuck in an office all morning,' she volunteered unexpectedly. She headed for the nearest bench and sat down. Out of her bag she extracted a sandwich box. Deftly she removed the lid and waved the box under his

179

nose. Paris had never felt less like eating in his life.

'Thanks,' he croaked, helping himself, sitting as close as he dared, wanting to tell her how desperately hard he'd had to work to find her. How he'd feigned injury this morning in training and bunked off so he could be here with her now. She'd think he was mad! He couldn't bear it. 'I couldn't believe it was you last night . . . ' he began cautiously.

'I'm surprised you remembered me. I'd no idea it was you . . . ' Her tone was mocking.

Crestfallen, he searched his mind for something else. 'Tell me about yourself?' he pleaded.

'What's to tell?' Clear, startlingly green eyes, seeing far more than he liked, turned in his direction.

His heart skipped a beat. 'Tell me anything . . . or everything!'

Something about his expression must have amused her. She smiled at last and bit into a sandwich, considering how best to put her life into a few brief words. There wasn't much to tell.

'I'm eighteen. I have three brothers, all older. My dad died shortly after I was born so my mum brought us up single-handed. I'm on a gap year before university.'

'Doing what?' he demanded.

'General dogsbodying!' Her face was alight with a sudden good humour. 'Working's meant to help pay my way whilst I'm studying and give me some idea what I want after uni. It's important to feel you're making a difference, don't you think?'

Paris nodded uncertainly, only sure it wasn't anything he'd ever considered. He munched on his sandwich, considering it now.

'You play football?' she prompted when nothing was forthcoming. She finished one sandwich and started another. She had a healthy appetite; he had to give her that.

'I thought you didn't remember me,' he teased, delighted that she knew him after all.

'There's enough in the papers.' Abruptly, the warmth left her voice.

'Nothing good, I hope?' he joked, wishing instantly that he hadn't.

'No,' she answered flatly. She snapped the lid back on the box and dropped it into her bag. 'It seems to me . . . not that it's any of my business of course but . . . '

'Say it!' he muttered, wishing she wouldn't, knowing it wouldn't be anything good. 'Why abuse your talent?' She tilted her head, scrutinizing him as if he was an object in an exhibition. He wriggled back against the bench.

'You have talent!' she pointed out. 'Isn't it making a mockery of what you do?'

She watched him as if what he said next was important.

'I love what I do!' he protested, colouring up and miserably aware of it. 'But there are other things in life!' Fame, money, adulation was what he meant, though some saving grace stopped him from saying as much.

'None of which is important,' she scolded, as if he'd spoken anyway. 'If you stopped giving the papers so much to write about, concentrated on your football . . . you'd be a better player, surely? Don't you care?'

Who was she? His teacher? Paris frowned, unaccountably annoyed and looking quickly away. This wasn't turning out at all as he'd hoped.

'Of course I care!' he cried, clearly wounded. He threw the remains of his sandwich to the swans. She clearly had no idea. Even Ronnie, his manager, journeyman footballer though he'd once been, knew nothing of the buzz when he took to the pitch. The rush of adrenaline just before scoring, the feeling that nothing else mattered, not his teammates, the crowd, nor Ronnie doing his nut, on the sidelines. He experienced an inner joy he couldn't explain to anyone, not even to this girl, who was at least trying to understand. Just him and a football and belting it into the back of the net. How could he find the words to tell her that? She'd laugh.

'I can't be doing with this serious stuff,' he cried, frustrated but mostly with himself. Reserve slid over her face like a mask. He would have taken the words back if he could.

'I'd better get back! I'll be late . . . ' She sprang up and began to gather her things. She'd been right; she should have followed her first instincts. It had been a mistake to come.

'I'll walk back with you!' He jumped up too, startling the swans, which scattered upwards, a flurry of wings and bright water through which the sunshine gleamed.

'Really . . . it doesn't matter . . . '

'I thought we could meet later . . . after work if you like?' He was throwing the words at her back. She walked on briskly, not taking the trouble to look round and yet, despite herself, wanting to look round very much.

Paris stood, hands thrust deep in his pockets, staring after her, willing her to turn round. Didn't she want to see him again? How could she be so careless when he felt so . . . overwhelmed? As if nothing else mattered in his life!

Anna was surprised to find herself smiling, her mind winging swiftly back to the summer, a hotel in St Tropez and a room bigger than the whole house in which her family lived. He'd never know that after their first chance meeting she'd returned and found him asleep, arms flung above his head, long silky lashes brushing the curve of his cheek. She'd stood an age, half-scared he'd wake up, unable to tear herself away, the one thought in her head being that he wasn't the conceited idiot she'd first, mistakenly, taken him for. He looked too vulnerable. A crazy mixed-up kid who'd had too much too soon. She'd wanted to comfort him. Or slap him. She still wasn't sure which!

All at once, on impulse, a thing she was experiencing far too much of lately, she turned and grinned, her heart lurching as she was rewarded by the biggest, most dazzling smile she'd ever had the misfortune to receive.

★ ★ ★

'Oh my, I wasn't expecting to see you two!' Bobbie and Babs had arrived together. This was a first! Eleanor was on her knees in the hall polishing the floor, a job that allowed full vent to her feelings. She rocked back on to her heels, brushing the hair from her face, her expression one of astonishment.

'Morning, Ma!' Babs announced cheerfully, plunged back to her childhood by the comforting scent of beeswax and fresh-cut flowers.

'Dad's asked us both to discuss the takeover,' Bobbie explained, taking a sensitive liberty with the truth.

Eleanor climbed to her feet, rubbing her knees. 'Hasn't it been talked out enough already? Do you want some lunch? It is good to see you both . . . ' She murmured the last remark, hiding her annoyance at Landon's arranging a family conference and never thinking to tell her. She led the way through to the kitchen where a burst of sunshine flooded through the large double window. The units gleamed. She'd been busy since she'd got back from Susie's. 'I hope he's come to his senses. Giles can't believe he's being so stubborn,' she muttered waspishly. She flicked the switch on the kettle, opened the fridge and reached for bread, cheese, radishes, butter. She hadn't even known Landon was coming home. The thought was making her unreasonably angry.

'I've already told you what I think.' Bobbie lifted down mugs. 'Mum, what is it between you and this . . . this Giles man?'

Eleanor sliced the bread and buttered it, refusing to answer though she knew exactly why she found Giles so attractive. He made her feel better about herself. As if what she said was something worth listening to. Something the rest of the family might do well to emulate! The furrow between her brows deepened: she was aware that she was on the verge of feeling sorry for herself. If Landon didn't want her, didn't care enough to ask her opinion, she must fill her life with other, different things. 'Giles was round at Susie's,' she began, feeling the need to say something. 'They were full of the takeover. Is it my fault if I believe what they're saying?'

'Giles Barnard is in cahoots with Eddie!' Bobbie cried, pausing in the act of pouring milk out. Eleanor knew this well enough. 'He's his right-hand man, if you like,' she went on patiently. 'Of course he'll try to persuade you to sell the shares. Susie too. It's in their interests. You should talk to Dad. I'm beginning to think there's something wrong with you two . . . ' It was said light-heartedly though they both knew it was true. It was becoming obvious, even to her children.

'Don't be silly, love! We just want different things . . . ' Though she couldn't bring herself to say it, it seemed, nowadays that they wanted different lives entirely. What if saying it made it true? Startlingly, Eleanor's eyes were full of tears. Distressed that she'd been the cause, swiftly Bobbie crossed the room and flung her arms around her.

'Sorry! That was tactless! I don't want to see you getting hurt, Mum, that's all. I just wish you'd talk things over with Dad.' She cast Babs a worried glance. The ructions in their parent's marriage were beginning to trouble them both. Despite Eleanor's numerous eruptions, she and Landon had always managed to present a united front. They all knew Eleanor was volatile but this, this time, was different. Eleanor was different.

'There you are.' It was a timely interruption. Landon stood beaming. Under his arm he carried a bottle of champagne which he placed carefully on the table, throwing Eleanor a look in which concern was uppermost. 'Are you all right, love?'

'Of course I'm all right,' she snapped, finding her hanky and blowing her nose. 'I'm coming down with a cold, that's all.' She noticed the champagne and frowned. Landon grinned.

'For a celebration, I hope.'

'What did Jimmy say, Dad?' Bobbie came towards him.

'Everything you thought was right, love!' He pulled out a chair and sat down. It had been a long morning, closeted up at Jimmy's, getting to the truth of things turning out to be anything but what they appeared on the surface. He exhaled heavily, in a clear state of excitement. 'Jimmy wants out!'

'I knew it!'

'Is this conversation closed or can anyone join in?' Babs demanded drily, joining them at the table.

'He's never got over the fans having a go at the start of the season, or so he says.' Landon frowned. 'As if a little thing like that would turn a hair of the old curmudgeon's head!'

'It must be something else?' Babs murmured, not believing it either.

Landon nodded, his mind spinning back to the morning . . .

★ ★ ★

'You at least owe me an explanation, Jimmy.' He'd sat uneasily on Jimmy's sofa in his immaculate sitting room, hands clenched together, watching as the old man eased himself up from his favourite chair to stand with his back to the room, gazing out of the French windows at the grounds beyond.

'Melchester want me on board,' he barked, suddenly swinging round, the picture of the self-made man, the man who would never be satisfied no matter how much he had.

'United!' Landon's shock was palpable.

'It's my chance, lad!' Age hadn't dimmed Jimmy's ambition. Jimmy was a man who would always want to get on. 'Every thing I've ever wanted,' he enthused. 'You know FA rules! One club at a time and no conflicting interests. I've no option.'

'But where does that leave Rovers?' Hang Melchester and Jimmy's ambitions, the Rogues were all Landon cared about. The thing dearest to his heart, save for his family.

'Eddie wants the Rovers!' Jimmy said complacently, thrusting his hands in his pockets, jiggling his change, daring Landon to spoil his plans.

'Over my dead body!' Landon sprang up, heart pounding, crashing a crescendo in his ears. Stubborn old fool, letting down the club, refusing to listen to reason! Anyone else might have given up there. Never Landon!

★   ★   ★

He reached for the champagne, his eyes seeking Eleanor's and an understanding he knew already she'd never give. 'I've offered to buy him out,' he admitted, unable to suppress his excitement. His football club! Who else should have it if not himself? He deserved it

189

more than anyone.

'Dad, you're joking!' Babs's face dropped.

'What do you think, Bobbie?' Landon's glance swung to his elder daughter, who stifled her first ecstatic response and instead cast a quick and worried glance towards Eleanor. What did Eleanor think? Did she need to ask? 'Isn't what Mum thinks more important?' she demanded, shocked that she had to tell him. He should have talked this over with Eleanor first.

She felt like an intruder, an interloper, party to something not her business. Here was proof, if she'd needed it, that the thing wrong with her parents' marriage, whatever it was, was far deeper than either she or Babs had ever imagined.

Landon recollected himself, his gaze reluctantly and belatedly returning to Eleanor, who stood, arms folded, perfectly and ominously still. Her grip on her arms tightened. Something was holding her together, if she wasn't sure what.

'You're supposed to be taking it easy, cutting down on things!' Her voice came from a way away. There was a strange buzzing in her ears. Was he being deliberately obtuse? At last, irretrievably, the temper she'd been hanging on to for far too long, spilled over. 'It doesn't even make sense!' she cried, heatedly.

190

'How can this family afford a football club?'

'There are ways . . . ' Landon frowned, determined not to go into it now and hating it when Eleanor adopted this tone. A hard knot of defiance rose, tightening painfully inside him. There was a way out, the only way. She'd have to listen. 'We should put it to the vote.'

Babs laughed nervously. 'You're asking us to decide now?'

'Why not?' came the reply. His gaze sought Bobbie's, his one ally in this family, if ever he had one. Reading the response in her face, he relaxed. Bobbie would do what was expected of her. 'We have to do what's best for the club, love. It's not difficult.'

It felt like a betrayal, and, at this moment, all Bobbie could think was of her mother. Though acknowledging that it wasn't really Landon's fault either, a wave of anger still rose in her against him for putting them in this position. Why did Jimmy have to sell his blasted shares now!

She sucked in her breath, her slim figure tensing. But this was Rislington Rovers, their life blood! What else could she do but go with Landon. Her every sense told her it was the only thing to do.

'I'm sorry, Mum,' she muttered, hardly able to look at her now. 'I know precisely how you feel. I wish I could make you understand.

The club's too important. We have a responsibility to the fans. I just don't see what else we can do.'

'There we are, then!' Landon reached for the champagne bottle and, taking firm hold of it, began to twist the cork. 'Try and understand, love. The idea's not as bad as it seems . . . '

'Haven't you forgotten someone?' Babs scraped back her chair and sprang up, unable to believe he'd ignored her again. On top of all he'd done already!

She was her father's daughter. Swiftly she crossed to her mother's side and laid an arm protectively round her shoulders, looking to Bobbie almost in sorrow. Just when they'd seemed to be getting back to how things used to be!

She braced herself, her gaze shifting to her father. This family, her mother, her life at Cedars were important too.

'Sorry to spoil the party!' she stated acidly. 'But I'm with Mum on this. I've never heard such a ridiculous idea in the whole of my life!'

7

Bobbie passed Landon a fresh mug of coffee. He was upset, the stubble on his chin was telling her; her father, a man so capable that nothing fazed him, had been in such a hurry to get out of the house this morning that he hadn't even shaved. Things must be bad. She pulled out a chair and sat down; acknowledging the shadow that the takeover was casting over her family. Her parents at loggerheads, their daughters settled in opposing camps. Things couldn't be much worse.

'I'm sorry, love. What were you saying?' Thoughtlessly, miles away, Landon wrapped his hands round the mug and lifted it to his lips. What was he thinking about? It was obvious he'd fallen out with Eleanor and, even worse, didn't want to talk about it. A curt 'leave it, Bobbie', was all she'd got out of him so far. Even Sam, his favourite, rushing off to work and cramming toast en route, had had little success.

'I was telling you about Ronnie . . . ' Bobbie persisted, attempting to drag him back to the present. 'Who else could have told the lawyers about Alan?'

'Alan?'

'Campion! You know the situation, Dad!' Patiently she explained again. 'The club has so much evidence against him, it's hardly worth taking it to court. I should be siding with them.' She frowned. If only life was ever so easy! She couldn't stand back and do nothing when her every instinct screamed it a miscarriage of justice?

'Alan's a good man!' Landon uttered fiercely.

'He is and I can't abandon him,' she agreed. 'Bayfield can issue as many warnings as he likes. I don't care!' She did of course. She took a gulp of coffee, her pride still smarting from the visit Evelyn Bayfield, the club's lawyer, had paid her yesterday. He was self-possessed, diplomatic and sharp as a box of knives. She didn't trust him an inch. 'So long as I know we're singing from the same hymn sheet, Bobbie . . . I should hate to think further action was necessary.' The words came with a smile but the warning was clear. Continue helping Alan and she'd be in trouble.

'I could kill Ronnie!' she wailed.

Her words drifted across the table, unacknowledged. Landon was staring into the depths of his mug, his expression tugging at her heart-strings. What did club affairs matter when her parents' marriage was disintegrating before her eyes and she couldn't, seemingly, do a thing about it? This man, throughout her childhood, had always been there for her. They'd always been close. Her face softened, her hand covered his.

'Dad, don't worry . . . You and Mum . . . we'll sort something out?'

'All right if I collect the rest of my stuff, Aunty Bobbie?' Paris's head appeared around the door. He came in to stand by the table, his fingers thrumming against its edge, a bundle of restless energy. She hadn't even heard the door. She nodded, abstractedly. His stuff was upstairs in his room, left there from the time when he'd been placed under house arrest by Ronnie. She'd been as relieved as he so obviously was when eventually he'd been allowed to return to Cedars. How did Babs cope with him permanently? Problems there too, she guessed. He was keen to move into his new flat in Nottingham. He was growing up, needing to strike out on his own.

She gave Landon's hand a last squeeze and stood up.

'Do you want a coffee? Shouldn't you be at training?' Shouldn't she be at work!

'Ronnie's given us time off . . . ' He threw himself down, watching her whilst she busied

195

herself about the kitchen, his expression, for once, serious.

'It's a business about the shares?' he proffered tentatively.

'It's a worrying time,' she answered guardedly, hating the way it made them so on edge.

'Don't bother the lad's head,' Landon interjected.

'Its OK, Grandad. Mum's filled me in already — '

'You're not to say a word.'

'She's told me that, too.'

'I bet she has,' Bobbie observed wearily, putting a mug in front of him, uncomfortable with discussing a subject he was bound to report back to Babs. There was trouble enough.

'Don't assume that . . . I necessarily agree with Mum.' He leaned back, drinking his coffee. 'I understand her feelings but . . . I care about the football club too!' His face coloured up, full of a surprising emotion.

'Of course you do, love.' Bobbie smiled for the first time that morning. He was a Vernon too, deep down, even if he'd only just realized it. Great-Grandad Albert would be proud! Paris smiled, relaxed, more his usual self.

'You are buying Jimmy out? Or have you already?'

'It's not that easy, lad.' The subject at least revived Landon. He leaned forward, rubbing his chin, the thin rasping sound accompanying it, jogging his memory: he hadn't shaved. 'Ray Lovett's promised to put up half if we can match him. He's a good man, dependable, but even if we're successful and buy Jimmy out, Eddie would still have the upper hand. We need one of the others on board.' He didn't need to spell it out. They were in a tight corner with no room for manoeuvre. Having the board's self-made millionaire and avid club supporter on their side was something, but was it enough?

'It's a lot of money, Dad,' Bobbie fretted. No wonder her mother was so worried! She curled her hands around her mug and leaned back against the units. Her parents had never been rolling in money. Given the undeniable fact that they were getting on in life; this was no time for Landon to be wreaking such havoc with their finances. Not for the first time, she conceded, her dear football-hating mother did have a point.

'I'm not sure we have enough money,' Landon muttered, his voice laced with tension. Was money all it was about? Bobbie sighed, not understanding, only knowing she wanted to throw her arms around him and tell him, somehow, that everything would be all right.

Someone had to be strong! They'd suffered other, equally difficult crises over the years. She couldn't help the way she felt and neither could Landon. How could she see her dad, whom she loved, go down without a fight? Much as she loved Eleanor too!

'I've some savings,' she offered, regarding him carefully. 'Not much, admittedly but what there is . . . I want you to have it, Dad.'

'Nonsense!' Landon blustered, eyes suspiciously moist. He found his hanky and blew his nose, fooling no one.

Paris rocked back in his chair, glancing curiously from one to the other. They'd forgotten he was there. 'I've got money,' he announced abruptly. The chair rocked back to the floor with a clatter. He'd got more than he knew what to do with! Why shouldn't he do some good for once? He sprang up, smiling happily, his words shocking them both. 'You can have it, Granddad, if it'll help! I want to help you buy Jimmy out.'

★　★　★

'Is Steph in?' Sam smiled grimly, determined that even George wouldn't guess just what it had cost her to come here, to this run-down

198

old house on the other side of Rislington and the top-floor flat the young men shared.

'Sorry Sam, I'm not sure where he is . . . only out! Why don't you come in?'

He flung open the door. A smell of burning recalled him hastily to the tiny kitchen where he was cooking lunch. Sam followed, absent-mindedly noting the used cups and plates on every available surface, the crumpled garments thrown carelessly over the chairs. A mess, waiting only a passing female with the urge to tidy up. She'd imagined Steph would be different, but there again, she'd imagined too much of late.

It was her lunch hour. She'd come on impulse, even though she'd sworn that running after him was the last thing she'd ever do.

Her heart was beating too fast, a fact not just occasioned by two flights of stairs.

'I haven't much time, George.' She stood, staring around her miserably, questions crowding her head. It was so long since she'd seen him. Was he avoiding her and, if so, why? What other conclusion could she draw?

Since he'd returned from his leave in Italy, their contact had been reduced to work or the occasional phone call. Once he'd turned up at Bobbie's, insisting they go for a drink. She'd gone, only too willingly, hoping that this time they'd sort things out. He'd been so on edge, avoiding her every question, so she'd ultimately lost her temper and stormed home, piqued then that he hadn't followed to apologize. That should have been that. She wasn't normally so slow to take a hint, so why exactly was she here?

George jammed his foot down on the pedal-bin and tipped cremated remains into it.

'There's always the chip shop down the road!' he murmured, ruefully.

She couldn't help smiling.

'I thought Ronnie was big on healthy eating? Salad, pasta, that kind of thing?'

'You could . . . come with me if you like?' A gleam of hope sprang into George's rather handsome brown eyes. She hated to disappoint it. She did, instantly.

'I have to get back. I'm sorry, George. It's college tomorrow and I haven't even packed!' She rolled her eyes. The truth was, she hadn't time for this and yet how could she leave for Loughborough the way things stood? Whatever she and Steph had once had, it at least needed to be resolved. 'What's wrong with him, George?' she blurted out abruptly.

To her dismay, he turned away, busying himself clearing pots from the table but not before she'd seen the tell-tale colour rise to his cheeks. His demeanour quashed any faint lingering hopes. He tipped a pile of pots into the sink, swearing softly under his breath.

'It's none of my business, Sam!' He spun round, leaning back against the sink and folding his arms, his expression one of embarrassment. He obviously knew more than she did. He and Steph had obviously talked. Sam frowned, unable to bear the thought of Steph discussing their relationship with anyone, even George.

'Do you think I haven't guessed there's someone else?' Her voice was small, revealing her worst fear and yet, even now, desperately wanting George to deny it.

'You two need to talk . . . '

He must know she knew that!

'Perhaps you'd tell him so!' she answered sharply.

It wasn't fair to take it out on George. It wasn't George's fault.

'You deserve better, Sam . . . '

She knew that too. Her shoulders lifted. She was doing no good here.

'Tell him I called?' Not giving him a chance to reply, she turned on her heels and fled, banging out of the flat and clattering downstairs, her eyes full of tears she couldn't bear anyone to see, least of all George, who would only tell Steph. She wouldn't give him that satisfaction! She dashed them away angrily. Where was her pride?

Coming here, so desperate to see him, pride hadn't seemed to matter.

A light drizzle had fallen earlier; it had turned now to a sharp rain which stung her face. It was over. She'd have to get over it. What other option was left?

She'd walked the distance from Rislington Park. It loomed on the horizon, a comforting fact of life, solid and reassuring, unlike Steph who so patently wasn't. She pulled up her hood and began to walk, concentrating on the sound of her shoes striking the wet pavement. Traffic roared, spraying water. College tomorrow. Back to normality . . .

Her mobile rang, bringing her skidding to a halt.

'Sam? What exactly have you and Todd been saying to your father?' Her mother's voice, clearly irate, came bouncing over the airwaves. Sam turned her head, shielding the phone, her thoughts spinning.

'Why, nothing! I . . . '

'He rang me whilst I was with your granddad!' she interrupted crossly. 'Can you imagine? Where's he got this idea we could possibly get back together? I'm sorry, love. I know it's not your fault but . . . I'm beginning to wish he hadn't come back!'

There was a pause in which Sam could imagine her mother's pained face, only too clearly.

'Mum, we haven't said anything! At least . . . ' The fog that was her mind sprang abruptly into action. 'I might have suggested . . . not that I meant to exactly but . . . Oh Mum! I wouldn't exactly be against the idea!' she concluded miserably, her thoughts winging swiftly back to the previous evening and her father's insistence that he should take both his children out for dinner. His over-exuberant praise of Bobbie's qualities, whilst undeniable, had no doubt been fuelled by too much wine. Even so she and Todd had been only too willing to listen. They'd egged him on. She realized that now.

'Would it be so very bad, Mum?' she coaxed, into the rain, distance lending her courage. A man passed, walking his dog, watching her curiously. Her face flamed red, knowing the importance she attached to the answer, knowing even without answer, that it wasn't any good.

'Sam, how could you?' Bobbie no longer sounded angry, only perplexed. 'I know he's your dad . . . I know you love him! But come on, love. It wouldn't work . . . '

There was a bitter, pain-filled silence. What could she say? Her mother and father together didn't, couldn't work and it wasn't fair. Even now, no longer a child, she wanted her parents together. She'd wanted it all her life . . . more than anything.

'I'm sorry, Mum.'

She heard, or imagined, Bobbie's heartfelt sigh of relief.

'Don't let's fall out. I'll see you teatime?' She clicked off. Sam dropped her phone back into her pocket. It was over. Another dream gone. Was that what growing up was about? If it was she didn't like it.

Hunching her shoulders against the rain she carried on into work.

★ ★ ★

'There's no need to look so surprised!'

Anna Kirkby jumped from the car, her young face alight with amusement. To her right, Belfield House shivered in the murky cold of a late winter's afternoon that was only just beginning to clear. Ahead, at the top of the car park, lay Blueberry Wood, leading up to the huge man-made reservoirs feeding the waterworks and the fountains in the gardens below. These were a visitor attraction which brought the crowds flocking in the summer. Now it was quiet, dreamy almost, a throwback to a bygone age.

'I'm not . . . really . . . it's cool!' Paris grinned, only too happy to be here.

He'd followed directions since he'd picked her up in Brookfield, still unable to believe his luck that she'd agreed to come. Stopping only to hoist the haversack on to his back, he hastened after her, remembering now he'd been here before, many years ago, on a picnic with his Aunty Bobbie. How odd that Anna should choose here over all other possible destinations!

It had been raining all day. Puddles of water squelched underfoot, telling him it was no picnic weather. He didn't care and neither, by the looks of it, did Anna. They were here now, and together, surely the most important thing.

'We're in luck, the sun's coming out!' Anna cried, turning impatiently. 'Hurry up, there's not much time! We'll eat by the lake at the top.'

What was the rush? Intrigued, he ran to catch up.

'I hope you like smoked salmon,' he called. After his meeting with Bobbie he'd returned to Cedars, standing an age in the kitchens, getting under Babs's feet, trying to make his mind up what to take and deaf to her pleas that he should let one of the cooks take over. It had never crossed his mind that he ought to tell her: he'd thrown his lot in with Granddad. It would wait. Unlike Anna! 'There's egg if you'd rather! I wasn't sure which . . . '

'Smoked salmon will be lovely.' She laughed.

They entered the wood and followed one of the tracks that criss-crossed upwards, underneath trees with branches already showing promise of spring to come. Spring and Anna! He relaxed. Anna was in his life. It must mean something.

She threw him a shy glance, wondering for the umpteenth time that afternoon just what she was doing here. Was she crazy? Lost all sense of reasoning? Yes and yes! Her heart leapt. Sensible Anna who'd said yes on instinct, even knowing all she'd read in the papers. If she believed even a small part of that she'd have run a mile!

'They were OK at work about time off?'

'Just this afternoon,' she agreed pleasantly. 'I am due for a break.'

How serious, grown-up they sounded. Water dripped from the trees, accompanying their every step. Soft patterings like distant music. 'I'm really glad you've come!' he blurted out suddenly. The track had broadened. He drew level, staring down into her face. 'I wasn't sure you would . . . '

'Me neither!' There was the hint of laughter in her voice. Paris halted, seizing his courage and slipping his hand round hers, delighted that she made no resistance.

'I really like you, Anna,' he whispered shyly. Was he saying too much, too soon? Recklessly he plunged on. 'I can't stop thinking about you!'

She nodded, amused that he should imagine that she didn't think about him too. 'I like you too, Paris, only . . . Don't you think we're too different?' she suggested cautiously, hating to put a damper on things.

'Not so very much,' he urged.

She'd have to spell it out.

'I come from a single-parent family. We've never had any money — '

'Money doesn't matter.'

'You say that because you've always had it!' She tugged her hand free, walking on more slowly. Money was bound to make a difference. They had nothing in common. 'You wouldn't fit into my world,' she warned. Nor me yours, the thought sprang, unasked.

'I can change!'

'How can you?'

Words and easy to say. He sounded sincere but how well did she really know him?

'Please don't give up on us before we've even started!' he cried, sensing her wavering.

'Oh, come on, Anna! At least give us a try?'

'I suppose . . . I could put you on probation?' She grinned, her voice full of a sudden delight. She had nothing to lose. They were young, the afternoon's length: a lifetime.

Clambering on, over terrain slanting steeply upwards, they followed the course of a stream, a musical accompaniment to their progress, bubbling over stones and tree roots, in reality, a man-made feature directing the water from a deep reservoir on to a broad slope from where it powered the waterworks in the garden below. Through the trees, the sun began to shine. Anna's cheeks glowed; suddenly she was glad she'd come.

'Hurry, there really isn't much time.'

But what was the urgency! They'd arrived at a point where the water was directed down a sheer rock face, falling in a roaring crescendo of bubbling froth at their feet. Beyond it, they rejoined the path and followed it round and upwards until they came to a series of stone steps, cut into the limestone. They climbed and emerged moments later, breathless and laughing, high above the house and on a level with the water crashing over the rock. What they saw looked like toy cars parked by a doll's house.

'I wish you'd tell me what you're up to!' he grumbled good naturedly.

She laughed, tugging the haversack from his shoulder in answer and stooping to lodge it against a rock before, wonderfully to him, grabbing hold of his hand. 'Don't let go,' she whispered.

The waterfall he saw now, on closer inspection, left a gap between the rock face and a stone ledge directly in front of their feet. Her grip tightened. She stepped on to it, pulling him quickly behind. He followed, too shocked to do anything else, turning with his back against the rock and the world at his feet to face a sheet of tumbling water. There was room to stand there, but not much. The roar of tumbling water thundered in his ears. For one sickening moment fear transfixed him to the spot.

'Don't worry, I've got you . . . '

Anna's voice came, calm and reassuring. He relaxed, leaned back and felt the reassurance of cold stone against his back and water spraying his face like rainfall. Her hand burned in his, more wonderful to him than anything.

The sun was going down over the hills. To his amazement, little red chinks of gyrating light reflected through the sheet of curved water, turning to rose, indigo and a bright glowing gold, like shoots of liquid fire.

'We're inside a rainbow!' he breathed,

awestruck. 'Beautiful!' he shouted, turning towards her, not even meaning the water, finding himself looking down into a face radiant with sparks of moving, multicoloured light.

Her body was too close, they were too confined. Gently, scarcely daring to breathe, he pulled her to him, his free hand rising to touch her face. She caught it, pulling it quickly to her lips, her eyes alive with an expression that even now he hardly dared to acknowledge. She wanted him too. She was beautiful. His senses quickened accentuated by the sounds all around, filling his head. He closed his eyes and held her, convinced they'd flown upwards and gone to heaven.

★ ★ ★

It was the weekly up-to-date with Ronnie, following on the back of precisely the kind of a day even the thoughts of which had made Bobbie quake. After the phone call from Gerry events had quickly spiralled out of control, filled with accounts which wouldn't add up, a lost shirt deal she'd taken as read and a steady barrage of abuse from fans disgruntled at the team's mid-table mediocrity. If they didn't start picking up points soon, they'd lose any chance of the play-offs.

Ronnie obviously didn't see the last of these as a problem and this time, no matter how Bobbie longed for the chance to put the day behind her, she was determined to put him straight. Presenting herself as a vulnerable woman would cut no ice with this dour old Yorkshireman.

'We're six points adrift, if you haven't noticed?' Borden United having been dispatched, the fifth round loomed; disaster as far as Bobbie was concerned. Her tone was firm, in control, sustained by a desire to do what was best for the club. Her football club, dash it, and it was time he understood.

'I'm the manager! The Cup's the only thing . . . ' Ronnie, fresh from training and filling her office with his track-suited presence, reared to his feet, face brimming with the assumption there was nothing she could do. She could do more than he expected, she mused, her eyes narrowing, flints of hostility, matching his.

'And I'm the chief executive, a fact you choose to forget.' She sprang up and moved smartly round the desk, wishing she owned another six inches and could meet him eye to eye. It was bad enough that he'd gone behind her back to Jimmy about Alan. The thought lent her voice added force. 'It's in my power to fire you, Ronnie!'

Something else he'd chosen to forget. Nothing would give her greater satisfaction. She watched the colour drain from his face.

'You'd never dare . . . ' he blustered.

'Try me!'

His reply was choice, but he was shaken.

The door burst open, revealing Colin Peterson, club secretary, clutching the early edition of the *Evening Telegraph* and obviously in a state of shock.

'Have you read the papers?' he demanded, hurrying in to thrust the offending article into her outstretched hand. Quickly she scanned the headlines, then returned to her chair to read the rest, her spirits failing with every word.

ROVERS SHARE BATTLE.

Championship Club Rocked to Foundations! 'Rislington Rovers, famous old football club in existence since the football league first formed, is in danger of imploding after Jimmy Proudfoot, the club chairman, announced the shock decision he wants out . . .

'Eddie Lamoure . . . ' she growled, passing the paper to Ronnie, who didn't look surprised. Was he in on this too? Nothing would surprise her. The treachery all around them thickened the air like a London fog. Her legs were trembling. She thrust them under the desk, jamming her feet to the floor.

'It had to come out some time . . . ' Despite the volcano of emotion raging inside, her voice, at least, was calm. No one would guess she was shaken.

'Why does no one tell me anything?' Colin's lean features were creased with anxiety. 'How long has this been going on?'

'A few weeks,' Bobbie answered honestly. 'Dad's doing his best to sort things out.'

'He'd better, Bobbie . . . '

He had better, and there was no need for Colin to say so. At that moment the phones began to ring. Colin pulled a face and shot back downstairs. Ronnie picked up the extension in one large hand, mouthed 'BBC' and engaged in heated conversation. Bobbie lifted her phone to a local reporter wanting a quote. It rang again as soon as she put it down whilst Cheryl from admin poked her head round the door, with the news that one of the nationals was downstairs. Pandemonium had broken out. 'I'll go!' Ronnie snapped. Bobbie returned to her phone, more relieved than she would care to admit to hear Landon's voice. A warm tide of gratitude flooded through her, bringing her calm when she needed it most.

'Dad, how did you know I needed you?'

'Chin up, love, we'll get there . . . Bad is it?'

'Do you need to ask?' She smiled for the first time, it seemed, for a long while. 'The place's gone mad . . . '

'We'll have to move quickly.' His voice was threaded with emotion. 'We'll meet up back home. I'm hoping I'll have some news.'

The call, never mind that it was so brief, steadied her. Deftly she fielded calls, arranged press conferences and drafted statements. Outside in the quickening gloom the vultures gathered, illumined by the bright lights of Sky TV. The phone rang again.

'Bobbie, are you all right?' Babs's voice, the last Bobbie had expected. She sounded sincere but gauging her little sister's moods had been something Bobbie had found difficult of late.

'Just about all right,' she admitted shakily.

'I do understand what you're doing, even if I don't agree . . . right?'

Bobbie relaxed. A phone call of support. Her family rallying. A family after all. 'Hey! Aren't those my lines? Just who's the big sister here?' she joked. Things blurred. She rubbed her eyes, determined not to give way. 'We need to talk,' she urged. 'You need to talk to Paris at least . . . ' The words were out of her mouth as soon as thought. How would

Babs feel when she learned of Paris's offer to his grandfather? She didn't know about it, Bobbie sensed.

'What's gone off now?'

'Please Babs, talk to Paris.' She sounded as guilty as she felt. Paris and Babs would have to sort this out between them. Better that she didn't get involved. 'Why don't we meet up at home later and have a chat? Dad said he might have news.'

'Too right we need to chat!' Her sister's voice was filled with a sudden excitement, thoughts of her son forgotten in her haste to tell Bobbie what she'd really rung about. 'I've been looking into this Aldergate Holdings — '

'Babs, I'm not sure I've time — '

'Listen, Bobbie, this is important!' Babs's voice rose. 'I'm sorry to tell you this. I really wish there was some other way but . . . I've been down to Company House and seen a list of directors. It's turned up a very interesting name.'

'Go on. I'm listening.'

'One G. Mansfield?'

'Gerry? Babs . . . what season are we talking about here?' Bobbie's voice was sharp.

'Ninety-six, ninety-seven?'

Bobbie was shocked, a sickening certainty building inside. 'But Gerry was the accountant here, at the club, at that time!'

'Mmm . . . ' Babs's voice bristled with indignation. 'You have to ask yourself, Bobbie, why would he pay club funds to a company in which he held a large number of shares? Worse, the profits from Aldergate were creamed off into an account on the Isle of Man. Whilst he worked here, he was fiddling the books. There's no other way of explaining it . . . '

It had been one of those days, culminating in something so awful it didn't bear contemplation. Bobbie replaced the phone with shaking fingers, the mayhem around her falling into insignificance, the one thought thundering in her brain. Sam and Todd would be devastated. How could she tell her children that their father was a crook?

Her shoulders slumped, her eyes squeezed shut. If only she could make it go away!

★   ★   ★

'Either of you know where your mother's gone?' Landon turned from the window where he'd been staring into the garden, too keyed-up to remark upon the sight of his daughters together. They'd arrived together by chance, lingering on the drive to discuss Gerry and, more important, what Bobbie was going to do next. Confront him? It went

216

without saying. She owed Alan Campion that much at least.

She couldn't stop thinking about her children. Grown up as they were, they still worshipped their father. 'I've always tried to put Gerry in a good light, Babs,' she moaned. 'There's no mistake?' One look at Babs's face and the last lingering hope faded.

'I'm sorry. I've checked and checked again.'

The two women linked arms, wandering through the back door and into the house, surprised to find Landon in the kitchen and Eleanor out.

'Dad — you've news?' Bobbie hurried across, laying a hand on his arm, forgetting her own problems in a concern for his. He looked washed out. Something had happened.

'You'll not believe it, love — '

'We ought to wait for Mum,' Babs cut in, the look she threw Landon making clear exactly where she laid blame for the family rift.

'There's her car now,' Bobbie cried, glad of the interruption. Whatever the news, it was bound to end in argument. They might as well wait until Eleanor was here.

Feeling no better than when she'd first gone out, Eleanor Vernon jumped from her car and walked smartly into the house. She'd been cooped up all morning, depressed following another pointless argument with Landon. She'd done some shopping and called on Susie. Eddie had been out. They'd sat drinking tea, putting the world to rights, Landon included. Should she feel guilty?

'Where've you been?' he demanded almost before she'd got through the door.

'I am allowed out!' She laid her car keys down carefully, aware she'd spoken heatedly. She modified her voice. If she told him about Susie it would only cause more upset. 'I've had a walk round the shops.'

'It'll have done you good, Mum.' Bobbie's tone was placatory, awkward about this share business, Eleanor sensed. It wasn't Bobbie's fault.

'Dad has some news,' Babs cried.

'I bet!' Eleanor muttered, instinctively aware that it wouldn't be anything she wanted to hear. She pulled out a chair and sat down, staring fixedly at the daffodils in the blue vase she'd arranged earlier and oddly remembering the times when Landon used to pick them for her. The first flowers of spring! After winter's gloom she'd always loved that first bright splash of colour in her home.

He'd always been so caring. Where had it all gone wrong?

He sat down opposite, resting his elbows

on the table, watching her uneasily.

'There's no easy way to say this, Eleanor. You and Babs will be furious but . . . ' He glanced towards Bobbie, his gaze filled with a sudden excitement. 'We've pulled it off. It's wonderful, darling! Believe it or not but this family is now a major shareholder. The Rogues are ours!'

His voice shook with emotions of which pride was uppermost.

Clearly in pain, Eleanor screwed up her eyes. Babs's sharp intake of breath was audible.

'Dad, that's wonderful,' Bobbie breathed, even then, in that first moment of joy, thinking of Eleanor. She must be devastated.

The silence became unbearable. All eyes of one accord centred firmly on the woman with the blonde hair, threaded with grey, who sat so silently, head sinking into her hands.

'Say something . . . please?' Landon's voice was reduced to a strangled croak.

'What do you want me to say?' Her head snapped up. 'You've got exactly what you want, haven't you?'

'Please don't be like that, love. You know what it means to me.'

Oh, she knew! She knew and hated it. He'd no concern for his health, their marriage, anything but his blessed football club!

'But how did you manage it?' Bobbie cried. There must have been more support than he'd reckoned. Given the way things had been weighted against them, she'd steeled herself for bad news.

'I bought some shares from Ted Hillier,' Landon countered, uneasily.

Ted was one of the board's quieter, less volatile members. The first faint stirrings of alarm surfaced on Bobbie's face. The look she gave Landon was a sharp one. Even given her small contribution and the tidy sum Paris had so unexpectedly offered, buying Jimmy up should have cleared him out completely.

'What have you been up to, Landon?' Eleanor demanded, her body stiffening visibly.

Some of the euphoria so buoying Landon up since Jimmy had put pen to paper began, slowly, to evaporate. He'd set in motion a procedure he'd had in place for some days as back-up, a last resort, never in his wildest dreams imagining he'd be called upon to use it!

He should have talked it over with Eleanor. It was unforgivable. He saw that now, too late.

'There wasn't time!' he blurted out. 'Things moved so fast. Melchester were pressing, Eddie was ready with the money.

Jimmy couldn't wait longer.'

'Landon, what have you done?' Eleanor's voice was heavy with dread.

'Please believe me, darling! If there'd been any other way — '

'Dad tell us, for goodness' sake!' Even Bobbie sounded worried. He looked away, unable to meet her gaze, finding himself staring instead at the silver birch outside the kitchen window. Wanting pruning, it had grown too tall, blocking out the light.

'I had a meeting with the bank manager,' he admitted quietly. 'I've remortgaged the house.'

The words were easy, their implication stunning, falling into the warm confines of Eleanor's domain, shattering its cosy domesticity irrevocably. Tight-lipped, she scraped back the chair and stood up.

'Say something, darling,' he pleaded.

'Don't darling me!' she snapped. 'There's nothing to say, Landon.'

Home, Eleanor, their life together, everything she'd thought he'd held dear had been weighed against football and lost. She'd never forgive him. Straightening her shoulders, head held high and without another word, she stalked out of the kitchen.

'How could you, Dad!' Babs cried, turning on him furiously.

Landon pushed back his chair and stood up. 'I'll go after her.'

'I'd leave it, Dad.' Even Bobbie who understood, recognized that this time he'd gone far beyond anything even Eleanor could reasonably be expected to swallow. He appeared to have forgotten: Eleanor was important too.

A soft sigh escaped Bobbie's lips.

'You could at least have talked to her first!' Babs sank down into a chair, thinking for once, not of herself, but of the effect this was going to have on her parents' marriage.

'You've no need to tell me!' he ground out miserably. 'There didn't seem any other option.'

He was making excuses where there was none to be made. Automatically, Bobbie began to move about the kitchen, making coffee, finding mugs, milk from the fridge, something, anything to do with her hands whilst she tried to marshal her thoughts into some kind of order. Euphoria, misery, two extremes, jangling her nerves into frenzy. They owned the football club! And in the process they'd managed to tear their family apart? How could they recover from this?

For the first time Eleanor's viewpoint was crystal clear. What right had Bobbie and her father to do this to their family? Football was

222

a game, a silly foolish unimportant one, some would say. How could it be weighed against her parents' marriage, the bedrock of her life?

She stood, milk jug in hand, relieved when Eleanor reappeared. The relief didn't last. To Bobbie's dismay, Eleanor was clutching her overnight case, her coat slung over her arm. She stalked into the kitchen and grabbed her car keys from the table.

'I'll call round for the rest of my things in the morning,' she stated in a cold voice that none of them recognized. 'I don't see how we can go on after this, Landon. I'm leaving. I'm sorry. I simply can't take any more.'

Throwing him a last reproachful glance, leaving them all speechless, she stalked from the kitchen and slammed the door.

8

'How could he, Giles?'

Eleanor's face was full of a painful reality that was only now sinking in. By selling their house from under her, Landon had demonstrated that he cared so much for his precious football club he was prepared to put everything else in his life, even their marriage, at risk. She couldn't understand now why she'd been so shocked. It was as if she'd spent her married life asleep and only now woken to the reality of the self-obsessed man she'd married.

'We all do things when we're desperate.' Giles Barnard eased his lean frame from Susie Lamoure's plush sofa and stood up.

The last thing she'd expected was sympathy for Landon. The morning sun climbed high, promising a good day ahead. Eleanor shot him a curious glance before returning to the view of the landscaped gardens she'd been staring at so helplessly before Giles arrived, seeking Eddie. Giles must be furious with Landon too, spoiling all his plans! Spoiling everyone's plans, even Eleanor's, when he should have cared about Eleanor

224

and her hopes for their future most of all.

She'd been in turmoil ever since she'd stormed out last night. Blindly she'd fled from the house. Even now she didn't know how she'd managed to drive herself over here, to Susie's, the one place she could have chosen that would drive Landon crazy if he had known of her choice. She took warped satisfaction in the thought. Something had to get through to him!

Susie was a good friend. 'Stay as long as you need,' she'd murmured. She'd taken her in and made up a bed in one of the guest rooms, tactfully not asking unnecessary questions. One look at Eleanor's face had been enough. She'd packed Eddie off and out and opened the wine. The two women had sat up half the night drinking more than was good for either of them, trying impossibly to put the impossible right.

'I shouldn't be here, Giles,' she cried, turning towards him, pushing the hair from her eyes. She was tired. Her head thumped. She hadn't slept a wink. Worse, she couldn't see any way forward.

'If there's anything I can do . . . '

Giles crossed the space between them and drew her gently to him. She was too much in need of human comfort to back away. Grateful, blinking back tears, she leaned into him, relaxing for the first time since she'd got up.

They were alone together. Susie had gone reluctantly, and at Eleanor's insistence, to a committee meeting of a local children's charity which she was chairing and couldn't put off, Eddie was closeted in his office taking flak over the failed takeover bid. Everything was a mess. Landon had made a mess of so many lives.

'There's nothing anyone can do.' The realization stared her firmly in the face. After long and basically happy years, her marriage was over. She'd yet to come to terms with it.

The sun was shining on the last of the winter pansies. The garden looked peaceful, their happy smiling faces giving her an odd, strange hope. She must be stronger than she'd realized. She'd find a new life, move somewhere else, love someone other than Landon who didn't deserve that she should give him another thought.

'The man's a fool,' Giles whispered, so close she felt his breath on her face. The look in his eyes was unmistakable and for one long, wonderful moment she battled with temptation. Why shouldn't she? Giles wanted her and part of her wanted him too, and not just because of Landon's unforgivable behaviour. He was still a good-looking man. He listened to her. He cared for her! Why shouldn't she have some love in her life? Everyone needed love.

The thought made her feel faintly ridiculous. She was too old for this, certainly for starting an affair with another man. She was old and worn out and she'd never forgive Landon for what he'd put her through!

Reluctantly she moved away.

'I'm sorry, Eleanor. It was hardly fair.' Giles's voice was laced with concern.

'Sorry, Giles. I do like you, only . . . '

'Just liking's not love?'

She nodded, not even sure of that much, only he was right about one thing, Landon was a fool.

'Mum? Eddie said to come through . . . '

Bobbie stood in the doorway, her troubled gaze moving from one face to the other. Her initial euphoria in discovering that her hunch was right and Eleanor was here, at Susie's, faded as she saw them together, looking so intimate . . . so much a couple. She came into the room, dropping her bag on the sofa, unable to shed the thought that she'd interrupted something. But Eleanor had always sworn that Giles Barnard meant nothing to her!

Her father would go crazy when he knew that this was where she'd come.

'Don't be so ridiculous, Bobbie. Eddie's is the last place to go looking for her. She cares more about me than that!' he'd snapped, too obviously exhausted by a sleepless night spent ringing all their friends, everyone they could think of, all to no avail. She'd forgiven him his ill humour, seeing only his remorse, his desperation to put things right after the crazy way he'd been behaving of late.

'I'll see you later, Eleanor?' Giles dropped a light kiss on Eleanor's cheek. Treating Bobbie to a thin smile, he stepped past her and hastened up the corridor in search of Eddie.

'Mum! If only you knew how worried we've been!' It was some kind of understatement. Bobbie hurried over, looking tentatively into her mother's face, unsure how to treat her when she seemed, oddly, almost a stranger. A woman at a crossroads in her life. She longed to throw her arms around her and assure her that between them, somehow, they'd sort this mess out. Yesterday she could have done it without a second thought. Today, it felt too much like treading on eggshells.

'Dad's out of his mind with worry . . . '

'He should have thought of that before he sold our house,' Eleanor answered sharply, some of her anger returning. Of course Bobbie would side with Landon. Bobbie always sided with Landon. The fact put distance between them, almost palpably cooling the atmosphere in the room.

'You're tired, Mum, we're all tired. We've none of us had any sleep.' Bobbie persisted, wishing she could explain how things really were back home. Babs had eventually and reluctantly gone back to Cedars, leaving Bobbie to stay on and keep an eye on their father who, the girls had decided between them, was unfit to leave. He hadn't been fit to cope with the press pack besieging the house either, seeking interviews with the new owner of Rislington Rovers. The football world, it appeared, was agog over the takeover bid. If she told Eleanor as much she'd only take umbrage again.

'Mum, you must come home.' She hadn't time for this. She should have been at the ground long since, fielding the media frenzy she'd be bound to find there too.

Problems never came singly; more usually piling in en masse, like a rugby scrum.

'I haven't got to do anything!'

'You must talk to Dad! Let's ring him, shall we? Tell him we're on our way back ... You haven't seen him. I really am worried ... '

Alarmingly, Eleanor shook her head.

'Don't tell him I'm here, Bobbie,' she cried. He would storm over, causing all kinds of complications when things were bad enough.

Even Bobbie grasped that Landon's knowing her mother was here, at Eddie's, would only inflame the situation. She was unsure what to do. What a mess things were, when this should have been one of the best days in her life. They owned their precious football club and yet, if anything could have shown her where her priorities lay, this was it. Her parents should be together for always. Anything else was unthinkable, sending her world spinning out of control.

'Promise?' Eleanor demanded, her voice, so often raised in temper at home, momentarily unrecognizable.

'There must be some way forward, Mum?' Bobbie responded, miserably aware that if she gave up now, without a fight, things might never return to normal. Eleanor seemed so determined that things were broken beyond repair.

Her mind drifted to her childhood, filled mostly with happy memories, but she was aware that there'd been arguments aplenty there too; she and Babs had been like a series of miniature volcanoes on the point of explosion, each demanding their parents' undivided attention. What a handful they'd been!

'Remember what you used to tell us when we were children?' she murmured, her eyes shining. 'You said we had to stick together! Family was family and that's what families did.' For always, no matter what the provocation.

Eleanor conjured up a tired, weak smile.

'Stop looking so worried' she chided. 'I don't blame you for this, Bobbie, or Babs, come to that. You'll always have each other, just as you'll always have me and your dad.' Just maybe not together. Wishing she could make her understand, Eleanor's hand brushed her daughter's cheek. This was between her and Landon, no one else, not even Bobbie. No one had asked Landon to sell the house, treating her feelings as if they were of no consequence. He'd no right to rampage through their marriage destroying all in his path.

Her next words took Bobbie's breath away.

'I'm sorry, love, please believe me. I can't see any other way round it. I can't come back. I can't ever come back. I'm afraid your father and I can never be together again.'

★   ★   ★

Paying scant attention to the strangely muted lunchtime noises emanating from the restaurant, Babs Vernon hurried across the foyer of

Cedars towards the office, into which Taylor had just disappeared. Trade was slack and somewhere she registered the fact, but for the moment she had other, more important things on her mind. On top of this wretched share business, her mother's disappearance and Bobbie as usual taking over and pushing Babs out, there was the perennial problem of Taylor!

There was more to this than feeling rejected, Babs concluded. Frowning, she pushed open the door and stepped inside. At the sight of Taylor, reading the paper, feet up on her desk, her mood plummeted even further. He looked up and smiled.

'Good time last night?' she demanded, swinging his feet round and on to the floor, her tone frosty enough so that even Taylor sensed the atmosphere. His welcome smile disappeared.

'So-so,' he admitted guardedly. 'Russ's OK, better than I thought. We had a few beers, chatted over old times. You know how it is?'

Russ Packard was an old teammate whom Taylor had been out with the previous evening. He had blown the money earned during a lucrative playing career and was now surviving in a crumbling bedsit. Taylor had seen a lot of Russ lately.

Babs had never realized that Taylor was so benevolent.

'Oh, I know how these things are, Taylor!' she retorted, not meaning to sound quite so accusatory. Or maybe she did?

He threw down the paper and sat watching her through narrow, hostile eyes.

'What's the matter?' he demanded.

'Did you listen to a word I said last night?' she enquired icily.

He'd arrived home late, too obviously the worse for wear, too oblivious to Babs's despair, hardly listening to her tale of woe concerning events back home before falling into bed and straight into a deep and peaceful sleep. Babs, left tossing and turning the night away over Eleanor and what her father was going to do now he'd succeeded, at last, in bringing his marriage crashing down around his ears, hadn't slept a wink. The wreck of her parents' marriage was too close for comfort. Something was sadly wrong with her own marriage and, bad as things were, that fact overrode everything else.

'Eleanor's one tough cookie. She'll be OK,' Taylor responded, proving he had been listening after all. If he thought it would gain him brownie points, she couldn't wait to disabuse him.

'Everything's fine in your book, Taylor!' she responded, her eyes full of hurt.

Ignoring his frown, she removed herself to

the window in time to see Tessa Cunningham, The Cedars' bright and too-attractive new receptionist, appear from the direction of the car park and hurriedly cross the yard. She was late; a habit of which the girl had too often been guilty nowadays. The sight triggered suspicions that Babs had been harbouring for too long.

'There's something about that girl' she muttered, swinging round to look Taylor full in his handsome face. The truth was, Babs had never taken to her. Taylor was the one who'd been so insistent that she should be taken on. Babs should have read the warning signs. When had Taylor ever been concerned with the hiring of staff?

'She seems OK to me,' he answered guardedly, his eyes roaming past his wife and falling uneasily on the slim figure disappearing inside.

'I don't trust her,' Babs responded, too aware of the glance, her thinly worn patience snapping. 'You should have heard the untruths she told me yesterday about needing time off. According to Tessa, her young brother was playing an away match for the Rogue's youth team and she had to ferry him to the ground. Just her bad luck that I bumped into Nigel Jennings, and it turns out the youth team haven't had a match for ages.'

Babs's face flushed at recollection of the deceit. She'd yet to tackle Tess over the issue and boy, was she in the mood! She smiled bitterly. Even Taylor couldn't argue with this. Nigel was the youth team coach. As so often of late, following a stint at the ground catching up on admin work, he'd called round at Cedars for his morning coffee. Naturally she'd asked him how things had gone last night; naturally, he'd told her straight away that there had been no match for the youth team.

'I wonder why she felt the need to lie?' she fretted, staring hard at Taylor.

'Probably found herself a date,' he countered, too smoothly for Babs, who could detect guilt at point-blank range.

'You've been seeing a lot of Russ lately, Taylor?'

She stood her ground, her body tense, accusation written in her face. One word from Nigel this morning and everything had clicked too frighteningly into place. Taylor's frequent ventures out, coinciding too often with Tessa's shifts off or the times she rang in ill. Taylor wouldn't hear a word against her. It was time to have this out.

'What are you implying, Babs?' he cried heatedly, springing up, the picture of injured innocence. He could be astute when he wanted. If Babs hadn't been so hurting, she could almost have stood back to applaud.

'Do I have to spell it out?' she muttered, bracing herself, perversely wishing she hadn't started this now. It would have been better to let things lie; pretend she didn't think what she thought. Where was her pride?

'You think I'm having an affair with Tess?' Incredulity laced his voice.

'Aren't you?' she demanded, her voice small and full of pain. They could put it behind them, start afresh if only he'd promise never to let it happen again? So far she'd managed to hold back the tears but one escaped now, spilling over and trickling a lonely furrow down her face.

It was too late. Taylor, being Taylor, as always took the easy way out. Throwing her furious glances, he stormed past her and out of the office, slamming the door with a passion that made his feelings all too plain.

★ ★ ★

'Meet me at the police station on Prospect Way. I'm on my way there now. Double quick, Harry. I need you!'

Prospect Way? What prospects had he now, other than a lengthy prison spell?

Gerry Mansfield dropped his mobile into

his jacket pocket and turned towards Bobbie, who was driving. A smattering of shops and houses were starting to appear along a tree-lined street. They'd reached the outskirts of Rislington. The roads were busy with post-lunchtime traffic.

'Harry's a good lawyer, one of the best.'

'You'll need him there, Gerry.'

'It's good of you to take me,' he admitted humbly.

He'd turned up at the ground barely half an hour since, edgy, surprisingly contrite, full of, as he'd thought, a confession that Bobbie knew nothing about. Years ago he'd swindled money from the football club. He needed to put things right. More than anything, he needed Bobbie to come with him to the police. He'd looked so helpless and sorry for himself that, despite her anger at the effect all this was bound to have on their children, Bobbie hadn't the heart to do anything else.

'Why own up to me, Gerry?' she murmured, still puzzling over it. Worse, why now, when everything else seemed to be going wrong too! Her parents' marriage, the takeover, her own marriage split in two. She was worried sick about Eleanor. Her hands tightened on the steering wheel, longing suddenly for Davie's arms around her and the sheer joy of having someone to share her problems with. Worryingly, they'd hardly seen anything of each other lately.

Gerry rubbed his face. He looked washed out.

'Who else should I own up to besides you, Bobbie? I've been working up to it. Why else did you think I've come back?' he muttered. He lit a cigarette and inhaled deeply, not asking her whether she minded. He dropped the match to the floor.

'You heard about the police investigation?' she prompted, trying not to sound too impatient, needing to understand.

'A tourist left his morning papers at the monastery,' he explained, as tendrils of blue-grey smoke filled the car. 'Ill-luck, I suppose . . . or divine retribution. The back pages were full of it and Alan's apparent implication. I was horrified! I might have behaved badly, Bobbie, but . . . I couldn't let anyone else take the blame for something I'd done. I had to come home. I have to put things straight.'

'You can hardly do anything else,' she agreed.

'You do believe me?'

She nodded cautiously, prepared this time, for her children's sake, to give him the benefit of the doubt. Whatever emotion her husband engendered, compassion was, for the moment, uppermost. But what a mess he'd made of his life — and now, by implication, his children's too. She ought by rights to be furious with him.

'I still don't understand . . . ' They were coming up to traffic lights. The car slid gently to a halt. It must have happened just after they'd split up. Heaven forbid any one should think she'd known about it, that she'd somehow been involved too.

'Our divorce was messy, remember?' he muttered, his gaze fastening on the car in front. 'I had the children's future to think about. It was my bad luck that the property deal in Spain came along at virtually the same time. My one big chance. My savings were way short — '

'It still doesn't excuse — '

'Jimmy always had it in for me,' he interrupted, his voice filled with emotion. 'He always held me back. I was stuck in a dull job with no prospect of getting on. No wonder I wanted out of the club. It seemed a good way of getting back at Jimmy, too . . . '

Put into words it sounded bad and he knew it. His shoulders lifted helplessly. Bobbie grimaced, remembering, in that instance, the man with whom she'd been so unhappy and the reason why they'd split up. Always wanting more, nothing ever enough. Greed

239

cloaked as ambition. Gerry Mansfield had never quite been what he seemed.

He flushed.

'I'm not trying to blame anyone else, Bobbie. Please believe me. What seems to be done with good reason at the time, with hindsight turns out the craziest thing you've ever done.'

'It isn't I who have to forgive you, Gerry,' she suggested gently. Red changed to amber. She let off the handbrake, moved on. His children, Alan Campion, the people he'd cheated — no wonder he felt bad. What ever he did now, he couldn't change the hurt he'd caused.

He was watching her closely, trying to read the expression on her face. 'How are the children going to cope with the fact that their father's a thief!' he exclaimed miserably. 'I've let them down so badly. I've let everyone down.'

He could have thought of that before he embezzled the money. Bobbie's hand slid from the wheel and found his, giving it a brief and reassuring squeeze. 'You're doing the right thing. The children will manage. You'll be surprised how resilient they are.'

'We'll have to tell them?'

'First things first, Gerry. We'll get the police over, shall we?'

For once, she was afraid that her children would have to wait. She swung the car from the main road on to Prospect Way and pulled up in the double parking bay outside the redbrick police station. They got out of the car. Gerry's face visibly drained of colour. He dropped his cigarette to the floor and ground it under his heel.

'What shall I say?' he muttered, hand lingering on the door-handle, obviously longing to cut and run.

She couldn't blame him. He'd committed a crime and must be punished for it. He was trying to put things right. Impulsively, she came round to the passenger side and took his arm. 'You'll think of something,' she answered, trying to infuse her voice into a confidence she didn't feel.

Smiling encouragement, she headed them up the steps and inside.

★   ★   ★

The sun was already sinking over the university building as Sam, with an enthusiasm she'd almost, but not quite, forgotten, propelled her body forwards and into the massed defenders milling inside the penalty box. Her foot connected instantly and satisfyingly with the ball, propelling it over the line and into the net.

The coach blew; Loughborough women's first training session of the new term was officially ended. Sam hauled herself to her feet and scraped the mud from her knees. True, on her first day back, training had been the last thing she'd felt like, but it had done her good, releasing a tension which had been building up for too long.

Rislington with its myriad of problems seemed comfortably distanced away.

Her teammates crowded round.

'Well done Sam . . . save a few for Saturday . . . are we going for a drink?'

'You bet!'

The throng parted, revealing a familiar figure: the last person she'd expected to see. Sam's heart, already beating fast from her exertions, measured an extra beat. She stood, hands on hips, breathing hard, her smile of pleasure in the goal fading. But she'd put Steph firmly behind her! What was he doing here now?

'We need to talk . . . ' He stood, watching her anxiously, his warm brown eyes contrite, indifferent to the glances of approval that her teammates, who were tactfully dispersing, threw his way. He'd always been too handsome for his own good.

'You're telling me!' She spoke heatedly,

unsure for the moment exactly how she felt. Shocked? Angry? Anger, she decided, was uppermost.

'What are you doing here?' she demanded.

'I've come to see you . . . who else?'

She forced herself to remain calm. They couldn't talk here.

'Give me a few minutes. We'll meet in the student's bar.'

He'd come all this way, it must mean something. Her head buzzing as she ignored the banter from her teammates, she still hadn't arrived at an answer by the time she pushed open the door and stepped inside the cosy, dimly lit room in the university block that was set aside for the students' relaxation. She had showered and changed in record time, and her hair was clinging in damp curls around her face, but at least she felt more in command of the situation.

'You're surprised to see me.' His eyes were warm with an appreciation, giving her hope instead of the anger she was so desperately trying to hang on to. She'd forgotten just how good he made her feel.

He'd already got the drinks in, wine for her, orange juice for him; they sat, huddled over a table in the corner of the bar-room around which members of the women's football team were already grouped, throwing curious glances their way and giving voice to their prospects for Saturday's match. A match that Sam, up until then, had been looking forward to.

'Can you blame me?' she answered quietly, bracing herself for his explanation. 'I thought we were over, Steph! What else was I supposed to think?' What gives you the right to hurt me again? This last she kept to herself. She sipped her wine, aware that her hand was trembling. Hastily she put down her glass.

Was she being unfair? When they'd been together she'd never found the courage to tell him exactly how she felt, aware from previous experience that she had a habit of assuming too much too soon, and then scramming before things got too deep. But even given the first initial awkwardness over the language barrier, he was sensitive enough to pick up on her feelings without the need of words. She'd liked him far more than she should have. She'd thought, wrongly it seemed, that he'd liked her too.

One of the students perched himself on a spare stool at the bar and began to play the guitar, strumming out chords of a romantic melody that she could have done without.

Steph sat, his finger tracing circles round his glass, watching her sorrowfully.

'Sam . . . life's maybe . . . different where I come from. These things are arranged. Parents play a part in their children's lives even when they grow up.'

His hand shifted from his glass towards hers, lying on the table. Hastily, she pulled it out of harm's way, ignoring his pout of ill-humour. Making the rules as she went along, she'd always set the pace, she realized. Had she simply set it too fast? He sat back, visibly bracing himself.

'Our village back home is a poor one,' he went on quietly, 'but my parents are happy. They are friendly with many people, but spend more time with one couple in particular. Their daughter, Sophia and I, are of an age. We grew up together . . . ' The pause before he proceeded was too long, making Sam only too uncomfortably aware that she wasn't going to like what was coming next. She was right, she didn't. He sighed heavily. 'The understanding has always been . . . Some day, we'd be together! You understand what I'm saying? A couple, for always, and what our parents have always wanted . . . '

'Marriage you mean?' she murmured, her heart beating painfully hard.

He nodded awkwardly. 'It's just the way things are.' He took a gulp of orange juice before continuing, staring fixedly at a space some way over Sam's head. 'Things were fine when I went back to Italy. I thought Sophia was pleased to see me but later, when I returned to England, she follow me to tell me she's fallen in love! A boy from the next village. A boy she wants to marry so they can spend the rest of their lives together. Her parents aren't happy . . . my parents aren't happy! But that's what she wants . . . '

'You mean, all the while we were seeing each other, Sophia was back home, supposedly, as you thought, waiting to marry you?' Hot colour flooded Sam's face, her voice gathering a heated strength. 'You didn't think I'd need to know?'

His duplicity, so casually revealed, was stunning and too much to take in at once. He nodded uneasily, his reply left her breathless.

'Why should you? We were so good together, you and I, Sam. I knew you'd misunderstand. Me and Sophia . . . we never loved each other — '

'Why didn't you tell me?' she blurted out. Any talk of love had nothing to do with this! He'd let her go on in ignorance, knowing all the while that things could never work out the way she'd wanted. Marriage, children. Shock had cleared her mind. She hadn't realized she was quite so conventional. There were things she'd always meant to get round to but only when the time and the man were right. How ludicrous it seemed that she'd thought that man was Steph.

He'd come back because things had fallen through with Sophia; that much was clear.

'I thought I'd done something wrong,' she muttered, still too shocked to take it in.

'Sam, I had things to sort out!' He leaned forward eagerly, his face flushed. 'What's holding us back? Don't you see? Nothing's in our way now! We have a good time like we did before?'

'A good time was all it was?' She'd never thought she could feel such hurt.

Too late he realized what he'd said. 'No! Sam! Of course it was more! How can you think . . . '

She scraped back her chair and stood up, too worked up to realize that she was trembling from head to foot. She didn't believe him and couldn't bear to think now that she'd been no more than a girl to have a good time with, whilst the woman he meant all along to marry waited for him back home.

How blind she'd been! She shook her head, anger rising to the fore.

'We're finished, Steph. I don't want to see you again — ever!'

She spun on her heel and ran from the room.

Landon stood waiting in Bobbie's office, gazing through the window to the pitch below. Something he'd eaten was disagreeing with him. Absent-mindedly, he rubbed his chest. He'd felt it off and on all day, a dull squeezing pressure, all his problems seemed to be packed too tightly inside and were now waiting to burst out: the mess he'd made of his marriage, Eleanor's disappearance, his desperation to know where she'd gone. Where was she? Why, when he needed her more than ever, had she disappeared from the face of the earth?

'I thought you'd be out celebrating?' Colin Peterson, the club secretary, poked his head round the door. Landon swung round and stared at him glumly.

'I was looking for Bobbie. It's late. She must have packed up and gone home.' Bobbie more than anyone might shed light on Eleanor's whereabouts. He'd evaded the press lingering outside and called in on the off-chance, determined to winkle her out.

'She went off with Mansfield a while back,' Colin told him, coming into the room and, unknowingly, deepening the older man's gloom. 'No one seems to know where they've gone.'

'Gerry?' The older man looked nonplussed.

'I take it you've not seen the evening papers?' Colin's tone was dry. He stood rifling through the clutter scattered over Bobbie's desk. He exclaimed in triumph when at last, he unearthed the early edition of the *Evening Telegraph*. He passed it over, studying Landon's face while he read the ominous headlines splashed across the front page. The grainy black-and-white photo accompanying it was of Paris and his agent, Stevie Bentnall, sitting at a restaurant table with someone too suspiciously like Reginald Faraday, the Melchester United Chief Executive to be anyone else. Something in Landon's heart sank. Weren't things bad enough?

'Rogues star Paris Pryce-Martin in fresh FA probe . . . ' he muttered, reading aloud. Now he was alarmed by the thought that if ever he'd needed proof Bobbie had followed Eleanor's example and disappeared, this was it. If she'd had one sniff of this she'd be here now, trying to sort it out. Quickly he scanned the report. Paris, it appeared, quite undoubtedly given the photograph, had broken every rule in the FA book in an apparent effort to land himself a transfer to Premiership highfliers United. It was known as tapping up, a cardinal sin. 'The FA'll throw the book

249

at him. Melchester too, and serve them right!' He looked up angrily. The pain in his chest had moved inexplicably to his arm. He rubbed it irritably.

'Melchester know we're strapped for cash,' Colin murmured, propping his lean frame against the desk. Landon snorted, not needing his club secretary to spell it out. Everyone connected with the club knew that, given an in-coming chairman with cash-flow problems, harsh economies would have to be made. It was going to be a rocky ride from now on.

'What's Faraday's game? He knows we're not in the business of selling our star players!' Landon growled, provoked beyond reason. He'd assumed, not unnaturally, that his reckless grandson was at last beginning to settle down. The phone rang. He leaned across the desk and picked it up.

'Aunty Bobbie?' Paris's voice sounded young and anxious.

'This is your granddad!' Landon snapped, his colour deepening. He hooked his foot round the leg of Bobbie's swivel-chair and sank down. 'What the deuce have you been up to now?'

'Granddddad, you've got to believe me. I was set up! I was meeting Stevie for a business lunch. I'd no idea Reginald Faraday was going to turn up. I want to play in the Premiership with the Rogues! What's Anna going to think?' His voice rose a decibel. 'I promised her — no more trouble. I need to talk to Bobbie!'

'Who the blazes is Anna?' Landon held the phone from his ear, glaring at it scathingly. Something about the earnestness of his grandson's tone rang true. 'You'd better get yourself over here,' he cried, resuming the conversation, modifying his voice. 'And sooner rather than later. Don't talk to anyone else.' He dropped the receiver back on its rest. The media would have a field day. Breathing heavily, he retrieved his hanky from his top pocket and mopped his face.

'Can't I leave this place five minutes?' At that moment, Bobbie hurried through the door. Her gaze swept the room, some of her tension visibly relaxing at sight of Landon. It had been a toss-up whether to go home or return to work. News on the car radio had decided her. Paris and trouble went together, hand in hand. At least she, unlike Landon, knew that Eleanor was safe.

'Have you heard from your mother?' he demanded.

'Not exactly,' she replied, evasively, hating herself, even more hating that Eleanor had sworn her to such unreasonable secrecy. An impossible situation. She felt herself torn in so many ways she didn't know what to think. She seized the paper.

'Where've you been?' Landon demanded, waiting with thinly veiled impatience whilst she read the report.

'Don't ask,' she answered flatly, praying he wouldn't.

'I'll get on to the FA,' Colin retorted briskly. 'I'll do it from my office and get back to you.' Sensing that the two wanted time alone together, he threw Bobbie a reassuring smile and disappeared.

'Paris is on his way in.' Landon's eager eyes searched her face. 'Bobbie, where have you been?'

News of Gerry would at least deflect him from asking awkward questions, she decided quickly. 'You're not going to believe this, Dad . . . '

He didn't and she had to run it past him twice. 'Babs had worked it out anyway, long before Gerry turned up wanting to confess. He's on a charge, out on bail. I've taken him round to Cedars and dropped him off — '

'The deuce you have! Have you told the children? And what about Alan? This lets Alan off!'

'I've told no one,' she told him firmly. She'd told only Landon, the one person she told everything to. So how come she hadn't told him about Eleanor yet?

'Where is she, Bobbie?' He buried his face in his hands, his despair at Eleanor's disappearance overriding everything, even football. Football most of all. What a fool he'd been!

Instinct, compassion, Bobbie's innate desire for truth, took over. How could she not tell him? She sprang up from her chair and hurried round the desk. Quickly she knelt in front of him and gently pulled his hands from his face.

'Dad . . . it's OK. Mum's OK. I know where she is. I've seen her and we've talked. You need to talk to her too. Whatever you've done, it's not irretrievable . . . '

She prayed that that was so. The glad light of joy flew to his face.

'But where . . . why didn't you say? Tell me, for God's sake, Bobbie! I must go to her.'

He was already pulling away.

'She's at Susie's.' She spoke in a rush, hoping, stupidly, that it might lessen the bad news. He froze instantly, staring in blank incomprehension. 'Where else should she go?' Bobbie cried, beginning to gabble. 'Susie's her best friend! Don't make something of this when there's nothing in it — '

'She's gone to Eddie's!' he cried, having

none of it. The ultimate treachery. Eddie the man who would trample on his every dream! A sigh of pain escaped him. If anything told Landon exactly how Eleanor felt about the state of their marriage, this one action told him above all.

His hand flew to his chest to massage the pain which flowed with a terrible clamping certainty, spreading outwards into his jaw and neck. He couldn't think. He couldn't breathe. 'Eleanor, I need you . . . ' His lips framed the words though no sound came. Too late he understood, his shocked gaze locking on to Bobbie's as his world closed in, lost colour, went black. Unaware of her sharp cry of terror he pitched forward and into her arms.

9

'Mum!' She'd never been so glad to see anyone in her life. Bobbie rushed across the visitor's room and into Eleanor's arms. Some of the panic threatening to overwhelm her since Landon had been admitted here, to Rislington's bright new coronary care unit, began to subside. Her mother was here. Everything would be all right. Eleanor always made everything all right.

'You've made it,' she breathed, heartfelt, her gaze flickering unsteadily towards Babs, who'd arrived with her. No need of the sign by the door urging quiet. Her voice was unsteady, highlighting the strain she'd been under. Tough, resourceful Bobbie Vernon, who could stand up to the best of them in the boardroom, was falling to pieces, would have done so already if it hadn't been for Paris arriving at the same time as the medics she'd so frantically called. Paris, who'd been so calm, so not like the Paris she thought she'd known. He'd held her hand in the ambulance, whispering encouragement. 'He'll be all right, Auntie Bobbie. This is Granddad remember. Tough as old boots!'

She turned, flashing him a grateful look.

'The doctors are with him now. No one's said anything yet, I don't know what to think . . . '

'Hush, love, he'll be all right!' Eleanor murmured, unsure why she felt so certain. Landon's voice, almost dreamlike, had been with her all the way over here. Earlier, she'd been consumed by an overpowering sensation that her husband had need of her. Had she been dreaming? She didn't believe in premonitions. Eleanor caressed her daughter's cheek.

'It's more than he deserves,' Babs muttered crossly, hugging her son, still catching her breath from her mad dash across Rislington to the Lamoure's. The sisters had quickly decided between them on the phone, that news of Landon's collapse would be better imparted to Eleanor face to face. Babs hadn't even known Eleanor was at Susie's until Bobbie had filled her in. 'You might have told me where Mum was!' she had blurted out, a thing she'd already grumbled to Eleanor about in the car. Now Babs felt ashamed of herself for grumbling, after all her father's collapse was far more important.

'Darling, do keep your voice down,' Eleanor remonstrated. People, others' relatives, were beginning to look. The Vernons closed ranks, huddled together, drawing strength from each other. Landon would be all right, they'd make him all right!

'Sorry,' Babs whispered, shamefaced. 'I'm just worried.' She was upset, they were all upset. Her lips trembled, her eyes filled with unwanted tears.

'I should have told you. I'm sorry.' Bobbie let go of Eleanor and hugged Babs instead.

Paris grinned. 'There's a first, Gran!'

Eleanor's gaze was elsewhere, settled on the white-coated figure emerging through the swing doors leading into the unit. It was a fresh-faced young woman, no older than Sam! She, Eleanor, was getting old. She moved swiftly, planting her body firmly in the girl's path. The white-coated young woman saw a faded, yet still attractive older lady, determined on her own way. Landon was still Eleanor's husband, despite all he'd done.

'We're waiting for news of Landon Vernon,' Eleanor began, hurriedly. 'He's been brought in with a suspected heart attack. I'm Eleanor, his wife . . .'

'Dr Adams,' Eleanor's hand was grasped in a surprisingly firm handshake, candid blue eyes were summing her up and evidently liking what they found. The young woman's tone was friendly. 'We've run a few tests already, Mrs Vernon. Fortunately the attack's a mild one. More a warning, if you like — '

'Is there a chance he'll suffer another? Is he awake? Can we see him?' The family, with a clamour of eager voices, in collective need of reassurance, gathered round. Two young nurses emerged from the direction of the wards and headed towards the way out. They exclaimed excitedly over Paris. One grabbed the other's arm. A faint smile played across the doctor's face.

'I'm sorry, that's all I can tell you. We're keeping a careful eye on him and yes, you can see him. Only two at a time, I'm afraid. Like all our coronary care patients, he needs peace and quiet.' A hand flapped apologetically towards the door and the notice on visitor quota that was prominently displayed across the glass. 'Try and not worry. We're doing our best . . . '

She was gone, hurrying up the corridor. Babs fumed after her.

'Trust a doctor. They tell you precisely nothing . . . '

'I'm sure they try their best, love.' Things could have been so much worse; Eleanor's shoulders slumped in relief.

'You and Babs go, Mum . . . '

Bobbie's face was full of emotion too much mirroring Eleanor's own. Why should Bobbie feel guilty? Eleanor frowned; the vestiges of her marriage were clinging to her, refusing to let go.

'What if he doesn't want to see me?' she asked quietly. Given the circumstances of their last meeting, why would he want to see her? She was uncertain, torn two ways at once. 'It's all my fault!' she moaned softly. 'I've driven your father to this — '

'Nonsense, Mum!' Babs spoke firmly.

Bobbie shook her head. 'I told him you were at Susie's,' she cried, agitated. Eleanor would have every right to be furious, never speak to her again. 'It's my fault! You told me not to tell him . . . '

'He was bound to find out some time,' Eleanor murmured, understanding at last. Poor Bobbie! But it really wasn't her fault.

Babs frowned, exasperated but at the same time oddly touched by Bobbie's offer. 'Are you sure . . . Dad, I mean?' she murmured tentatively.

'Give him my love.' Bobbie pushed her forward.

Without further argument Babs took Eleanor's arm. The doors swished behind them, cutting them off in an alien world peopled by gowned figures going efficiently about their tasks. A capable-looking woman sitting at a desk and wearing a cap denoting high rank, looked up from her papers and frowned.

'Landon Vernon . . . he was brought in earlier . . . ' Babs murmured, wishing herself somewhere else. Her voice trembled. She couldn't bear it if he was attached to tubes, helpless like a child. He'd hate it!

The woman's eyes widened in sympathy.

'Third door on the left. I'm afraid he's very tired. You mustn't stay long. Five minutes maximum.'

'Best foot forward,' Eleanor whispered, sensing Babs's unease and, as usual, taking charge. Once that had been Landon's favourite saying, always on a cheerful note, usually when one or the other of the girls had met with difficulties. A change of schools, dreaded exams, even boyfriends who never quite came up to the mark. How long ago it seemed now.

They'd reached the door to his ward. Through the glass partition, allowing a view into the room, they could see his figure lying motionless. So not like Landon, who was always so full of life. Too many tubes, drips, hospital paraphernalia. Eleanor caught her breath. His eyes were closed, his breathing reassuringly deep and even. She pushed open the door and stepped inside. The monitor bleeped, making them both jump.

'Why didn't he listen?' Babs moaned, squeezing Eleanor's arm for comfort. Steeling herself, willing him to wake up, she stared down at her father's face.

Eleanor's shoulders rose helplessly. If only this hadn't happened now, when they were so at loggerheads! One hand lay on the top of the covers. She picked it up, held it gently between her own.

'Why didn't you listen?' she whispered softly, the tears she'd held in too long, at last, filling her eyes. Because he always liked his own way? Wasn't that one of the reasons why she loved him? She laid his hand against her cheek, trying to impart through it her own resources of strength.

At that moment, startlingly, his eyes snapped open. Even more startlingly it was Landon's voice, irrepressible as ever. 'Eleanor . . . darling. Where are my things? Let's get out of here and go home.'

★   ★   ★

'Babs's car's arrived!' She'd seen it through the bedroom window. Eleanor hurried downstairs, her arms full of the flowers she'd bought in town, in anticipation of Landon's homecoming. It was mid-morning, several days later, days in which the various members of the family had, in their different ways, done their best to keep the invalid in hospital

261

until he was well enough to be discharged. They'd had their work cut out. Sam had eventually returned to University, and was expected home again today. Todd constantly popped in and out; Bobby was due any minute, when she could spare time from work. The family was rallying round, giving her strength just when she needed it most.

She'd taken the flowers upstairs; sure that Landon would be exhausted and ready to take to his bed. She might have known. She put the vase on the table in the conservatory, where he was settled with the papers, flashing him a small, quick smile. Warm sunshine spilled on to his face suffusing it with colour.

'Aren't these beautiful?' she cried gaily, giving the arrangement a quick tweak. Daffodils, narcissus, tulips, tall elegant iris a gorgeous shade of blue. Spring flowers, their presence giving her hope things would soon be back to normal.

She could not remember their ever having been through such a time as this. The thought brought with it a too familiar pain.

'Beautiful,' Landon murmured, not looking at the flowers. He reached across and seized her hand. Gently, hating to hurt him, she pulled herself free, exposing her careful show of happiness for what it was.

'I do appreciate your being here, Eleanor,'

he declared, huffily. 'I am aware it's more than I deserve. I only wish ... ' His expression softened, tugging at her heartstrings in a way of which he was perfectly aware. 'What I did was unforgivable, darling. I'd do anything, if only I could make amends!'

'Hush, don't talk about it now,' she soothed, contrite. She was here. Where else should she be when he'd been so ill?

He shook his head. 'I can't bear it that you've come back only because I'm ill,' he continued doggedly, determined to have this out. 'I don't want your pity, Eleanor!' He forced the word out. He'd been sitting here, pretending to read, working himself up to this. What else should he do? Accept that she'd come back and it didn't matter how she felt?

'But it's not pity I feel!' she cried. With one swift movement, unmindful of her earlier hesitation, she knelt and took his hands. She felt angry, yes, and she'd every right to be. His illness hadn't altered that. But sorry for him? 'Landon, I love you,' she murmured quietly. Whatever he'd done. Whatever he chose to do in the future. It was the simple truth. It had taken his illness to remind her.

'There you both are,' Babs's voice, filled with warmth at the sight greeting her, broke the spell. 'Good to see you love,' her mother murmured. She sprang up, rubbing her eyes, fooling no one, least of all Landon, whose own eyes were suspiciously bright.

'I'll make fresh coffee!' she murmured. 'Stay and talk to your father. I won't be long.'

Babs sat down gratefully; relieved to take the weight off her feet, delighted to see her parents getting on so well. She hadn't been sure what to expect. 'It's good to have you back, Dad,' she proffered, prepared now to forgive him even the business of Paris and the share money. Seizing the opportunity, assuming — and rightly, that she'd be too worried about his granddad to care, Paris had eventually told her. The whole unsettling business, she'd quickly decided, was best forgotten. Landon's gaze was already wandering towards the kitchen, where he could hear Eleanor filling the kettle, finding cups.

'You don't realize . . . ' he muttered, shaking his head.

'Realize what? You are all right, Dad?' Babs demanded, alarmed. Something was on his mind. Heaven forbid the doctors had told him more than he was letting on? 'I know I'm not Bobbie, but if there's something troubling you . . . '

How like Eleanor she looked. A part of himself, his daughter as much as Bobbie was, he considered, wondering what had put the thought into his mind. Her words broke through their more habitual reserve. 'Blasted quacks have told me no work for three months,' he volunteered, needing to share this with someone, sensing that the sentiment would find scant sympathy with Eleanor. 'What ever shall I do?'

So that was all! Babs stifled an unforgivable laugh. 'There is life after football, Dad,' she suggested gently. 'Look around, you'll be surprised.'

'Why did you say that, you know you're not Bobbie?' he demanded testily, the sentiment, expressed so earnestly, belatedly sinking in.

Babs shifted uncomfortably. 'I only meant . . . well . . . you and Bobbie . . . you've always been close, that's all. She's always the one you've told your troubles too. I'm not saying I blame you, Dad!'

Landon's face fell. Was that what she was saying? Did she think he didn't care? Why hadn't he picked up on it? She stood, looking awkward, so much the child he remembered; it made him wince. 'You don't think we're close?' He frowned.

'Not as close as I'd like,' she declared doggedly, pink-cheeked, aware that she shouldn't be talking to him about this now when he'd been so ill.

But he'd never meant . . . Landon exhaled heavily, all at once understanding. He folded his paper, laid it carefully on his lap. What a ham-fisted fool he was! Unexpectedly, startling them both, he fumbled for her hand, holding it tight, remembering then, too late, how once he'd held it so naturally. 'I can change, Babs,' he urged gently, with perfect sincerity. They could both change. Babs nodded, her face clearing.

'There we are!' Eleanor beamed, bringing in coffee, smiling to see things arranged so satisfactorily. Carefully she eased the tray on to the table, sat down and began to pour.

★ ★ ★

Bobbie dropped the phone back on to its cradle and buried her head in her hands. She'd come in so determined to get things done, clearing the decks to spend some time with her dad! Despite Ray Lovett's taking temporary control in the boardroom, since Landon's illness, events at the club were spiralling viciously out of control.

'Problems?' Colin Peterson poked his head round the door.

'Reg Perry, from the FA,' she growled, raising her head and glaring at the phone. The ultimate indignity in a morning of similar such occurrences. 'Paris's inquiry is set for next week.'

'Reg isn't so bad. He'll at least get a fair hearing.'

'After all that the papers have made of it?' Bobbie shook her head, not so sure, her gaze wandering to the morning's tabloids, spread across her desk. 'The *Planet* says Melchester are offering wages of a hundred k a week. It must be getting to him, Colin. He was a shadow of himself at the weekend.' No doubt worry over Landon had played its part in Paris's poor showing in the Rogues most recent match, but she was wondering now if something else was bothering him too.

'Precisely what you'd expect from the *Planet*,' Colin was quick to point out.

She found a smile, spreading her hands, encompassing the mess that was littered all over her desk. She wasn't sure what she expected any more. 'Have you seen Ronnie? We set up a meeting for an hour ago.' Supposedly to discuss the club's ignominious FA Cup defeat to Premiership glamour boys East Ham. Her father being still in the infirmary at the time, Bobbie had found herself uncaring, one way or another. But now he was back home and out of danger. Ronnie's disappearance was annoying; that the morning training session had had to be taken by the club's more senior players was an even greater cause for concern. She frowned thoughtfully. It was time to make Ronnie Hubberfield face reality.

'He's here now!' Colin muttered, glancing down the corridor. He turned back quickly and rolled his eyes. Colin's opinion of Ronnie was pretty much the same as her own. 'Good luck,' he mouthed silently as the burly figure of the Rogues manager, breathing heavily, brushed past him and into the office.

'I haven't much time,' Ronnie growled, by way of greeting. He stood and drummed his fingers impatiently on the edge of her desk. Colin disappeared. Her manager's eyes slid quickly from hers but not before she'd gathered that he'd been drinking. She'd always known he liked a whisky with his lunch, or wine with his opposite number after the end of a match but she was horribly afraid that recently it had become much more.

Bobbie's spirits, already lowered by her manager's belated appearance, sank further. She was in no mood for conciliation. She stood up and came round the desk.

'We need to discuss the Cup defeat,' she began coolly.

'I thought you'd have summat to say about that!' he snapped defensively.

'It's fortunate we have been knocked out!

You do realize how important this makes Saturday's game?' This was a home fixture against high flying Midwich, that they needed to win to stay in touching distance of the play-offs.

'The fans will understand we're below par,' he answered complacently. 'The lads have given their all in the Cup — '

'And decimated the squad in the process!' she reminded him angrily. 'The fans won't thank you for an early end to the season.'

'The fans aren't interested in the Premiership,' Ronnie snapped, red-faced, obviously having lost his composure. 'The Championship at least gives us chance of winning.'

Saturday's result had hit him harder than she'd thought. How defeatist he'd become.

'You're scared!' The thought came to her of a sudden, explaining so much! His bluster, his air of overconfidence, his refusal to listen to anyone else's point of view. Why hadn't she seen it for what it was, a façade hiding his incompetence? He knew he'd lost it and now she knew it too. The Premiership would find him out. He had no intention of letting the team anywhere near it.

The knowledge decided her, jolting her into the uncomfortable awareness of things to be faced. Drastic action had to be taken, whether Landon was around to back her or not. She spoke with genuine sorrow, hating what she was about to do, knowing there was no alternative. Unpalatable decisions came with the territory. She took a deep breath, forcing her voice to sound calm. 'This can't go on any longer. I'm sorry, Ronnie. The club appreciates everything you've achieved here but I'm afraid it's time we parted company. We'll pay up your contract. You'll not lose out financially.'

'You're sacking me? Why you little . . . ' Ronnie's hands balled into fists. He stepped closer, pulled up short, his mouth working strangely.

'Do you want me to call security?' Her legs were trembling. She'd no idea how she was managing to appear so calm. She stared him out, determined he wouldn't see how alarmed she'd become. 'I *will* call security, Ronnie!' she repeated firmly, sickeningly aware of her vulnerability. She braced herself, almost expecting a blow. Instead and to her heartfelt relief, he spun on his heel and stormed away. At the door he turned, his face unrecognizable, a last and bitter invective flowing from his lips. 'Everyone knows you only got the job because you're a daddy's girl! You're a laughing-stock! By God, you're going to regret this. The whole country's going to know you've just sacked the club's longest serving stalwart!'

He crumpled, leaving him what he was, diminished, an old man long out of his depth. He hurled away and slammed the door viciously behind him. His footsteps resounded as he made his way along the corridor.

Bobbie stood for some moments, staring at the door, transfixed, unable to believe what she'd just done, an undeniable pity welling up in her heart. But a football club couldn't be run on pity; of course she'd had to do it! He'd left her with no other option. The wonder was she hadn't done it long before now.

The realization that her legs were still trembling, at least galvanized her into action. Ronnie was on the loose, and hurting so badly that she had to act — and fast. She ran out into the corridor, turning sharply right and down the stairs towards the tunnel leading on to the pitch, where the players were going through the last of the morning's training session. This was the leisurely wind-down with which procedures were always terminated. A small knot of senior players stood near by, discussing tactics for Saturday's match, Davie amongst them.

'Mr Mackenzie I'd like a word.'

Davie Mackenzie trapped a stray ball neatly under his foot and stood, hands on hips, looking at her in astonishment. They both knew the score. Public contact was kept strictly to a minimum.

'Now?' He sounded offended.

'If you wouldn't mind.' She fixed a smile on her face, turned on her heel and stalked away, all too aware that he was following quickly, aware too, of the ribald comments of his teammates. 'She's taken a fancy to you, lad . . . keep your shorts on. Davie, put a good word in for me!'

'What's this about?' he hissed, catching her up easily.

'My office, Davie . . . please.'

He glanced at her face, then walked with her quietly, not speaking again until they were upstairs and the door closed safely behind them.

'What's wrong?' he demanded.

Desire, determination, uneasy bedfellows, were flooding through her in equal measure. Which was uppermost? How could she feel both things at once? She stepped back, out of harm's way, determined that this, at least, must remain strictly professional. 'I've sacked Ronnie,' she admitted quietly. Davie's face dropped, the magnitude of what she'd done too obviously shocking him. He didn't seem to realize that it had shocked her too.

'But where does that leave the team?' he

cried heatedly. 'And when the play-off places are still up for grabs! We'll never get anyone worthwhile in at this late stage of the season.'

'You're wrong, Davie!' She folded her arms, at long and wonderful last beginning to enjoy herself. Ronnie's departure, she realized now, was a release that left a resolution bursting cometlike into her firmament at the same time. She'd always known Davie Mackenzie was a man going places, a rising star. 'I want you to take over, Davie,' she cried, experiencing a great swell of relief now that it was out in the open. 'Player manager until the end of the season. I'll get on to the legal people; have the contract drawn up . . . '

His expression was one of bewilderment. 'Oh no!' he cried, throwing up his hands, backing away. 'I've no experience. The fans will never wear it.'

'The fans will get used to it!' she persisted, determined. 'They'll forget, once we start winning matches. The rest of the players respect you. What's the problem?' Why did it sound so easy when she said it quickly? 'New and exciting times, Davie! You have until the end of the season to get us into the Premiership. Prove you can do it! Or, are you too scared?' Of course he was and so was she. She laughed shakily.

'You really mean it?' he groaned, bemused.

She held out her hand, aware that he was still weighing up the pros and cons. That was Davie. A man who'd never commit himself until he was sure. She could see he wanted it, she recognized instantly the excitement springing into his eyes. She knew it because she'd felt it once too. His hand fastened clamplike on hers. A grip of iron. There was steel in Davie Mackenzie. She'd known it all along.

'Deal!' He grinned.

At once the door burst open, revealing an agitated Colin Peterson. 'Bobbie! Please tell me you've not sacked Ronnie?'

Things were moving, the Rogue's former manager was apparently already letting rip.

'You'd better believe it, Colin!' She laughed, reckless with relief. 'You're looking at our new manager. Davie's about to take us into the Premiership. You'd better believe that, too.'

If only she'd had a camera. Joy surged through her, overwhelming all else. Bobbie Vernon became what she was, a woman working to her full professional capacity. The Chief Executive of Rislington Rovers Football Club. She'd never looked more like Landon in her life.

'We need to get our story out before Ronnie does,' she murmured, galvanized into action again. Already she was reaching for the phone. 'Get a press and TV call set up for one o'clock, Colin. I'll speak to Ronnie's agent and the *Telegraph*. You deal with the tabloids. Here's the release.' A slight bending of the truth, but this was business! She meant her father to be proud. She took a deep breath, her voice, steady, determined, her father's voice. 'Ronnie Hubberfield has left Rislington Rovers with immediate effect and by mutual agreement . . . '

★ ★ ★

She'd been mad to come. Dismayed, Babs stared through the car windscreen. She'd turned off through a tumbledown housing estate and on to a patch of scrubby ground over which a wild-looking bunch of boys were playing football, albeit enthusiastically. That was the last thing she'd expected to find when she'd followed Taylor in here, hanging back until he'd parked and got out of his car. The roads were full of home-time traffic; twice she'd lost him, then found him, then trailed him here, to the back of beyond, it seemed to Babs, who was still recovering from the shock.

Returning to Cedars from her parents to the sight of her husband's car turning out of the car park when he'd promised faithfully he'd spend the day in the office, catching up on accounts, had flattened her euphoria, as if it had never been. She'd followed on impulse, determined this time to face him with the truth.

Tessa Cunningham had the afternoon off too. Wearily, still afraid of what she might find, Babs slid out of the car. How often of late had Taylor not been where he was supposed to be, where he'd faithfully promised he would be, filling her head with untruths?

A thick cloud of smoke bellied out of a crumbling chimney, reaching high over rooftops and obscuring a sun that was, in all probability, relieved to remove itself from the sight. The air reverberated with the sound of young lads letting off steam. Why exactly was Taylor here, talking to a track-suited figure looking too much like Russ Packard, his old teammate? Had he been telling the truth when he'd insisted he'd been seeing so much of Russ lately?

Yells of triumph jolted her out of her reverie. One of the teams had scored. Taylor clapped his hands in encouragement, leaving Babs even more confused. He turned and saw her, startled astonishment flooding his face. Unsure how she was to explain her presence, she felt her heart begin to thud. She'd just happened to be passing and happened to notice the car? He'd see through that at once. Grim-faced, he was marching towards her and if ever she'd wished the proverbial ground would open and swallow her, the time was now.

She shivered, trying a smile.

'What are you doing here?'

Startled at his angry tone, words deserted her; her gaze wandered beyond him to a pile of training bibs, and a tired-looking starling, pecking the ground in search of food. She'd followed him because she no longer trusted him. She couldn't believe she'd done it now. This was worse than anything. The bird flew away, flapping its wings against an ugly sky.

'You followed me!' he growled, his voice ominously quiet, his injured innocence hitting out at her. It was no more than she deserved.

'Oh Taylor, I'm sorry. I truly am!' The words tumbled out in a rush, startling them both. To her horror, hot tears spurted under her eyelashes, rushing down her face unchecked and filling her mouth. Everything was crowding in on her, her dad, Taylor, her rivalry with Bobbie, Paris even. The feeling that nothing she ever did was right. What kind of a hopeless case was she? How could she have been such a fool!

Tears dripped from the end of her nose. Helplessly she fumbled in her pocket for a hanky. Exasperated, Taylor found his and waited impatiently whilst she mopped up before seizing her arm and marching her, his expression tight-lipped, back to his car. 'Get in!' he snarled, his voice not one whit mollified. He slid into the driving seat beside her and slammed the door.

'This is a boys' club — Russ's baby!' he cried, twisting towards her, his expression suggesting that he was hanging on to his temper, but only just. 'He was on the dole, at a loose end. He wondered if I'd like to help out.'

'But why didn't you tell me?' she demanded, not understanding. It explained so much, so many of his recent absences. She couldn't believe they'd grown so far apart that he couldn't have told her something as simple as this.

'If we can help only one or two of these lads, it'll make it worthwhile.' His eyes filled with an enthusiasm that she only longed, forlornly, he'd directed to her.

'Taylor, why didn't you tell me!' she repeated, exasperated, not getting anywhere on her own. Unexpectedly, unnerving her, he smiled.

'Ruin my image? I'm not supposed to give a toss about anything, remember?'

'No one thinks that!' she protested, too hotly, averting her gaze, afraid he'd read the truth. He carried on as if she'd never spoken.

'This is something I can do,' he went on, giving voice to something to which he'd obviously given much thought. 'It helps make up for everything else I've messed up in my life.'

Did he mean his career or, worse, his marriage? She couldn't bring herself to ask. 'But I thought you were seeing Tess!' she wailed, the suspicion too much to keep to herself.

'Babs, she's young enough to be my daughter,' he snapped, his temper returning. He sucked in his breath, visibly making an effort. His words, when they came, were considered and spoken with surprising sincerity. Her heart leapt. 'I'm sorry I haven't been all you want, Babs. I've left too much to you. Cedars, Paris. I've hardly been fair . . . '

Amazingly he'd taken her hand and was holding it quietly in his own. 'I was angry. I know it was wrong to take it out on you just because you were making such a success of Cedars — '

'But Taylor, I needed you!'

'It didn't feel like it.' He sounded resigned. 'Admit it, Babs. This hang-up you have with your family. You wanted to do it on your own.

Prove something, I expect?'

'I needed to prove to myself I could do it,' she admitted. And thereby and inadvertently pushing her husband out? An unforeseen consequence.

'I needed to prove things too.' He smiled, his free hand flapping, indicating his young charges. 'I can do some good too! It's given me back my self-respect.'

She'd got it so wrong! She watched him humbly, wishing she could put back the clock and somehow make things right. Was it too late? This was her marriage! Whatever mistakes they'd made, it was surely never too late to try.

'We need to talk,' she began falteringly, thinking for once, instead of letting her emotions lead the way. Wondrously, the pressure on her hand increased. His fingers laced into hers.

'Too right!' he agreed, heavily. There was no mistaking the irony. She smiled faintly.

'We've been feeding off each other . . .'

'And in all the wrong ways?'

'But that's it exactly, Taylor!'

Her face was shining with excitement. Why hadn't they talked like this before? Why hadn't each thought more of the other? They'd loved each other once, madly, never wanting to be apart.

He kissed her gently. Her heart thumping with joy, still unable to believe it was happening, she leaned forward and into his arms.

★ ★ ★

'So all the while you were supposedly arranging the best deal for the football club, you were setting up a false account and creaming off the profits into an off-shore account?'

Sam sounded what she was, scandalized. Her granddad's illness, finding out about Steph, all the trouble at the football club, none of it was as bad as this. Her own father! Unable to meet her gaze, Gerry Mansfield hung his head. Todd had yet to say a word; he was listening in with a resigned look that suggested he wasn't even surprised. Bobbie wished he'd say something. She reached across the table and squeezed his hand, determined that having already let him down so badly, this time she'd be around to give him every support.

They'd reached coffee. She'd begun to think Gerry was going to chicken out; she'd have to tell them herself. It had been a huge relief when at last he'd put down his cup and stutteringly begun to explain. She stood up, stacked pots, brooding on how, once news of Ronnie's dismissal had broken, the day had descended into chaos. The press didn't know the half and she could imagine the furore if they had. The evening news on the portable TV in the kitchen, where they'd eaten, had shown film of her emerging from the ground, surrounded by a phalanx of reporters and fans alike, seemingly cool and composed when in reality she'd been anything but. Following hot on the heels of a sympathetic interview with a clearly bewildered Ronnie Hubberfield, it had hardly shown her up in a good light. The coverage in the morning's press would be vital if she was to get away with her job as chief executive still intact.

She'd dealt with it, her every ounce of professionalism stretched to breaking point. She'd even squeezed in a visit to Landon to give him a carefully abridged account of the day's events. She'd only just got home in time to cook them all supper. Gerry had picked Todd up on the way over, home seeming the most obvious place to tell their children the truth which, given the certainty that the papers would shortly have a name to put to the shadowy figure charged over embezzlement of club affairs, couldn't decently be left any longer. It would have been unforgivable if they'd found out any way other than from their parents.

'Will you get a prison sentence?' Sam demanded, determined to meet things head on. Todd's hands clenched tight.

'We're hoping not,' Bobbie intervened quickly. She dumped the plates on to the draining board and returning to her chair. 'Your dad's made a full confession. He's repaid every penny, plus interest. It's a first offence. We're hoping a hefty fine, community service. We've employed a good lawyer.'

'Someone to get you off?' Sam asked coldly.

'Not exactly that, darling,' Gerry muttered wretchedly. Whatever grilling he received in the courtroom, it surely couldn't be worse than this. Some of Bobbie's sympathies shifted to include her ex-husband too. He looked so crushed, so much as though he wished himself somewhere else and who could blame him? He'd let his children down and worse, for once he was being made to face the fact.

'Your father accepts the blame!' she cried, springing to his defence.

'And what about Alan?' Todd demanded, speaking up at last.

'Alan's why I came back!' Gerry's head shot up, unable to bear the thought that his children should think quite so badly of him.

'Alan knows he's in the clear,' Bobbie stated firmly, relieved that she could at least reassure them of this. When, at last, she'd prised herself away from Landon and gone to see her old friend, it was only to discover that whilst not telling him the name of the real culprit, the police had already told him he was in the clear. The joy on his face had been only too evident. He'd been surprisingly unsurprised upon the discovery of the real culprit, agreeing readily to keep the knowledge quiet until her children were told. 'Your father really didn't know,' Bobbie murmured, hanging on to the fact, the one thing decently to be said for him.

'What a mess,' Gerry groaned, shooting her a grateful look before pushing back his chair and wandering over to the fire-place, where he stood, shoulders slumped, resting his hand on the mantelpiece. Sam stared at him thoughtfully. Bobbie's heart skipped a beat. Long seconds passed.

At last Sam stood up and crossed the room.

'Come here,' she whispered, at last throwing her arms around him. He was her father; whatever he'd done, she still loved him. Todd joined them, standing awkwardly, his hand resting on his father's arm. Typical

Todd, needing prompting, needing Sam to take the lead. How proud Bobbie was of them! Tears pricked the backs of her eyes; Gerry's too, much as he tried to hide them. His children, and more than he ever deserved.

★ ★ ★

Had she really meant to sack Ronnie? Shouldn't she have advertised, interviewed, put anyone other than Davie in his place? Bobbie opened her eyes, blinking against the sunshine streaming through a chink in the curtains and on to her face. She was late. The night's rain had stopped, the world beyond her window was full of light and warmth and a promise that made every nerve in her body alive. Sam was already up, throwing things together for her return to Loughborough and the week ahead. Calling a cheery good morning, curiously light-hearted considering how little sleep she'd had, Bobbie threw back the quilt and jumped out of bed. Quickly, she rammed her arms into the sleeves of her dressing-gown and ran downstairs to gather the morning's papers from the hall floor before heading kitchenwards. She flicked the switch on the kettle and scanned the contents of the back page. 'Rogues sack Championship's longest-serving manager,' informed the headlines over a picture of a tired-looking Ronnie, the article beneath giving a strongly worded summary in his favour. The press were doing their best to show her precious football club in the worst possible light. No more than she expected!

The kettle boiled, switched off. She turned the paper over, reaching for tea bags, her hand abruptly freezing in mid-air. Disbelief and horror fought for ascendancy. A picture of herself and Davie at the table of a restaurant they often visited stared back at her. A discreet upmarket watering hole promising a chance for the two of them to spend time together without fear of discovery, so she'd thought. But they'd been so engrossed in each other they hadn't even realized that the shot had been taken!

'Bobbie Vernon, the Rogues chief executive enjoys an intimate moment with newly appointed manager Davie Mackenzie,' informed the caption beneath, its implication obvious. She and Davie were an item, hot gossip, front-page news and now the world knew it too.

Her happiness evaporated instantly. Their secret was out and in a way designed to show it in its very worse light.

10

The sun was shining. May had all the makings of a glorious month. Bobbie Vernon eased the car into the space marked Chief Executive and jumped out, throwing her jacket on to the back seat before walking smartly towards the ground. Confidence rang in her every step. She'd gained so much of late. Wonderfully, her dad was on the mend, the Rogues were in the play-off finals whilst, most stunningly of all, she and Davie had surmounted their difficulties and were together at last.

A group of supporters hanging around the main entrance sprang into instant life. 'Ready for the final, Miss Vernon . . . Wembley here we come . . . just wait until we're in the Premiership!' 'Not long now!' she agreed, laughing, shouldering her way through, enjoying the good-natured banter, so different from the abuse, her more general lot, when first she'd sacked Ronnie Hubberfield. How she and Davie survived after she'd made him manager, given news of their liaison so quickly hitting the papers, was anyone's guess. They'd brazened it out, adopted a devil-may-care attitude. 'Publish and be damned,' Davie had said, and he'd been proved right. It seemed so long ago now, though in reality only a few short weeks. The club's unexpected surge up the Championship had silenced fans and critics alike.

'There you are, miss!' A beaming Fred Vinter threw the door wide. He hustled her through and planted his burly frame in the way of the more enthusiastic of the supporters.

'Wonderful morning, Fred!' she murmured, walking smartly across the hall, past the glass-fronted trophy cabinet and the bust of Great Uncle Albert on its marble plinth, just as the last of the players, studs clattering, left the changing rooms and made their way pitchwards to the morning's training session.

She paused, one hand rested lightly on the banister as a track-suited Davie Mackenzie emerged. He was the kind of young manager who liked nothing more than to get stuck in with the rest of the lads. Whatever his regime, it was proving wildly successful. His position was unassailable. He saw Bobbie and his face lit up. There was no one around, why should he hide his feelings? What was the point when everyone knew and cared little? The Rogues were on their way to Wembley! A soft swell of feeling which she recognized instantly for the happiness it was, bubbled up inside.

'I was just thinking about you.'

'Only just?' she teased.

'All the time!' he quickly corrected, taking her arm. He hustled her back towards the deserted changing rooms and took her into his arms.

'Davie, someone will come!' she cried, failing to sound shocked, then not trying hard enough to extricate herself for long and delicious seconds, leaving her only wanting more. Reluctantly she pulled away.

'Let them come! The papers have already done their worst and much good it's done them,' Davie growled, then laughed too, yet accepting the sense of her words and making no further move.

'It mattered when we lost your first match,' she reminded him, remembering, too, all the accusations, mostly unfair but, at the time, enough to drive her to consider giving up. She was too much her father's daughter; the thought, a fleeting one had quickly been dismissed. She knew why she'd sacked Ronnie and taken Davie on. Taking the Rogues into the Premiership was why! Being in love was nothing to do with it, despite all the rubbish in the papers.

She stood back, conscious of a nagging uncertainty, the one cloud in her sky of a deep and stunning blue. She'd never told this man exactly how much she loved him, nor had he told her. Did he really love her? Or was he merely allowing Bobbie's enthusiasm to propel him to places where he didn't want to go? They'd been so wrapped up in the Rogues lately that there'd been no time for anything else and certainly not talk of love.

'Davie I — '

'Bobbie I — '

They spoke simultaneously, stopping in confusion as the thickset figure of Mike Strange, the goal-keeping coach, appeared in the doorway. 'Ready, Davie? The lads are waiting.' Davie Mackenzie's shoulders lifted; what he'd been about to say, what he'd been steeling himself to say since he'd woken this morning, was reluctantly consigned to a back seat. Again! Would he never get round to telling Bobbie Vernon exactly how much he loved her? Would he ever have agreed to do this job if he'd had the slightest notion it would so consume him, and, he'd have no time for something as important as this? Yes, yes and yes and Bobbie, more than anyone, would understand.

He threw her a resigned look, one that, he hoped contained at least some of his feelings, before following Mike down the tunnel and on to the pitch where the players were already well into the throes of their pre-training warm-up.

One figure stood apart, foot resting listlessly on a ball, hands thrust deep into the pockets of his track-suit, his gaze fixed on the goal-mouth ahead. Suddenly Paris burst into life, flicking the ball with his foot into the air and slamming it into the back of the net. If only he could do the same on the pitch! Davie frowned. No need to blame Paris for the team's presence in the play-off final. His star-player's form had been way off beam lately. This morning the sight proved too much.

'Pryce-Martin! Get yourself over here!' he bawled, clearly irate.

Amused glances followed Paris's reluctant slouch across the pitch. His manager hung on to his temper but only just. It was time this young man was made to face the facts. 'Glad you've deigned to join us for once! Like to share the problem?' he snapped, taking no trouble to lower his voice, keen that everyone else should hear this too.

Paris's booted foot traced a circle in the turf, his shoulders lifting into a shrug, which only infuriated Davie the more.

'Dunno what you mean.'

'Missing training. No effort when you do get here. You'll know perfectly well, come

291

Monday and the Final, when you're left warming the bench!' His unexpected display of temper caused heads to turn. Paris's hands shot out of his pockets. He stepped back, visibly shocked.

'You're dropping me?'

'Give me one good reason why I shouldn't!' Davie's voice fell. Something in the young man's expression extinguished his anger as quickly as it had arisen. 'What's going on, Paris?' he demanded quietly.

Show over, the players returned to their exercise. Paris looked uncomfortable.

'Nothing . . . I . . . It's not my fault, gaffer! There's stuff going on. Things over which I've no control!'

His manager softened, torn between amusement and exasperation. If only the following match wasn't the final. Brigham United, their opponents, had been unlucky not to go up automatically, unlike the Rogues who'd scraped into the play-offs in sixth place. They really did need their star player firing on all cylinders.

'Who is she?' he asked tiredly.

'I've never felt like this about anyone! I can't eat, sleep — '

'Who, for goodness' sake?'

'Anna! Her name's Anna!' Paris answered miserably, finding no comfort in the name.

'After all the business with the FA hitting the headlines, she won't have anything to do with me,' he muttered, conceding that, given the promise he'd made to keep out of trouble, he could hardly blame her.

'I thought that had been dealt with?' Davie's tone was sharp. Despite the consensus of opinion in the boardroom that the lad had been set up, the FA had still come down hard, fining Melchester, who should have known better, an astronomical amount and Paris a hefty two weeks' wages. He'd been lucky to escape a ban. Steve Bentnall had yet to be dealt with. Paris sighed so heavily that Davie could have shaken him.

'She doesn't think I'm serious.'

She sounded a sensible girl.

'Have you told her how you feel?' An image of Bobbie sprang unbidden to Davie's mind. The star in his heavens! Who was he to lecture when he'd never yet got round to telling Bobbie exactly what she meant to him.

Paris looked quickly away, aware that he was treading on new territory and hadn't a clue how to explain to anyone, least of all Anna. He stumbled on, trying it out on Davie. 'I . . . I can't imagine being with anyone else. I'll never want anyone else! It's just . . . unthinkable.' Somehow he had to find a way to be with her. All the time. That about summed it up, but how could this man understand? He was way too old and even if, unbelievably, he had ever conceivably felt like this, it must be so long ago, he'd have forgotten it long by now.

Davie's face twitched.

'Try asking her to marry you,' he suggested.

'What?' The young man's head shot up.

Surely Paris couldn't be so dim-witted? And surely neither could he. Davie's smile faded. 'Ask her to marry you,' he urged quietly, seriously, an ache inside, finding instant solace at the thought. 'You're no good to me in this state. Go and do it now . . . and don't come back until it's done!'

This last he shouted out loud, too late. An idiotic grin plastered all over his handsome face, Paris was already running at breakneck speed, back towards the changing rooms.

★ ★ ★

'Take these bibs down to the lads, there's a good lass. Extra training? No one thinks of all the extra washing.'

Not giving Sam a chance to say no, Ellie Darbyshire, the Rogues' laundry lady, happily piled high into her arms the garments she'd just that moment finished ironing. She'd been busy. The very idea that her precious boys should wear anything allowed out of her laundry room other than in pristine condition was utterly unthinkable!

On her way to an early lunch before tackling the remaining Wembley tickets awaiting dispatch, good-naturedly Sam did as requested, making her way down to pitch level and musing on the truth that every employee in this football club, from financial director to tea lady, mucked in and did their bit. A large and happy family. A well-oiled machine, each cog as important as another.

The sun was shining, an omen for Wembley if anything was. Smiling happily, she walked briskly towards the players, her smile quickly turning to laughter as they descended en masse, seizing the bibs before she'd a chance to dish them out, and shared them out between themselves. Shortly a hotly contested football match was under way.

'Good to see you, Sam.' Davie strolled across the pitch. Sensitive enough to wish his presence didn't make her quite so uncomfortable, some of her happiness instantly oozed away. She was only just back from college. She'd hardly had a chance to catch up with anyone yet, least of all Davie Mackenzie.

'It was good news about your dad?' Davie proffered tentatively.

'I suppose,' she admitted, not meaning to sound so grudging and trying desperately to rediscover her smile. He'd been given a suspended prison sentence and community service, as Bobbie had always predicted. It had been a huge relief, and to her father most of all, but she wasn't sure she wanted to admit it to this man, his rival. Being so wrapped up in the court case, she'd hardly had a chance to think what, as yet, she felt about her mother's new boyfriend.

Davie stood, watching her uncertainly, unsure of his reception, she guessed; she found his diffidence oddly touching. He'd done her mother good. She'd no right to make things difficult. That thought decided her.

'Davie, I am pleased you and Mum have got together,' she murmured, nodding thoughtfully. 'And so is Todd. We've never known Mum so happy.'

Visibly, he relaxed and she was glad she'd spoken.

'You don't know how much that means to me,' he admitted quietly. 'I am aware how difficult things have been for the pair of you recently . . . ' He broke off. A cry had gone up from the players as Paris belted the ball gleefully into the back of the net. Davie's face broke into a wide smile of approval. 'Hope he's saved one for Monday! The lad's on fire this morning, blessed if I know what's got into him.' He could take a pretty good guess. He blew the whistle round his neck, signalling the end of the session. Short and sharp this morning. After lunch, they were travelling to the secluded five-star hotel that Bobbie had reserved as team base for the Final. 'I'll catch you, later.' He patted Sam's arm awkwardly, yet feeling oddly light-hearted. Another bridge crossed and only Wembley to go.

The players trooped from the pitch. Davie hurried away. A familiar arm snaked round Sam's shoulders. 'How's my favourite cousin?' It was Paris, too obviously pleased with himself. Grinning, she disengaged herself.

'Good goal' she conceded, amused that something so simple could account for such a ludicrous amount of self-approval. Typical Paris, vainglorious, conceited. Nothing had changed.

'Who cares about a stupid goal?' he cried, startling her, bouncing back, happiness exuding from his every pore. 'Hang the goal, Sam! I'm in love! The most wonderful . . . the most beautiful — '

'Anna? Your mystery girl!' she cried, shocked, delighted, many things at once. She'd never seen him like this. She grabbed his arm. 'Come on! Spill the beans!'

He made an effort to calm but quickly gave it up, swinging her round instead, scarcely waiting for her world to stop spinning before he burst out. 'I've asked her to marry me . . . Oh Sam! She's said yes!'

★ ★ ★

Wonderfully, Paris was plunged back to the grim social services building, the most beautiful building in the whole wide world. He was running upstairs again, taking the same wrong turnings, trying the so many different doors, discovering the right one at long and wonderful last, uncaring of the startled faces or the fact that he'd interrupted some kind of meeting, already under way. Seeing only Anna! Her shocked expression registered. Delight? Despair? He rushed towards her and then did something so wildly improbable, he couldn't believe it, even now. He was down on one knee, his hand fumbling for hers, taking no notice of the amused expressions, the bursts of startled laughter, too full of the overwhelming instinct that this was the most important moment in his life.

'Anna, please marry me,' he murmured. The words sounded so strange on his lips that he didn't know, even now, how he'd found the courage to force them out. 'I love you. I can't live without you. I want us to be together more than I've ever wanted anything in my life.'

His grip on her hands tightened. She must have heard his heart thudding so wildly, read the desperation in his eyes. Miraculously, her eyes were full of bright tears and she was laughing crazily and to loud cheers was saying the one wonderful little word he'd never in his wildest dreams thought to hear.

★ ★ ★

'Paris, I'm so pleased.' Delighted, Sam extracted herself, still unable to help wondering what her Auntie Babs would make of it all. What would the press make of it! The poor girl would need nerves of steel.

'I see he's told you?'

George jogged towards them, eyes only for Sam, his appearance oddly that of someone unhappy with his lot. Something was wrong. Not sure why it should bother her so, Sam's smile quickly disappeared.

'Are you all right, Georgie?' she asked.

'Of course he's not!' Paris laughed, full of himself and jumping in before George had chance to answer. 'We're only short on full-backs. Davie's told him there's a chance he'll be playing on Monday. A virtual certainty, in fact!'

'But that's good, isn't it?' she cried, not understanding.

'His debut? Hah!' Paris retorted gleefully. 'I wouldn't fancy turning out for the Rogues, first time, at Wembley. The fans will eat him alive!'

George groaned, stood running his hands through his hair and watching Sam in despair.

'Shut up, Paris!' she answered sharply. No wonder George was so worked up and so she told him, over a coffee at Ted's café, where she'd taken him for the lunch he so patently had no appetite for. 'You'll be all right' she soothed, inwardly conceding that he might not. 'Once you're out there, you'll forget it's Wembley. It's only a game, after all!'

'Hah! One with fifty million riding on the outcome? Are you joking, Sam? What if I make a mistake, gift United a goal? I couldn't bear it!'

'You'll not let anyone down,' she reassured him calmly, sure of this at least. George was dependable, the sort of man who'd never knowingly let anyone down. Everyone at the club knew it, which was why Davie had picked him. He was as trustworthy as Steph so patently wasn't.

She sat back, startled at the thought, her expression, always open, hiding nothing. The noise around subdued to a stifled hum, the atmosphere suddenly seemed thick with things unsaid. George was watching her warily.

'What a fool Steph is!' he muttered, taking her by surprise. 'How could he have let you go? If you were mine, Sam . . . ' He stopped and flushed, seeming to realize what he was saying. She'd taken his mind off football. Her eyes began to twinkle. How interesting the conversation had become! 'Oh yes, Carter? If I were yours . . . ?'

He held her gaze steadily. 'If you were mine, you'd easily be the most precious thing in my life.'

How earnest he sounded. But he was earnest and straightforward and all those other things of which she was only, belatedly, beginning to appreciate the worth. He liked her and had no intention of hiding it. He took a deep breath and plunged on; his tone diffident and she guessed it took a lot for him to speak, guessed too, exactly what he was about to ask.

'Perhaps we could go for a meal or a drink sometime?'

Was she over Steph enough? Looking into George's steady brown eyes, Sam rather thought she was. So what if he was a footballer? So what if Steph had left her feeling she'd had enough of footballers to last the rest of her life?

She grinned happily, suddenly aware that the length of the summer holidays stretched invitingly. There would be time for them to get to know each other properly. If only there weren't the little matter of a play-off final to get through first.

★ ★ ★

Landon pressed the off-button on the video remote, consigned the Rogues' exploits in the semi-final play-offs to a welcome history. Eleanor yawned, tried to stop, giving it up for lost in a smothered laughter. He pulled a face. She was trying; he had to give her that.

They'd had sandwiches for lunch, eating on the sofa whilst watching the TV and temporarily forgetting their problems which, after all, hadn't become so entrenched that they weren't unsolvable. Their present strait-ened financial circumstances were only a part of it. They'd lived through worse! It was nothing permanent, Landon had explained over tea yesterday. Their money was tied up. It would go ceiling-high once they got into the Premiership — if they got into the

Premiership he added, with a troubled expression.

Eleanor stood up quickly, gathered plates and cups and stacked them neatly on the tray. Then she returned to the sofa. Football again. If only she could understand the pull it had on her family!

It lay, an unwanted presence between herself and a perfection she still saw tantalizingly out of reach. Landon's eyes were twinkling. 'So that's it! The four teams who finish the season third to sixth in the league enter a mini knock-out competition. Third plays sixth, fourth plays fifth over two legs, home and away. The winning teams go through to the final at Wembley. And the winner of that — '

'Plays in the Premiership next season.' This time she really did laugh. How complicated it all was and yet how ridiculously simple. 'Landon, I'm not a complete idiot.'

'I was only explaining,' he declared huffily, his expression softening. Fumbling, he reached for her hand. He'd nearly lost her and it would have been no one's fault but his own. What a crazy fool he'd been. 'I'm so lucky you came back,' he admitted humbly. 'It's more than I deserve.'

'Darling, we've been through this.' Many times. She frowned. All she really cared about was, was he was making progress? Was he graduating through inactivity to convalescence then light work round the house and garden and the sharp brisk walks recommended by the doctors? Un-Landon-like, he'd done everything they'd asked. His illness had shaken them both. 'We have to go forward, love,' she murmured softly, leaning into him and gazing up into his face. She needed to know he was taking this seriously. 'We've both made mistakes. It doesn't mean we can't learn.'

'Even at our age?' He shook her hand playfully, their minds were running on parallel lines. They had a marriage worth saving. It still had to be worked at. He'd let things slide for too long.

Football fled from his mind, his world centring on Eleanor, as it had so often of late. 'You're so generous,' he muttered, finding the thought too painful to bear. Under his dear wife's fiery surface there beat a heart overflowing with magnanimity. He'd always taken advantage, waiting for the explosion to die down as he knew it would, then seizing on the opportunity to get his own way. His selfishness filled him with contrition. 'I've thought a lot of things of late, love. All kinds of things you wouldn't believe!'

'Landon, it doesn't matter.'

'I do love you.'

'I know. I love you too.' They could still say it; even more, mean it and nothing else mattered. Anything else could be circumnavigated, dissolved, eventually overcome. Eleanor was filled with a sudden bright joy. 'I hope you've reserved my seat for Monday, Vernon, or you're for it.' His face expressed an amazement which would have made her laugh if she hadn't been so deadly serious. 'The little matter of a football match?' she prompted, stifling the desire to shake him. 'Don't tell me you've forgotten? And don't look so shocked!' she added sharply. 'If the doctors reckon you're well enough to cope with the trauma of a play-off final, I'm coming with you, that's all.'

She'd shocked him at last. Her free hand fumbled for his, gripping it tightly. If they weren't to meet the same problems, albeit approached now with different attitudes, somehow she'd got to get to the bottom of this football business. It had excluded her from enough of her family's life.

★   ★   ★

Bank Holiday Monday and London was thronging. Amongst all the car horns blaring, the shouts and cheers through hastily wound-down windows, the second of the two luxury coaches eased out of the sumptuous grounds of the Maybright Park Hotel and into the line of traffic on the slow and fateful journey to Wembley.

The first coach, containing the players and coaching staff, was already some vehicles in front. They'd be late, break down, they'd never get anywhere near Wembley Stadium! The knot of tension which had tied itself inexorably round Bobbie's waist sometime during the course of an early luncheon that no one had any appetite for, tightened relentlessly. A slim figure in a well-cut suit, she took one deep and calming breath and waved to the few supporters who'd managed to evade security staff and gain the hotel entrance in time to give their heroes a rousing send-off. She made her way down the aisle to the seat reserved next to Babs. Landon and Eleanor, Sam and Todd, Ray Lovett and his wife Rosie, Ellie Darbyshire and Fred Varney were all seated near by. Everyone was present and correct and as taut as the proverbial bowstring.

Her little sister was positively glowing. Unbearable tension seemed to suit her. Bobbie sank down gratefully, unaccountably pleased that they were going together and that Taylor was otherwise engaged, driving the minibus he'd hired, at his own expense, to transport Russ Packard's boys' club to the match.

'Nervous?' Babs grinned.

Bobbie exhaled slowly. She felt as nervous as she'd ever been in her life. 'I wished we'd never got to Wembley,' she muttered warmly. 'I wish East Ham had knocked us out in the semis! Oh Babs, what if we get thumped? Make fools of ourselves? Sky'll have a field-day!'

Babs squeezed her arm. 'For goodness' sakes, Bobs! We're here on merit. The team'll do us proud. Get a grip on yourself!'

She found a shaky smile. The last twenty-four hours had been too much: emotion piling on emotion. No wonder she felt so on edge. 'Can you keep a secret?' she blurted out impulsively, the wonderful news, even now vying for attention with the little matter of a play-off final, urgently demanding expression. If she didn't tell someone she'd simply burst, and who better than Babs? She used to tell Babs everything.

The rest of the bus was otherwise occupied, chatting, staring out of windows, or simply absorbed in thought. Bobbie's hand rose to her blouse collar, pulling free the chain fastened around her neck and revealing the ring she'd so carefully slipped on to it before she'd left her hotel room that morning. A gold band supporting a sapphire of the deepest blue. Like her eyes, Davie had said, before he'd kissed her.

'Please tell me that's an engagement ring?' Babs cried in delight.

'Can't you guess?' Bobbie laughed, experiencing again the deep and contented joy she'd felt when first he'd slipped it on to her finger. She wasn't sure she had the right to so much happiness twice in her life. They'd lost each other once. It seemed a miracle that they were back together again.

'Bobbie, it's beautiful . . . ' Babs's face broke into a wide smile of approval.

'Had you given up on us?' her sister teased, dropping the chain and its precious burden quickly from sight. Primly, she pulled the edges of her suit jacket together. 'We're not telling anyone until after the match. Win or lose, whatever happens. Davie reckons the team can't cope with any more distractions.' And neither could she! What could be more distracting than falling in love, resisting it all the way, at long last, frustratingly, giving in, only to discover, miraculously, that the object of your desire not only loved you too, but was desperate that you should spend the rest of your lives together? She leaned back against the seat and closed her eyes, her mind wandering gladly back to the previous evening and Davie's proposal.

They'd long since finished dinner. The players had decamped to bed, the rest of the Rislington party had removed to a lounge that Bobbie had suddenly found cloyingly hot and from which she'd escaped through the French windows and on to the veranda. The night was warm, the moon was golden, the colour of sand washed by waves, and so low in the sky she could have touched it.

She leaned against a pillar, staring out on to the ghostly shapes of trees and the endless lights of the metropolis beyond, thinking about Davie and where the two of them went from here. Had she told him she loved him? Oddly she couldn't remember. Things had become jumbled, fused inextricably during the long years that had passed since last they'd been together.

Hands slid round her shoulders, pulling her round. Davie was looking at her quietly.

Bobbie's heart skipped a beat. Davie had followed her out. A man who knew what he wanted and was at this moment wanting Bobbie more than he'd ever wanted anything in his life. 'Marry me, Bobbie? I love you,' he'd murmured, his heart beat so loud it embarrassed him.

She'd imagined him saying it so many

times, chiding herself for a fool to imagine he'd want to marry her now.

'Our world'll go crazy,' she warned.

'I don't care and neither do you.'

'You'll be sorry you asked. I haven't changed a jot. I'm as bad to live with as ever.'

'Ssshhh . . . ' First laying a finger across her lips, he pulled out the ring and slipped it on to her unresisting finger. He'd not needed an answer because, deep down, they both knew the score. Laughing, he'd pulled her back and into the shadows . . .

★ ★ ★

'I can't understand why you've taken so long!' Babs grinned inanely, as though there was more to her joy than the simple fact of her big sister getting married at long and wonderful last.

Bobbie knew her too well. Something was definitely up. Infuriatingly, Babs only grinned the more, relaxing her head back against the seat and wondering if now was the time to impart her own delicious and unexpected secret. Trust Bobbie to steal her thunder when she'd exciting news of her own to impart! She'd only just got round to telling Taylor. Her hands folded neatly over her stomach, fondly imagining it swelling with new life already.

'I hope you're going to enjoy being an auntie again,' she announced matter of factly.

'Babs, you're not . . . ?'

'I am!' She beamed, taking more delight in Bobbie's shocked expression than she could have believed possible.

'But that's wonderful. And so . . . '

'Unexpected?' Happiness exuding from every pore, Bab's eyes twinkled with unsuppressed laughter. 'It wasn't exactly planned,' she conceded, still amazed; for once she and Taylor were taking a chance. A pledge for their future. It had come as a shock that they actually had a future.

'But Babs! That's the best thing could ever have happened!' Bobbie cried.

Babs nodded happily, remembering how astonished she'd been, and yet delighted too. No second thoughts, nothing but a burning conviction that it was the very best thing. They'd needed a change of direction. Hang Cedars! She'd been in danger of becoming a single-minded career woman. It did her so much good to see Taylor planning how they were going to work their way round a new baby. 'You won't have to worry about a thing, darling. You're to rest, put your feet up. I'll see to Cedars, everything.' A man transformed. For the time being at least. 'I've no idea what Paris will say,' she murmured,

311

turning to Bobbie, suddenly worrying.

'It'll give him something to think about.' She laughed, thinking about Anna and wondering how her sister felt about that situation. 'I was really surprised to hear about his wedding plans,' she hazarded carefully, feeling her way. She needn't have worried.

'The best thing for him,' Babs announced airily, worry dissolving. 'Anna will do him good — and the new baby, come to that!'

'I'm going to be an aunt again!' Bobbie cried excitedly, the fact only just beginning to sink in and, if only to see her mother's face, wanting to jump up and announce it.

It was pretty unbelievable that things were going so right at last.

The bus had crawled to a halt, held up by the crowds cramming on to Wembley Way; a sea of black-and-white bedecked supporters, as if the town of Rislington had risen up and emptied itself out over the stadium. Young boys draped in flags, grandmothers in weird hats and face-paints, proud dads wearing the precious shirts of their youth. The forward impetus of supporters marching towards the Wembley Arch carried them all along and, they hoped, on to victory. But this was their family too, Bobbie realized. Not just Vernons but all those here on the bus, all around and spilling out on to the streets. One big happy family encompassing every one of the Rogues supporters who'd got themselves down here by whatever means available.

The sea parted, the crowds cheered. The bus eased through. There was no way they could let these people down. She offered up a silent prayer. They'd surely never come this far to fall down now?

★ ★ ★

The ground was bursting to capacity. The Vernons had taken their seats with the rest of the directors and staff, looking down from high over the pitch. Even Eleanor had to agree that the new Wembley Stadium was impressive. She sat next to Landon, amazed by the volume of noise and colour, leaving her senses spinning. She'd never expected anything like this; she was afraid she could feel the beginnings of a headache. She checked in her bag for headache pills, glancing up to a sea of flags and balloons and a cacophony of horns, drums, a band, cheers, yells, shrieks. The match hadn't even started yet. Why was everyone so excited?

It was contagious. She gripped Landon's arm, laughing at the ridiculousness of it all. Everyone had gone crazy. If only she could work out what the fuss was about!

The clamour intensified, swelling high over the crowd. Fireworks exploded, coloured smoke drifted across the pitch. Overhead a helicopter buzzed.

'The teams are coming out!' Landon cried, pulling her up and hugging her tight. At least that was what she thought he said. His mouth opened. Words came out. In the row in front, like the pair of giddy teenagers they once were, Bobbie and Babs jumped up and down. The Rogues appeared, splendid in their chequered black-and-white. United were all in red. A file of dignitaries followed. More men in suits. Eleanor waved to Paris, who couldn't possibly see her, nor could George Carter either, who looked so nervous. The anthem was sung by a large man in a blue suit, and everyone joined in lustily. Things blurred. The match was under way. The crowd swayed, absorbed, thousands of voices reacting as one. On the pitch there was a lot of huffing and puffing and honest endeavour that she didn't try to understand. Men kicking a ball about. What it had always been. At half-time Landon fetched tea in paper cups. She drank hers, surprisingly grateful.

'The mid-field's overrun. We're not getting the ball up to the front men,' he growled, looking glum.

'Aren't we, dear?' Must he speak a different

language? The crowd around them were subdued. Things, it appeared, weren't going as well as they'd thought. At once Landon cheered up.

'Keep at it, darling. You'll get there.'

Would she? Did she want to? Suddenly she did, very much.

'I wish you could understand,' he murmured gently into her ear. 'We could come to the matches together, whatever league we're playing in. Eleanor, I've been meaning to have a word . . . ' When better than now? He hadn't exactly meant to tell her here but why not? He took her empty cup, deposited it under her seat, then turned her gently towards him. He'd given this a lot of thought. 'I've decided to cut down on work,' he said firmly. 'Leave more to Bobbie. She's perfectly capable. If this illness has taught me anything, it's that, much as I love football, there are other things in life.'

Like Eleanor and his children. Eleanor most of all.

'Landon, are you sure?' She pulled away, uncertain, looking up into his face, needing to know that it was what he really wanted. A soft swell of joy expanded. It *was* what he wanted. She was crying. What would folk think? Heads were turning, Bobbie and Babs too, looking worried. Landon hugged her again so she couldn't even say what she wanted to say: that she loved him, that he'd just made her feel the most blessed woman in the world.

'We're going to enjoy life from here on in.' He smiled, deposited her back in her seat. Bobbie turned round, again demanding to know that she was all right. Of course she was all right; she'd never been more all right in her life.

Eleanor wiped her eyes, squeezed Landon's hand, paid attention to what was happening on the pitch. The sun was shining; the teams were coming out again. The game restarted and she felt an odd little stir of excitement. They'd have a life outside football! What more could she ask? Was there anything more? The noise of the crowd was rising again, swelling to a roar. Her eyes fastened on Paris running down the pitch, the ball at his feet. Thousands of voices screamed in unison. Paris still had the ball. Why did she want so desperately for him to knock it past the man in a green jersey, standing in front of the nets? All these people around about her would be happy, she expected, and so, she supposed, would she. She was a Rislington lass. Rislington was where she belonged. Paris had skated past a red-shirted figure and sure enough . . . She'd blinked. Had she missed it? How come the ball had found its way so cleverly into the back of the net?

There was a split second of silence, then the crowd rose as one, yelling crazily. An explosion of emotion burst into Eleanor's heart. She leapt up, yelling crazily too, flinging into Landon's arms, wild joy, deep love but most of all, in their onward march towards the Premiership, an understanding uniting them as nothing else.

We do hope that you have enjoyed reading this large print book.

Did you know that all of our titles are available for purchase?

We publish a wide range of high quality large print books including:
**Romances, Mysteries, Classics
General Fiction
Non Fiction and Westerns**

Special interest titles available in large print are:
**The Little Oxford Dictionary
Music Book
Song Book
Hymn Book
Service Book**

Also available from us courtesy of Oxford University Press:
**Young Readers' Dictionary
(large print edition)
Young Readers' Thesaurus
(large print edition)**

For further information or a free brochure, please contact us at:
**Ulverscroft Large Print Books Ltd.,
The Green, Bradgate Road, Anstey,
Leicester, LE7 7FU, England.
Tel:** (00 44) **0116 236 4325
Fax:** (00 44) **0116 234 0205**

MS. HEMPEL CHRONICLES

Sarah Shun-Lien Bynum

Ms. Beatrice Hempel has just taken her first job as an English teacher. Closer in age and sensibility to her pupils than to her colleagues, she spends her time outside of school hours reading, writing, listening to rock and roll, and wondering whether she really was right to get engaged. In the classroom, too, she feels 'in-between'. Still young enough to understand her students' way of seeing things, she wants to be their accomplice; but she also feels a terrible responsibility as the adult witness to their adolescent growing pains.

THE LONGSHOT

Katie Kitamura

Cal and his long-standing friend and trainer Riley are on their way to Mexico for a make-or-break rematch with the legendary Rivera, who has never been beaten. Four years ago, Cal became the only fighter to ever take Rivera the distance, even though it nearly ended him. Only Riley, who has been at his side for the last ten years, knows how much that fight changed everything for Cal. And only Riley really knows what's now at stake, for both of them . . .